GIRL, UNCONVENTIONAL

C000000426

SASHA LANE

Discover other titles by Sasha Lane:
Girl, Conflicted
Girl, Unhinged

First published in Great Britain in 2017 by Sasha Lane
This paperback edition is the first edition

Copyright © 2017 by Sasha Lane

The moral right of the author has been asserted.

All characters and events in this publication, other than those clear-ly in the public domain, are fictitious and any resemblance to real persons, living or dead, is purely coincidental.

All rights reserved;
No part of this publication may be reproduced, stored in a retrieval system, or transmitted, in any form or by any means, without the prior permission in writing of the publisher, nor be otherwise cir-culated in any form of binding or cover other than that in which it is published and without a similar condition including this condition being imposed on the subsequent purchaser.

ISBN 978-0-9934562-2-0

Chapter One

'Two lines means positive. Yes?' I ask. I should probably already know the answer to this question, but under pressure I feel like I need clarification.

'Yes, yes. Two lines means it's positive.' Sophie nods, a serious expression on her face as we both stare poignantly down at my coffee table.

'And there are two blue lines. Right? I'm not seeing things? There are definitely two?'

Sophie nods, pressing her lips firmly together.

I exhale noisily, the sound deafening in the silence of the room, before we both simultaneously erupt into whoops of joy. Sophie flings her arms around me and I squeeze her tightly.

There's a baby on the way. A beautiful little baby. And it's so exciting…and scary…and perhaps I haven't thought through the true implications of this momentous event. As Sophie pulls away and curls up lazily on my sofa, I feel the need to keep the stupid grin plastered on my face, but my heart flutters a little. The reality of the positive pregnancy test signifies change ahead, big change, and I'm not sure I'm completely ready for that.

After Sophie leaves I pace the flat, feeling a mixture of feelings. I'm tempted to have a glass of wine to calm myself, but think better of it. An hour later, once I've practically worn a track into the lounge carpet, I hear the front door to the flat open and close and the familiar sound of Joe's footsteps as he heads down the hallway.

After Joe and I split up last year and then got back together again at Christmas, he decided to move out of the house we had initially rented together and into the two-bedroomed flat I'd moved into. He loves the view over the park below and the fact that it's within walking distance of the centre of town, meaning he can walk to work some days instead of taking the car. Not the most prominent selling point for me, I must admit. The view, yes, but walk to work? No.

'Hey.' Joe appears in the doorway of the lounge, where I'm now positioned on the corner of the sofa, trying to portray a vision of complete relaxation. He immediately looks concerned. 'What's wrong?'

Damn. I guess I need to work on my poker face.

'Absolutely nothing,' I say over-brightly. 'How was football practice?'

'Nice try, Emma, but you're fooling no one.'

'I don't know what you mean,' I protest. 'Now, what shall we have for dinner?' I stand up to try to make my way to the kitchen, but fail miserably as Joe remains standing stoically in the doorway, blocking my path.

'Don't try to change the subject. You and Sophie had some sort of "pow wow" here earlier –'

'Pow wow?' I shake my head dismissively.

'Yes, and now I arrive home and you're all jittery and acting strange.'

'I can't.' I shake my head.

'Can't what?'

'Can't tell you right now.'

'Okay, and why not? Is everything alright? Are you alright?'

'Yes, yes, I'm fine, and Sophie's fine, it's just...'

Joe looks at me with raised eyebrows.

'Um, did Matt play football with you today?'

'Matt, yeah, he's on his way home now. Why, what's going on with him and Sophie? Come on, Emma, this is my brother we're talking about.'

'Nothing.'

'Nothing as in something big and life changing?'

'Er...'

Damn it, I can never keep anything from Joe, he always manages to drag it out of me. But this is big, and it's not my news to tell – there has to be an order to such things. Surely the father of the baby should find out first? Okay, maybe second given that I, the best friend, already know. I open my mouth to say something else deflective, but thankfully my mobile phone bleeps on the coffee table in front of me, buying me some more time. I see a text from Sophie appear on the screen and snatch the phone up quickly.

I've told Matt. He's ecstatic! Thank God. You can tell Joe now xxx

I glance up, unable to hide the huge smile on my face, and realise that Joe is looking at me expectantly.

'You're going to be an uncle!' I announce triumphantly. 'Sophie's pregnant!'

'What do you think about having kids?' Joe snuggles closer to me as we lie spooning in bed later that evening.

'It's incredibly hard work. Your life is no longer your own. I mean, look at Simon and James.' Simon and James registered to adopt the minute they were married, and they became the proud parents of gorgeous fourteen-month-old twin boys about four months ago. I laugh. 'Actually, maybe they're a bad example. They appear to have taken to parenting like gorillas in the Amazon, carrying them around everywhere they go, never letting them out of their sight and being naturally paternal overnight.'

Joe sighs 'I meant how do you feel about *us* having children?'

'Oh. Right. Um.'

I realise with a degree of nervousness that I actually don't know the answer to this question. I mean, I always thought I would have children – well, I always thought I'd get married too, but I haven't managed that yet, although technically I have been proposed to. Joe and I were engaged to be married eighteen months ago, but then I ended up becoming completely stressed out by planning a wedding and doing a new fashion course at college, along with dealing with my new boss at the boutique I work at, who makes Cruella de Vil look like Snow White. In short I flipped out, called off the wedding and Joe and I split up for six months. Although Joe and I haven't discussed getting married since we got back together, I figure it will be on the cards at some stage. But children? Babies? Small human beings that require all of your attention, twenty-four hours a day, and whom you are required to keep alive under all circumstances?

'Emma.'

'Yes.' I sit upright, feeling somewhat under inquisition.

Joe sits up too and leans over, turning on the table lamp at the side of the bed. 'Are you okay?'

'Me? Yes. Absolutely fine.'

'I know we haven't really spoken about having children together, but this situation with Matt and Sophie has kind of got me thinking.'

Thinking? Hmm...it's got me thinking too, or rather got my mind whirling. I can feel Joe's eyes on me but I can't meet his gaze, and instead stare purposefully at my hands clasped in front of me while I try to engage my brain and say something that won't make me sound inhumane. I fail miserably and decide the best course of action is to deflect the question back at Joe and then respond appropriately to whatever he says.

'Do *you* want children?' I bite my lip nervously.

'I think so.' Joe takes hold of one of my hands, which is clasping the other tightly, and he pulls it up to his mouth. His lips brush my knuckles. 'I think it would be pretty cool to have a little Emma or Joe running around the place.'

'Really?'

'Just the one, though.'

'An only child?'

'Yeah, so I can spoil him or her rotten.'

Joe grins and I can't help but smile too. Joe would make a great dad, of that I'm sure, but it's not him I'm worried about; it's me. I am the person who's had to replace the orchid plant that my mother bought me when she visited shortly after I moved in. Replacing it once might be perfectly acceptable, but I'm on my fourth version of the damned thing, although I'm sure my mum will never know. Who am I kidding – she knows me only too well.

'It's something to think about,' I say positively, and I mean it. It's definitely something that's going to occupy my thoughts, probably constantly over the next eight months as Sophie's baby bump grows.

'I love you.' Joe leans over and kisses me, before turning out the bedside lamp.

'I love you too,' I say back as we resume our position snuggled together under the quilt.

But I can't sleep now. The whole issue of a baby is swirling around my brain. If I'm honest, it's something that has kept niggling at me pretty much since the day I turned thirty. Somehow it feels like an expectation that you'll have children, especially when really inconsiderate people – okay, mainly my mother and my step-mum, Margaret – make passing comments relating to "missing the boat", "women of a certain age" and so on, insinuating with annoying terminology that my biological clock is ticking.

All that does is add unwanted pressure to a situation that's already a minefield. What if I choose not to have children? Will I regret it when I'm too old to change my mind?

But should I make a decision about parenthood based on what I think society expects of me?

I lay awake listening to Joe softly breathing, sound asleep, oblivious to my inner turmoil. As I watch the minutes on the bedside clock tick over I can't help but feel that the gods of reproduction are mocking me as the ticking of passing time simulates my diminishing body clock, which up until now, I had refused to acknowledge.

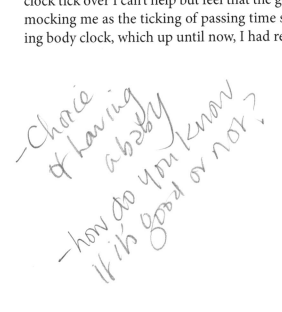

Chapter Two

Six weeks later

'Morning, Jenny,' I call, hearing the door to the back room of the shop open and close as I stand looking at the stock of handbags on the shelf. For once I'm the first one at work.

'Hi.' Jenny appears a moment later in the doorway, unravelling a pretty pink summer scarf from around her neck. 'Coffee?'

'The kettle's just boiled.' I put down the stock list I was tending to and head into the back room with Jenny. 'So how was last night with Scott?' I ask, trying and failing to hide a grin.

I know full well that last night Jenny had to meet Scott's parents for the first time. She'd been putting it off for ages, giving Scott every excuse in the book until she simply ran out of them and had to succumb. What she was so worried about I don't know. I've yet to witness anyone not being immediately enamoured by Jenny's bubbly personality and quick wit.

Before Jenny can answer the bell above the shop door jingles noisily and we both freeze, our eyes locked. There's still fifteen minutes until opening time, so that noise can only signify one thing.

'I presume someone is in here.' The sharp voice of Marissa Bamford reverberates through the shop, and Jenny's eyes widen.

Whatever reason has bought Marissa Bamford here, it can't be a good one.

The door from the shop to the back room swings open. 'Ah, there you are.' Ms Bamford appears in all her glory, large red wool coat swirling around her like a cape.

I hold my breath, waiting for whatever torrid news is about to be announced. Marissa Bamford stares at me and my stomach does a little flip.

'Emma,' she practically bellows, even though I'm only a metre away from her, 'as I'm sure you're aware, the Prince and his beautiful

Duchess will be descending on the city in four months' time.'

'Erm, yes.' I say vaguely, remembering some article in the local paper mentioning their visit to open a museum, or new town hall, or something to do with the cathedral. Anyway...

'Well, lots of our clients will be looking for something new to wear to such an occasion, something original, bespoke.'

'Right.' I nod along, wondering where this is heading. I glance at Jenny, who's nodding along also.

'So you can come up with something then?' Marissa's eyebrows disappear under her blunt-cut fringe.

'Come up with something?' I repeat, a little dumbfounded.

'You've completed your fashion design course, haven't you?'

'Um. Well, yes, but –'

'So you can design a range of dresses and jackets maybe, something new and stunning, something fit to greet Royalty in?'

'I'm not sure...'

Panic is rising rapidly inside me. I look to Jenny for some support, but find it lacking: Jenny merely stands frozen to the spot with her mouth gaping like a goldfish, which really doesn't help to calm my anxiety.

'I'll need some sketches by the end of the week, so I can choose the material.'

'Sketches?' I realise I sound like a demented parrot just repeating things back to her, but I have no idea what else to do.

'Yes, by the end of the week.'

'But I don't think I'm –'

'Right. I'm glad that's sorted. Now, I must dash. I'll be back in on Friday.'

And with that Marissa Bamford disappears in what might as well be a puff of smoke, leaving Jenny and I looking at each other completely bewildered.

'What the hell just happened?' I grip the worktop for support as my knees buckle.

'I think you just inadvertently agreed to design a fabulous range of outfits for our customers in preparation for a visit from the royal couple.' Jenny states matter-of-factly.

'Oh God.' I cringe, reaching for the instant coffee. 'Oh God, oh God, oh God. How did this happen?'

'It'll be alright,' Jenny tries – and fails – to console me.

'No, it won't be alright, Jenny. It will be a disaster, and not just your average disaster, I'm talking one of epic proportions. There's no way on earth that I can design several outfits that will meet the approval of Cruella de Vil, and certainly not within the next few days. It's completely unreasonable to expect that of anyone. Completely unreasonable!' My voice has become high and screechy.

Any creativity I could have possibly possessed has been completely zapped by Madam Bamford's unexpected arrival and demands.

'But –'

'No. I can't do it. I just can't do it.'

'Emma, calm down.' Jenny switches on the kettle. 'Let me make you a cup of tea.'

'Tea just won't cut it this morning, Jenny. It might only be eight fifty-five a.m., but I need cake, and copious amounts of it.' I fling on my coat and, leaving Jenny flustered and still mouthing something at me that I can't hear over the thudding of my heart, I head out of the back door into the cool morning air and gulp at it as if my life depends on it.

I'm so preoccupied with hurried thoughts of pencil skirts and cap sleeves that I literally fall through the door of the coffee shop I've been drawn to, tripping over the small step at the entrance. I land heavily on my right knee just as the contents of my handbag scatter across the tiled floor.

I'm torn between kneeling there in complete humiliation and crying loudly due to the searing pain in my kneecap. Complete humiliation wins, but is accelerated by the addition of the hot new barista helping me to my feet as I die inside.

'Are you alright, miss?' he asks, concerned.

'Of course,' I gulp, patting myself down and trying to remove my arm from his grasp so I can collect the debris of used receipts, lip glosses and old tissues that has swept across the floor.

'I'll have two skinny lattes and two chocolate muffins, please,' I manage to say while scooping up my belongings from the floor, trying my very best to ignore the stares and smirks from the other customers. Thank God it's early and the place isn't packed to the rafters!

'Are those to drink in or to go?' the hot barista asks.

'To go, definitely to go, please.' I force a smile, my cheeks burning, and pray for speedy service so I can get the hell out of here and back to the sanctuary of the shop.

'Emma! What on earth has happened?' Jenny is aghast as I hobble through the door, managing, miraculously, not to spill either drink or drop the brown paper bag containing the two chocolate muffins.

'Nothing.' I unload the coffees onto the worktop. 'I just tripped over a little, that's all.'

'Oh, Emma, how do you do it?' She tries to hide a smile. 'You're so clumsy.'

The answer is: I don't know. For some reason God seems to take every available opportunity to make me look a fool. The list of incidents that have caused me embarrassment is too long to mention. And I have no idea why. I'm a good person, or at least I try really hard to be. Maybe I was an axe murderer in a previous life.

'Just eat your muffin.' I hand the bag to Jenny and take a much-needed gulp of my latte.

I arrive home just after Joe. He's still wearing his shoes and coat as I hobble through the front door of the apartment (I have no idea how I just made it up two flights of stairs with my injured knee).

'Emma?' Joe steps forward and takes hold of my hand.

'I'm okay, I'm okay, I just hurt my knee.' I shake my head but tears sting my eyes. 'Sorry,' I mumble, 'it's just been a ridiculous day.' I sniff. I realise this sounds self-indulgent. I mean, in reality I've been asked to design a dress and I fell over. It's hardly the end of the world.

'Come here.'

Joe pulls me into a hug. Instantly the feel of his strong arms around me and the smell of his aftershave soothe my fraying nerves.

'Why don't you sit down for a minute?'

Joe walks me through to the living room and lowers me to the sofa. He disappears for a moment, but then returns with a glass of wine.

'I'll run you a hot bath. I'm sure you'll feel much better after a soak in some bubbles, and then you can tell me all about it.'

He leans down and kisses me on the lips before heading back out of the living room. I take a sip of my wine and think for the millionth time what a wonderful boyfriend I have.

Later that evening, I become perplexed as I try to explain to Joe the hideous situation I now find myself in – or, rather, have been unceremoniously dumped in by Marissa Bamford.

'This is a great opportunity, Emma. Can't you just get on board with it and see where it goes?' Joe smiles at me as I grip the kitchen worktop, trying to suppress my anxiety.

'It sounds like a great opportunity, but the reality is that I'm just lining myself up for an epic failure. I mean, who am I – Stella McCartney all of a sudden?'

Joe stifles a laugh. 'Why are you always so hard on yourself? Don't you see how talented you are?' He takes hold of one of my white-knuckled hands, prises if from its grip on the worktop and kisses it.

'It's just...I'm not...I mean...' I exhale heavily. 'I hope we have more wine.' The earlier glass of wine (and the hot bath) seemed to temporarily cure my painful knee.

'Come here.'

Joe wraps his arms around me, his warm lips find mine and I feel the familiar pull of him. Joe is by far my biggest fan, and no matter what it is I'm doing, or trying to do, his belief in me never wavers. Why, I'm not sure, as my own self-confidence wobbles constantly. Joe's complete faith in me is one of the many things that I love about him, and even after several years together I can still get turned on by just one kiss.

'Mmm...maybe I need a distraction first, to clear my thoughts,' I murmur.

'What were you thinking?' Joe asks between planting kisses on my lips.

'I was thinking that I'd like you to take me to bed.' I gaze into Joe's eye and he raises his eyebrows. I know what he's thinking – I'm usually not that forward. It's not that I don't enjoy sex, I just don't usually initiate it. There's something about the man taking control that makes me feel more desired somehow.

'Well, I don't need asking twice.' Joe scoops me up in his arms and I shriek as he carries me through to the bedroom. He lays me down gently on the bed and his lips meet mine.

Joe begins unbuttoning his shirt and I shuffle, slightly undignified, underneath him as I remove my own clothes. I enjoy the feel of Joe's muscular body pressing against mine as we begin to make love, and within moments I start to lose myself within him, until my whole body tingles as we climax together.

Chapter Three

I wake feeling slightly groggy even though I've had a good night's sleep. I glance at the alarm clock; it's six fifteen a.m. I can hear Joe breathing softly next to me as I snuggle back down under the warm quilt. But within seconds I'm wide awake, frustratingly, the replay of yesterday's request for designs by Marissa Bamford churning around my head. I slither as quietly as I can from under the bedcovers and tiptoe out of the room, grabbing my fluffy white dressing gown from the hook on the back of the door as I close it quietly.

I pad softly through to the kitchen and switch on my coffee pod machine. I have to admit, when I forked out the huge amount of money for this machine I half-expected the novelty to wear off quite quickly, but it has to be the most used item in the apartment, way ahead of the iron and vacuum cleaner, and it's got to the point where I don't function in the morning without my daily fix of proper caffeine.

I place a pod in the machine, press the button and enjoy the welcoming aroma of Guatemalan coffee as my drink is prepared. I take the cup and walk through to the living room. Standing at the large window overlooking the park at this time of the morning is very therapeutic. I see only birds, ducks from the pond on the other side of the park that are meandering about and the occasional jogger. As if on cue, a man clad in black Lycra shorts and, oddly, a bright-pink t-shirt zips by below me at quite a speed. I wish I was someone who enjoyed running, but I simply don't. I've tried it (perhaps only once or twice, I admit), but it's definitely not for me.

'Hey, you're up early.' Joe appears behind me and plants a kiss on my shoulder.

'I couldn't sleep,' I say, turning around to face him.

'Emma, stop worrying about these designs. It will be fine. Just find some time and make a start. You'll see.'

I don't share Joe's optimism, but I love him for having faith in me, so I just nod in agreement.

Joe kisses me on the lips. 'I'm going to head out on my bike for half an hour before breakfast.'

'Okay. I'll see you later.'

As Joe leaves the flat, I head back into the kitchen and place another coffee pod in the machine. I figure I'm going to need as much caffeine as possible to kick me into gear for these dress designs.

While I'm getting myself ready for work, I hear Joe come home.

'Emma, do you want a cup of tea?' Joe calls.

I wander, half-dressed, through to the kitchen and turn on the oven. 'I'll warm some croissants,' I say, taking a fresh packet of four from the bread bin. This is about as near to cooking as I get, but it makes me feel very domesticated as the smell of warm pastry fills the room.

Joe opens the fridge and takes out a variety of fruit – that I didn't know we owned, and I certainly didn't buy – and he begins chopping furiously, so by the time the croissants are ready to eat we also have a huge bowl of fresh fruit salad to accompany them. See, this is why we work, I think: yin and yang.

'How's Sophie doing?' Joe asks between bites of melon and mango.

'Okay, I think. I haven't seen her for a few days, but she texted yesterday to say she's got a date for the baby's first scan.'

'I know, Matt texted me too. He's so excited.'

'Do you think they'll find out what the sex of the baby is? I think Sophie would like to.'

'Hmm, she may have a fight on her hands. Matt wants to wait. But I don't think they can find out at this scan. I think it's the next one.'

'Oh.' How is it that Joe knows this and I don't? 'I might pop over to see Sophie tonight.'

'That would be good. Matt mentioned going to the sports quiz at their local pub tonight. I fancy going.'

'Then go, and I'll keep Sophie company. We haven't had a good gossip for a while. It will be good to catch up.'

Joe grins. 'You mean it's been at least a few days.'

'Anyway, I must get ready for work.' I eat the last bite of croissant, playfully ignoring Joe's last comment.

'Have a good day.' Joe kisses me on the cheek. 'I'm going to jump in the shower.'

I'm alone in the shop all day today, as Jenny doesn't work Wednesdays. A part of me wants Marissa Bamford to hire an additional person to help out, as it's hard being on my own for a whole day each week. But I kind of like it being just Jenny and me, as we get on so well. It's been just the two of us since Marissa's niece, Julia – who was equally as frightful – disappeared to work in the London store with her aunt.

To be honest, I'd be happy if someone came in once a week only to change the clothes on the stupid manikins. I push all thoughts of dress designing from my mind and focus on the job of re-dressing the manikins in the window display. Tomorrow is my day off, and I can spend it working on the dress designs so that I'm fully prepared for Friday, when Marissa will reappear demanding to see "some sketches".

As usual, dressing the manikins takes me about an hour. They're stiff and inflexible, and I'm puffing and panting by the time they're sporting new outfits. I head into the back room to make a well-earned coffee and to text Sophie to see whether she's free tonight.

The rest of the day passes without incident, and thankfully there's just a steady flow of customers to manage. As the clock ticks over to five thirty, I lock the shop door and grab my coat. Sophie has texted back to say she will be home from six, so I decide to go straight over to hers from work. We can grab some food together later: i.e. I'll call for a takeaway.

I arrive at Sophie's house just before six o'clock and bump into Matt on the street as I climb out of my car.

'Hey, Emma,' he greets me with a smile.

'Hi, Matt.' I smile back. 'Are you going out already? I thought Joe said the pub quiz didn't start until eight o'clock.'

'It doesn't.' Matt taps the bag thrown over his shoulder. 'I've got my running kit in here. Joe and I are off for a jog before we head out.'

'Ah.' I nod. That makes sense. Of course you need to go for a run before going to the pub quiz. 'Enjoy.' I grin as I wonder how Sophie and I, two people allergic to exercise, have managed to end up with two sporting fanatics.

'The door's open. Just go straight in,' Matt says as he jumps into his car. 'Catch you later, Emma.'

I push open the front door. 'Soph? Soph, it's only me,' I call as I take my shoes off in the hallway (something imprinted on me from a small age by my mother).

'Hi. I've just put the kettle on.' Sophie appears in the doorway to the kitchen and I do a double-take.

I take in this slightly dishevelled version of Sophie. A week ago she was positively glowing with her pregnancy. Now she looks pale with a slight green tinge, and her usually thick, bouncy dark-brown curls are limp and unstyled.

'Soph. Are you alright?'

'Yeah, I'm fine.' She waves a hand dismissively. 'It's just morning sickness.' She shrugs.

Okay, correct me if I'm wrong, but I thought morning sickness was, well, just as the name implies, sickness that you get in the morning?

'I know.' Sophie says, reading my mind. 'It's weird, but sometimes you get sick at other times too – everybody's different.'

'Right, well, you sit down and I'll make the tea.'

'Thanks, Emma. Make mine a ginger tea, please – the teabags are in the cupboard.'

'I can find them, Soph. Just go and sit down.' I usher her out of the kitchen.

Blimey. Poor Sophie, she looks so unwell. I make the tea (the smell of Sophie's ginger tea is enough to turn my stomach, so I'm not sure how this is going to assist her already nauseous state).

'There you go.' I place the mugs down on the coffee table and join Sophie on the sofa.

'Thanks, Emma. I was feeling perfectly fine up until a few days ago, but now I feel sick all of the time.'

I'm sure this is normal and I don't want to panic Sophie, so I just say, 'Are you still having your first scan on Friday?'

'Yeah.' She grins. 'I can't wait to see our baby on the screen.'

I feel an unexpected twang of envy. "Our baby." A little person she and Matt have created that is unique.

'When you can, will you find out if it's a boy or a girl? A little Jack or Jill?' I ask.

'I want to, but Matt doesn't, so I guess we'll wait and see.'

'So have you thought of any names?'

Sophie shakes her head. 'None that we particularly agree on. Matt likes really biblical names like Isaac and Lucas, but I want something more…modern.'

'If by "modern" you mean ridiculous, celebrity-style, made-up names then I'm afraid I'm going to have to side with Matt,' I state.

Sophie just giggles.

'I'm serious, Sophie. You might want an interesting name for your child, but he or she will prefer something that means not getting bullied to hell in the school playground.'

'Fair point.' Sophie nods. 'But enough of me. What's going on with you?'

I take a sip of my tea, then proceed to tell Sophie about Marissa's hideous request that I design some stupid dresses and matching jackets. Halfway through my tirade, though, Sophie turns a few shades greener and hurriedly leaves the living room.

I spend the rest of the evening alternating between making Sophie ginger tea and rubbing her back while she throws up in the bathroom. It's not the evening I planned to have with her, but she's my best friend and I love her. Plus, she's growing a human inside her and that's a whole lot more important than anything I'm doing right at this moment, so holding her hair while she's sick seems like the least I can do. That's just what best friends do for each other.

I make it home before Joe and, exhausted, I crawl into bed and snuggle under the duvet. I'm just drifting off to sleep when I feel Joe slide into bed beside me. He nuzzles into my back and fumbles playfully with my knickers, but I swat his hand away. Usually I'd be game, but not tonight. After the last few hours spent with Sophie, I want to have a check-up with my doctor to make damned sure that my contraception of choice is most definitely working before I let Joe anywhere near my naked body.

Chapter Four

Right. Okay. I'm going to focus.

I must focus.

It's the following afternoon and I'm staring down at a blank sketchpad, feeling a mixture of frustration at my lack of inspiration and crippling fear at…well, my lack of inspiration. The deadline to present my finished designs to Marissa Bamford is looming like a monstrous storm in the distance. Usually I can do this. For all of my coursework for my fashion diploma I managed to create works of art – well, perfectly acceptable designs for a fashion tutor anyway. But now, under pressure from the Wicked Witch of the West, my artistic creativity has become elusive.

Maybe caffeine will help.

I wander through to the kitchen and prepare a latte using my coffee-pod machine, and then resume my position on the sofa with the sketchpad on my knee.

I have no idea how long I sit there, but my hand aches from the constant scribbling and daylight recedes. I'm so consumed with fear and concentration that I don't even hear the front door open and nearly jump out of my skin as Joe appears, a shadowy figure in the doorway.

'What's going on in here?' he asks, flicking on the light switch and nearly blinding me with dazzling hundred-watt bulbs.

'What do you mean?' I squint, glancing around the room and taking in the large volume of screwed-up paper littering the floor.

'I take it the dress designing is going well?' Joe gestures towards my sketchpad. Instinctively I place my arms over it, covering the current scribbling. 'Come on, Emma. Let me take a look.'

'No.' I bite my lip.

'It can't be that bad.' Joe cocks his head to one side and smiles.

'Okay,' I concede. 'But I want your honest opinion.'

Joe nods. 'Of course.'

Reluctantly I hand him the pad and hold my breath.

'Huh.' He frowns.

'Huh? What does that mean?'

'Um…it looks a bit like…an ostrich.'

'An ostrich?!' I snatch back the pad.

Not helpful, Joe, not helpful at all. Lesson learned. Don't say, *I want your honest opinion,* when clearly I mean, *Please sugar-coat your opinion and tell me it looks great.*

Joe flails helplessly. 'I just mean that the skirt looks a bit, um, full, that's all.'

Too late to backtrack now, Joe.

'What about some of these earlier ones?' Joe starts picking up balls of crumpled paper and attempting to unfurl them.

'Don't look at those too!' I shriek. I'm already in a fragile state and I fear that further criticism may well and truly tip me over the edge into hysteria.

'This one's lovely,' Joe holds up a design I barely remember sketching hours ago, and I huff loudly in contempt 'and this one too.' He holds up a second crumpled sketch of a dress. But as I look closely at the designs I struggle to think of the reason I discarded them. The 'tulip' style skirt on the first one is flattering, and the shapely neckline on the second would complement any body shape.

'What was wrong with this one?' he asks, studying one of the drawings.

'I…um.' I stand perplexed, before exhaling loudly and feeling the tension I have been storing up over the last few days finally leave my body. 'Nothing.' I grin. 'Absolutely nothing. This is it, these are the designs I will develop the rest of the range from.'

I reopen the sketchbook and start to scribble at pace and before I know it I have four more dress designs, all variations of the original sketch, and two types of matching jackets.

See, that's all I needed. A little perspective. I'm perfectly calm now and ready to present my designs to Marissa in the morning. I feel totally at peace.

The shrill ring of my mobile phone interrupts my peace like a cattle prod. I glance at the screen. Oh no…

'Hi, darling.'

'Hello, Mum.'

'How are things?'

'I'm good, thanks.'

'And Joe?'

'Joe's fine, thanks.'

'What is it then, Emma?'

'What do you mean?' I frown down the phone, forgetting that Mum can't see my facial expression.

'I can hear it in your voice, darling – something's wrong.'

'Nothing's wrong,' I state, exasperated. 'Why should something be wrong?'

'Okay, Emma, you'll tell me in your own time.'

Oh. My. God!

'So how are things with you and Parker?' I ask.

'Don't change the subject, Emma.'

Really?

'I wasn't,' I say unconvincingly.

'Okay. So how are things with Sophie?' Mum asks.

I knew where this was heading and it's the conversation I was trying to avoid.

'Sophie's fine.'

'That's good, darling.'

Grrr!

'I know you know something,' I snap.

'I don't know what you're talking about, Emma.'

'Sophie's pregnant,' I blurt out. 'She and Matt are having a baby.' I'm pretty sure I'm allowed to tell mum now she's having her first scan. I know Sophie wanted to keep it to just her close friends and family knowing until they're sure everything is fine with the baby.

'Oh…I see. How lovely.'

Oh, I see? How lovely? She has to know. How does she know these things?

'Yes, she's nearly three months pregnant.'

'Well, that's wonderful, darling. The pitter-patter of tiny feet.'

'Yes.'

'And while Sophie is still…young enough.'

Here it goes, the guilt trip.

'How nice for her mother to become a grandmother while she's still young enough to enjoy her grandchildren.'

'Mum…'

'And how joyous for Matt's parents. Is it their first grandchild too?'

'Mum…'

'So is there any chance that I might become a grandmother before I'm too old and senile to recognise my grandchildren?'

'Mum…'

'I'm sorry, darling, but I just…'

'What?'

My tone is quite curt. Once you turn thirty, marriage and babies are all people want to talk to you about. Actually, that's not true, it's just parents and stepmothers who want to prod you relentlessly about your "living in sin" and your barren lifestyle. The thing is, my mother is so on-trend and glamourous that the image of her as a grandmother seems so farfetched it's laughable. Yet here I am being emotionally crushed by the guilt that's being forced down the telephone from however many thousand miles away New York is.

'Well, it's just that I *would* like to be a grandmother one day, preferably in the not-so-distant future. Have you and Joe even talked about children?' I can hear the want in her voice and its making me more uncomfortable by the second.

'We have discussed it, yes, but…I'm not…we're not there…in that place right now.' I'm rambling incoherently, I realise, but I can't stop it. 'I mean, I don't even know whether we want children at all.'

I hear a sharp intake of breath from the other end of the phone.

As soon as I said those words out loud I realised my mistake. People don't want to hear that you may be struggling with the idea of motherhood, and by "people" I mean my mother. Somehow it feels more pressurised and like I'm under a big, bright spotlight given that my best friend is with child.

'I'm sorry, Mum, I have to go. Take care.'

I dig my finger fiercely into the "end call" button.

Argh! Argh! Argh! I glare at the mobile phone in my hand with anger.

Actually, that's not fair. It's not just my mother. When you get to your thirties it becomes something of an expectation that you want a family. Yet you are judged either way. If you want children then you are "taking your eye off the game" where your job is concerned, but if you don't want kids then you're career-driven, somehow cold and unnatural, a monster who hates children.

And I don't – I don't hate children. I'm just really not one hundred per cent sure that I have the right capabilities for the job. I mean, keeping another human being alive – and a very small, totally dependent human being at that – twenty-four hours a day just seems like an impossible task to me. I have no idea how women cope with a husband, kids and a job.

It seems wholly unfair that a woman has to choose between children and a career in this day and age. See the problem is, with all the fighting that women did for equal rights to work I'm not sure they fully thought through the consequences. Instead of equal rights and equal lives, we've somehow ended up in the unfortunate situation of wanting it all and trying to have it all. But in doing so we need to be three different people – a wife, a mother and a career woman – when there is barely enough time in the day to manage two of these roles let alone three.

And why is it that just having a job isn't enough anymore, you need to have a career? And why is it that as soon as you find your career, the pressure is on to have a baby?

Okay. Rant over. I am neither a wife nor a mother. Well, the wife bit is probably just a technicality, as in most respects I am a wife, just without the ring and marriage certificate. But I'll just have to put up with the disappointing looks from mum who's dying to become a grandma – I'm just not ready yet and I can do without the unwanted pressure.

No, in fact *they* will simply have to deal with my decision to not have children…yet…at all…oh, I don't know.

I need wine.

I feel wide awake and not even remotely sleepy as I stare at the ceiling later that night with thoughts of my earlier conversation with Mum playing on repeat in my head.

'What's wrong, Emma?' Joe prompts from the pillow beside me.

'Nothing,' I lie.

Suddenly light fills the room, causing me to squint and pray for my corneas.

'Emma?' Joe props himself up on his elbow as he turns to face me. I roll over to face him too.

I bite my lip and feel myself frowning. 'Everyone's having babies.'

Joe raises his eyebrows, looking amused. 'Everyone?'

'Well, lots of people we know.'

'You mean Matt and Sophie.'

'Okay, so only one person we know, but she's my best friend and she's having a baby with your brother.'

'That's true.'

'And Simon and James have the twins.'

'They do.'

'So...'

'So what are you saying? Do you want a baby?'

'No...no...should I?'

Joe kisses me on the lips. 'It's not a matter of "should or shouldn't", Emma. No one can answer that question for you.'

'I know.' I force a smile. 'I just worry, that's all.'

'Worry about what?'

'Are you happy with the way things are – just me and you?'

'Happy?' Joe looks at me and grins. 'Emma, I love you, I'm in love with you, and if it wasn't just the two of us then I wouldn't be able to do this.'

He pushes me back down onto the bed and rolls on top of me, propping himself up on his forearms as he smothers my neck and shoulders in kisses. I squeal with delight as Joe gently bites my earlobe, before his lips brush my cheekbone until they find my mouth. He kisses me hungrily, his tongue pushing deep into my mouth, and every part of my body tingles with desire. Only Joe has ever made me feel this way, and even three years into our relationship his touch still has me instantly aroused. Our love-making has never waned; it's intense.

Joe devours every inch of my body, moving his mouth and tongue over each of my nipples, making me gasp, before heading further south. I clasp in his thick, dark hair as his tongue traces my inner thigh, and my insides instantly melt.

Chapter Five

The dreaded morning is upon me. I arrive at the shop half an hour early, my sketchpad clutched in shaking hands. I place it carefully on the worktop and fill the kettle for a cup of tea. I'm just dunking the teabag in my mug when Jenny wanders through the door.

'Morning.' She smiles, all carefree, and I envy her. I'm a jittering bag of nerves. 'So, let's see them then.'

'See them?'

'Your dress designs. Come on, Emma. I know they'll be fabulous.'

Okay. I take a deep breath and flip over the cover of my sketchpad to reveal the first design in all its glory.

'I love it,' Jenny states clearly as she clasps her hands together. 'I'd wear it, and I know I'm about ten years younger than its intended market.' Jenny continues flipping through the pages of sketches.

I exhale loudly. 'Thanks, Jenny. I'm so scared Marissa will just think they're crap and berate me for an hour before leaving in a complete huff.'

'Oh, Emma, have some faith in yourself, will you. They're great. You've done a really good job.'

'Really?' I bite my lip.

'Really,' she states emphatically.

I make Jenny a cup of tea and we both drink in contented silence.

'How are things with Scott?' I ask.

'Fine.'

'What does "fine" really mean, Jenny?' I raise my eyebrows at her.

'It means that everything is fine, in the literal sense of the word.'

I smile. 'Okay, no need to get tetchy.'

'I'm not tetchy!' Jenny protests. 'It's just…'

'You really like him?'

She nods. 'I really like him. But I'm scared of making a mess of things.'

'Why would you think that?'

'Come on, Emma. I'm almost as bad at relationships as you.'

Thanks, Jenny.

'I'm sorry,' Jenny says immediately.

'That's okay.' I know she didn't mean anything by that. 'And to be fair, I have had some disastrous experiences with men.'

'I know, but I –'

'Let's see, there was Chris who dumped me and admitted he'd been cheating on me when all the time I thought he was going to propose to me.'

'Emma –'

'And then there was "Johnny", with whom I had a one-night stand. He turned out to be Connor, who had just started dating my best friend, and he almost destroyed my friendship with Sophie and then nearly killed us both in a high-speed car chase.'

'Emma…' Jenny looks like she's trying not to giggle.

I realise that none of these circumstances are particularly funny, but described like this, they do sound quite amusing. I'm not sure that anyone, unless they knew me, would believe that all of these situations could happen to just one person.

'And then we get to Joe.'

I can't help but grin myself now, for two reasons: firstly because I know, after all those hideous things that happened, how good I have it now, and secondly because the night I met Joe, well…

'And if you recall correctly, Jenny, I met Joe because I knocked him off his bike and we spent the evening in the local Accident and Emergency department.'

Jenny's unable to contain herself now and she starts giggling, and I start laughing too. I realise it's not good at all that I maimed a cyclist, but it's not as bad as it sounds. Joe conceded that he wasn't paying attention and was listening to really loud rock music and he actually rode into my car. That didn't make me feel any better about the situation, until the doctor released him that evening to go home with just some bruises, no broken bones.

We're both laughing hard now and I'm leaning on the worktop for support; tears are trickling down Jenny's face. The bell above the front door of the shop jingles loudly and in an instant we're both silent and wide eyed. Then she appears, Marissa Bamford, bright-red coat/cloak swirling around her.

'Ah, I'll have a coffee, Jenny, black,' Marissa states rather than asks.

No *Good morning* or *How are you?*. I guess by now that shouldn't come as a surprise.

'So, Emma.' She looks at me expectantly. 'The dresses? Let's see them.'

Nervously I reach for my sketchpad and flip open the pages to show the dress and jacket designs. I made a few additional sketches, just showing tweaks here and there and to give a few options for the necklines. Marissa stares at the pages, flicking between them, her expression blank. I hold my breath so hard I think I might burst.

After what feels like an eternity, she flips the sketchpad shut and the tension in the small room intensifies.

'Not bad,' she says, lips pursed nodding slightly.

Not bad? Does that mean good? I daren't ask, but thankfully I don't need to as Ms Bamford elaborates.

'I like the shape. The skirts in particular are flattering.'

Wow. High praise from Cruella de Vil. She seems almost surprised to find herself saying something positive. But hey, I'm surprised at that too.

She flips open the sketchpad again and points a long, sharp, red nail at my first design, which has short sleeves with a triangle cut at an angle out of the edge. 'It has to be this sleeve design. I don't like the rest. They're hideous.'

Ah, there we are. The criticism that I knew had to be in there somewhere. Well, I don't care. She likes the skirts on the dresses and that's all I need – one compliment; just one.

'But some more work needs doing on it,' she continues, which is a shame as I thought we were done with the "Not bad" comment.

I bite the side of my mouth and wait.

'It needs more va-va-voom.' Marissa nods, and I find myself nodding back as though I know exactly what she means by "va-va-voom" when in reality I haven't a clue.

She daintily sips the black coffee that Jenny carefully puts down in front of her – made in a delicate china cup with saucer, not one of the "dreaded mugs" – and silence hangs in the air.

'Right. I must dash.' Marissa places her cup and saucer back on the worktop. 'I'll be at the material wholesaler,' she states, as though either Jenny or I would dare to contact her.

And with that she turns on her heel and disappears from the back room. We hear the jingle of the bell above the door again as she leaves and both exhale at once.

'Blimey.' I shake my head. 'I can't believe that's over. For three days I've hardly slept, I've chewed my fingernails to the point of disgrace, and that's it?'

'Just be thankful she liked them for the most part. Would you prefer it if she'd hated all the designs?'

'No! I guess you're right. Now I just need to figure out what "va-va-voom" means and all will be well.'

Jenny drinks the last of her cup of tea. 'We don't have time to figure that out now. It's time to open up.'

'I'll go,' I say. 'We have a delivery due at nine thirty today.'

Jenny and I are kept busy for most of the morning. As usual on a Friday, many 'well-to-do' middle-aged women come into the shop looking for a new outfit to wear to some posh social function on the Saturday night. Between dealing with the customers – some of them very demanding – and the delivery of new stock, we barely get a minute to pause until lunchtime.

I sit in the back room and eat a pasta salad from my Tupperware box. Looking down at the contents – it's far too healthy for me – I smile. Joe has taken to preparing my lunch, so I can just collect it from the fridge on the way out of the door. I think this is for two reasons: firstly because I was buying lunch on a daily basis, which, I have been informed, isn't that cost effective for our joint bank account, and secondly because my purchased lunch usually included a muffin of some description and flavour with a latte (a skinny one, though!) and I think Joe is concerned about my daily caffeine and sugar intake.

Well, we can't all be super-healthy like him. And anyway, I don't have the time for food preparation in the evenings. Okay, that's a lie – I don't make the time, but now I don't have to as Joe makes my food along with his. I must remember to thank him on a regular basis for this kind gesture. Maybe I'll buy him a muffin to say thanks.

I glance at my phone and notice a text message from Sophie. I've been so busy this morning I completely forgot that she was going to the hospital for her first scan.

I click on the flashing envelope on the screen and immediately a fuzzy black-and-white picture appears. I stare at it, my forkful of chicken and pasta paused mid-air, and my heartbeat quickens slightly. The outline of a curled-up baby is clear to see, and I suddenly feel overcome with emotion, overcome with love for this little baby who hasn't even been born yet but whom I can't wait to meet.

'Hey, are you okay?'

I didn't even hear Jenny come into the room.

'Um, yes, of course.' I wipe a tear from eye with the back of my hand.

'Emma?' Jenny sounds concerned.

I wave my hand dismissively. 'I'm perfectly fine, Jenny, I'm just being silly,' I say, turning the phone so she can see the screen with the picture on it. 'These are happy tears. I don't know why I'm suddenly feeling like this. I've known that Sophie's pregnant for over a month. I guess it's just now, seeing this, it's actually real.'

'I get that.' Jenny smiles and squeezes my hand.

'She's my best friend. We've been friends since we were five years old. I'm just a little...overwhelmed.'

'That's understandable. Things are changing, for everyone. Plus, that baby isn't just your best friend's baby. Matt is Joe's brother, so it's your niece or nephew too.'

I smile broadly now. 'I know, and that just makes it extra special.'

I text Sophie: *That's amazing. I'm so happy for you both xx*

She texts back: *Fancy a takeaway at mine tonight? x*

Sounds good to me. I'll come over around six. x

Great. See you later. x

Looking forward to it. x

As I finish work at five thirty and wave goodbye to Jenny, I decide to call in on Simon before heading to Sophie's. It's only a short drive, and for once the Friday evening traffic is light, so I arrive at his flat within ten minutes. I press the intercom buzzer.

'Hello?' his familiar voice answers.

'It's me, Si. Can I come up?'

'Hello, stranger,' he mocks.

'I know, I know, I'm a terrible friend. Are you going to let me up or not?'

Simon chuckles and I hear the door buzz open.

I climb the flight of stairs to his flat and Simon's already waiting in the doorway.

'Good to see you, Em.' He wraps me in a huge bear hug. 'It feels like ages since I've seen you.'

'It's only been a few weeks, Simon.'

We head through to the kitchen.

'Fancy a beer?' Simon asks, opening the fridge.

'A beer? You can't drink. You have two small children.'

'It's one bottle of beer, Em. It's not like I'm going to be drunk and incapable after one bottle. Believe me, I spent a lot of years building up a resistance to this stuff.' He grins, handing me a chilled bottle.

'Yes, I know. I seem to have spent many an evening trying, and failing, to keep up with your drinking habits.'

'Those were the days, Em.'

I shake my head at him but grin. We definitely had some good times.

'And anyway, I have another responsible adult in the flat. Are you forgetting James?'

'No, of course not.' I glance around. 'Where is he? In fact, where are Fitz and Theo?'

'Don't panic. James has taken the boys to see his mum for an hour or two.' Simon wanders out of the kitchen and I follow him into the living room.

'Oh, so you're all alone.'

'Well, I was. This is my "me" time, Emma, that you're disrupting.'

'I can see that.' I look pointedly at the numerous men's fashion magazines spread across the coffee table as I flop lazily down on to the sofa.

'What?' Simon shrugs perching next to me. 'Just because I'm a husband and a father, I can't keep up with the fashion trends?'

'Si, it will be a dark day when you aren't leading the way with fashion.' I smile kindly. And it's true. Even when we were kids, Simon always looked sharp and at least one fashion step ahead of the rest of the boys.

Just as I take a swig of my beer I hear my mobile phone buzzing in my handbag. I fish out the phone and cringe.

'Oh no.'

'Who is it?'

I bite my lip. 'It's my mum.'

'Well, answer it then. What's wrong?'

'Last time we spoke we had an awkward conversation about babies.'

Simon raises his eyebrows, looking a little amused.

'You know, now Sophie's pregnant.' I hover my finger over the "end call" button, but Simon swipes the phone from my hand.

'No, Simon –' I protest, but it's too late.

'Hi, Rosalind, it's Simon. How are you?' Simon puts on his posh telephone voice and I shake my head at him. 'I'm very well, thank you,' he continues, 'and the twins are perfect.'

There's a pause as my mother says something.

Simon guffaws. 'I know.'

Honestly.

'She's right here. I'll just pop her on for you.' Simon turns to me, a broad grin plastered on his face. 'You take care too.'

He hands the phone over to me and I stick my tongue out at him.

'Hi, Mum. Sorry, I was just in the other room,' I lie.

'Not a problem, darling. I was having a nice catch-up with Simon. Such a lovely boy.'

'Yes.' I glare at Simon and he giggles. 'Lovely.'

'I'm just checking whether you're free next weekend, darling.'

Oh no, this can only mean…

'I'm flying over, Emma, that's all – on business.'

I'm still none the wiser what "business" actually means. I know Mum does something with stocks and shares in New York, where she has lived for the last eighteen years, but despite asking several times I have no idea what, and we've passed the point of it being embarrassing for me to ask again.

'Flying over?' I say.

'Yes, just for three days.'

'Three days?' I repeat like a parrot, but nothing else springs to mind that's constructive.

I know already that this means Mum will be coming to stay with me and Joe. And it's not that I don't enjoy her visits, I do. I just wish I had more notice to prepare.

'So I can stay with you and Joe then?' Mum asks, but it's more of a presumption than a question.

'Of course, Mum,' I reply. 'It'll be nice to see you.'

And I know it will be. Once she's here, it will be fine.

'I'll call you next week to confirm times etc., darling.'

'Okay, speak to you then.'

'Take care, Emma.'

'Bye, Mum.' I hang up the phone.

'Why do you give her such a hard time?' Simon shakes his head at me 'She's not that bad.'

'No, she's not. It's just that she never gives me any advance warning of her visits. She simply announces that she'll be arriving within days, and Joe and I have to drop everything and entertain her.'

'How are things with her and that guy?'

'Parker? I don't know. She was a bit tetchy when I asked about him last time.'

'Maybe that's why she's visiting – man trouble.' Simon nods knowingly.

'Oh God, I hope not. I know my relationship with my mum has developed into a friendship over the last few years, but discussing her –'

'Sex life.'

'Thank you, Simon.' I whack him playfully on the arm. 'Well, that's not something I think I'll ever be comfortable with.'

'Oh, Emma, you're such a prude, always embarrassed at the mention of sex.'

'That's not true, Simon. This is my mother we're talking about, not you and one of your previous liaisons.'

Simon gives me a nudge. 'Hey, they weren't that bad.'

'Yes, they were. I was so relieved when you met James –'

'Not so relieved the first time *you* met him, from what I remember.'

'I don't call walking in on you two naked in your living room doing God knows what "meeting" someone.'

'It was funny, though, the look on your face.' Simon laughs.

'It's funny *now*,' I state. 'At the time I didn't think my eyes would ever recover.'

'I'm surprised that James recovered. He was so shy in those early days.' Simon smiles with the same warm expression that is his instant reaction the moment he mentions James.

I raise my eyebrows at him. 'And I'm guessing you've brought him out of his shell?'

'You could say that.' Simon winks.

'I just hope you behave yourselves in front of the twins.'

'Emma, don't be ridiculous.'

'I know, I'm just kidding.'

'It's not that. It's more like we're so exhausted looking after the little munchkins that, well...' It's Simon's turn to blush now.

'Oh. Right,' I stammer. This is an unprecedented conversation with Simon. In all the years we've been friends, and of legal age, not having enough sex has never been a problem for Simon. Having too many men on the go at one time, yes. But this? This is new territory.

'It's not like I don't love the twins. I do, so, so much.'

'I know that.' I give Simon's hand a little squeeze.

'It's just there's not always much time for me and James to –'

'To just enjoy being a couple.'

Simon nods. 'Yes. That's exactly it.'

'Have you talked to James about this?'

'Yeah, and he's not concerned. He's exhausted too, and he just keeps saying he loves me and that it'll be fine.'

'Well, it's good that he's not worried, and anyone who knows you two is in no doubt about how much you love each other.'

Simon swallows, a little emotional. 'I just don't want us to lose what we had. I miss the…intimacy. And I'm not just talking about sex.'

'I had no idea, Simon. I'm sorry.'

'What for, silly?'

I shrug. 'For not offering to help out at all.'

'Help out?'

'Yeah, you know, babysit Fitz and Theo.'

Simon chortles.

'What? That's funny why?'

'Come on, Em.'

'You know what, Simon, a girl could take offence. Here I am offering to do a nice thing and you're questioning my ability.'

'You're right. I'm sorry, Emma.' Simon clears his throat. 'That's very kind of you, but I wouldn't want to put you under that pressure. It's hard, incredibly hard. There are two of them, you know.'

'Yeah, I know Simon. The fact that they're twins kind of gives it away.' I roll my eyes.

Just then the front door opens and James appears in the doorway, laden down with a large carrier bag and a sleeping twin clutched tightly on each arm.

'Hi, let me help you, James,' I whisper as I jump up off the sofa.

With some difficulty he hands over a snuffling Theo, and I hold on to him like my life depends on it. He's warm, and as I hold him to me I can smell the distinct scents of talc and baby sweat. I look down at Theo, sleeping without a care in the world, which is exactly how it should be. He looks cherubic with his blond curls and ivory skin. It's a good job that Fitz has slightly darker hair or I would have absolutely no chance of telling them apart. Having said that, it's fine when they're together. If I only encounter one, then who knows?

I look up at James as Simon takes a dozing Fitz from him and kisses him. He looks tired. They both do. I glance down at Theo again.

'Hey.' I smile at Simon and James. I don't want James to know that Simon has been discussing their personal stuff with me, though I suspect he knows Simon and I have that kind of friendship. 'I've been thinking. Given that Sophie is going to have a baby in the not-so-distant future, I kind of need some practice with babies. Do you think I could borrow the twins a few times over the next few weeks and months, just to make sure I'm familiar with everything that a baby demands, so I can help Sophie out?'

Simon glances at James nervously, but James looks at Simon and smiles. I don't think I'm fooling anyone, but I continue persistently.

'I was thinking I could have them for an afternoon one Saturday.' I shrug. 'And you two could, I don't know, have lunch out, go to the cinema. It would really help me out.'

'That would be great, thank you, Emma,' James says.

'Just not next weekend, though. Next weekend I have to entertain my mother. But the weekend after is fine.'

Simon nods. 'Come on, let's get these two in their cots.' He looks much more relaxed now.

'I'll get us a glass of wine,' James says, heading into the kitchen.

'None for me thanks,' I say. 'I need to get going. I promised Sophie I'd look in on her.'

Simon and I tiptoe into the twins' nursery and Simon expertly lowers Fitz into his cot without the little one even opening his eyes. I don't quite trust myself with that kind of movement yet, so I just hover next to Theo's cot.

'Come here.' Simon takes Theo gently and puts him to bed then we tiptoe out of the room 'And you come here too.' He pulls me into a hug and squeezes tight. 'Thanks, Emma. You're a good friend. I love you.'

'I love you too, Si.' I kiss him on the cheek, feeling incredibly emotional.

We're all growing up, getting serious responsibilities. I wonder where the time has gone, from when we were carefree with only ourselves to worry about. Not that I prefer it that way. I wouldn't change having Joe in my life, or the extended family that just keeps growing, with James and also Matt, and the twins, and now Sophie's little addition.

'You okay?' Simon interrupts my thoughts.

'Yes, definitely.' I smile. 'We'll talk next week to make the arrangements.'

'Sure.'

'And Si?' I say in hushed tones.

'Yep.'

'If for the entire afternoon that I have your children in my care you and James are naked and sweaty doing God knows what, then please have the courtesy to lie to my face and simply say you went to the museum or something.' I flash Simon a grin.

He just laughs, which makes me think that I got it absolutely right.

We walk back through to the lounge. I say goodbye to both James and Simon and head back out to my car to make my way to Sophie's house.

As I drive I can't help but think of Simon and James. I guess it doesn't matter if you're gay or straight, married or just living together, having children has a massive impact on your relationship; it turns your world upside down. Yes, there are definite benefits, and I know how much Simon and James love the boys and how much Sophie and Matt are looking forward to being parents, but lack of sleep and huge demands on your time can put any relationship under strain. It's a good job that Simon and James are a solid couple, but I suppose it's easy to let that personal, intimate couple time slip away. Everybody needs that, though. It's what keeps you a strong couple.

I make a silent promise to help out Simon and James more, and to follow this through with Sophie and Matt once their little baby arrives. I feel a little guilty that I have time on my hands, but also grateful that I do so that I can be there more for my friends.

When I arrive at Sophie's, I note that she's looking much better. Last week's evening vomiting has passed and her pale-green pallor has been replaced with a soft peachy glow. In fact, she looks amazing.

'Do you want a cuppa?' Sophie asks as I follow her through to the kitchen.

'Sound's great. You look much better,' I say as Sophie presents me with a box of pink, sparkly cupcakes.

'I am, thanks. I feel much better, which on the one hand is great, but on the other it's not as I now seem to be craving cupcakes.'

I laugh. 'That's not so bad. It beats throwing up.'

'Definitely.' Sophie smiles. 'But if I carry on, I'll be the size of a house by the time the baby arrives.'

'I seriously doubt that, Soph.' I raise my eyebrows sceptically.

I've known Sophie practically her entire life, and I've never seen an ounce of fat on her perfectly proportioned curves. Sophie is blessed with the perfect body – boobs and a bum with a flat stomach. If she weren't my best friend, I'd be very jealous. Okay, so I am jealous, just a little. As I bite off a chunk of cupcake, I can't help but glance at Sophie's slight baby bump as she makes the tea. It's barely a bump, just a tiny roundness that if you didn't know better would only look like she's eaten a large meal. Or, simply put, it resembles my stomach on any given day. Hmm.

'So, what's going on with you? Wasn't today the day for you to show your boss your outfit designs?' Sophie asks as she hands me a cup of tea.

I swallow the last mouthful of my cupcake and grimace. 'Yeah.'

'That bad?'

'Yes and no. She likes them, but apparently there's more work to be done on them.'

'Okay. What does that mean?'

'Honestly I have no idea.' I shrug.

'Oh, Emma. How do you get yourself into these situations?' Sophie chuckles.

'If only I knew, I could learn to avoid them. Instead I'm left to flounder as ridiculous situations continue to seek me out.'

'Here, have another cupcake.' Sophie nudges the box towards me. 'You need them more than I do.'

I reach in and scoop up another sparkly cupcake. When it comes to cakes, I don't need asking twice.

'How was the scan? You both must be so excited!'

'We are. And seeing the baby on the screen just…I know it's a cliché, but it made it all real.'

'I get that.' I lick pink frosting from my fingers.

'I mean, I knew I was pregnant, but at this stage you can't feel the baby or anything, you just feel…different.'

'Have you thought any more about names?'

'No, not really. But we're going to start decorating the nursery.'

'That's lovely.'

'So you won't mind coming baby accessory shopping with me on Sunday?'

'Of course not.' I smile. 'I'd be happy to, but won't Matt mind?'

'Don't be silly. He wants to be part of all the important stuff, but picking out wallpaper and curtains he's more than happy to leave to me.'

'Fair enough. It's a date.'

'Great. Now that's sorted, I'll order us a takeaway. I'm starving.'

By the time I leave Sophie's house it's late, and Joe's already in bed when I get home. I tiptoe through to the bedroom and undress before sliding into bed bedside him.

'Hey, how did it go today?' Joe murmurs as he snuggles up to me.

'It went well. She liked the majority of the designs. I just need to figure out what "va-va-voom" means and it will all be fine.'

'What?' Joe mumbles into my hair.

'And prepare yourself. My mother's coming to stay next weekend.'

Chapter Six

The following Sunday is a complete eye opener for me. Never once had I considered the huge volume of items a baby requires – yes, I presumed you must go through a mountain of nappies and baby wipes, but I hadn't expected some of the more delicate items of kit required.

'What's this?' I hold up a weird bottle contraption with a tube attached to the end of it.

Sophie shakes her head at me with a look of amusement. 'It's a breast pump, Emma.'

'Oh…a what?'

'You attach it to your breast to extract milk so you can prepare bottles to take out with you – you know, if you don't want to, or won't be able to, breastfeed the baby where you're going.'

'Right.'

I slide the breast pump back onto the shelf, regretting asking what it was. In fact, I decide, maybe it's better if I stop being inquisitive and leave the baby-stuff shopping to Sophie, while I just look at the cute miniature clothes and stuffed animals.

'Look at this.' Sophie holds up a little stripy jumpsuit.

'You have to get that, and it's unisex so it's perfect.'

'You're right.'

Sophie places it into the already overflowing basket that I'm clutching with desperation, my arms numb from the weight of the bloody thing. I think they must have stretched three inches during the last hour – not that that would be a bad thing.

'I think we're going to have to remortgage the house at this rate.' She looks down at the pile of things flowing from my arms and nearly covering my face.

'Don't worry, Soph, it's best to get it all done in one go,' I state, thinking that maybe Sophie should do any future baby shopping with Matt, who will definitely reign her in, rather than me, who clearly just exasperates the situation. As well as three thousand babygros in a variety of colours appropriate for either sex, there are a number of rattles, dummies, blankets and an animal mobile to hang above the cot.

Sophie sighs. 'I think I'm ready for a coffee after all this shopping.'

'Me too.' I exhale, thinking I've potentially worked up more of a sweat than Sophie this morning – although that's absolutely the right thing to have done. Sophie protested, but I insisted that I carry everything for her. She keeps stating that she's pregnant, not ill, but I don't want to take the chance of her over-exerting herself. Anyway, it saves me a session at the gym. Who am I kidding? I never go to the gym.

We head over to the tills and Sophie pays for the items. I cringe as the shop assistant hands over three large bags and asks for somewhere near two hundred pounds. Jesus, Sophie wasn't wrong about having to remortgage!

We leave the baby store some hour and a half after we arrived there and walk across the street to a coffee shop. I'm laden with two of the three large bags, and inside, as we make our way to a comfy looking sofa that's empty, I nearly take out three small children and an old lady as I try to navigate through the small gaps between the tables.

I unload the bags onto the sofa. 'I'll get the drinks,' I say.

'Don't forget mine's a decaf.' Sophie plops herself down on the sofa.

'I know.' I walk back to the counter, making my apologies to the children and elderly woman on the way.

I order our coffees – soya milk, caffeine free for Sophie, skinny with an extra shot of coffee for me. I collect two blueberry muffins for good measure too. If Sophie can't eat hers then I'll more than happily eat both myself.

'There you go.' Back with Sophie, I slide her mug towards her on the table. 'I got muffins. Are you okay to eat those?'

'Oh, yeah. They're fine, thanks.'

Damn it.

I sit down on the sofa and take a drink of my coffee. 'Can I ask you something, Soph?' I take a deep breath, preparing myself for a delicate conversation.

'Of course, Emma. You can ask me anything, you know that.' Sophie picks up her muffin but just holds it, waiting for me to continue.

'Are you scared?'

'About what? Being pregnant?'

'Well…yes.'

'No, not at all. It feels…'Sophie grins. 'It feels perfect, even though I didn't exactly plan this right now.'

I take a bite of my muffin and nod.

'I mean, don't get me wrong' – Sophie nibbles her muffin – 'I'm terrified of giving birth.'

'Aren't you scared of what happens after that?'

'After that?'

'Yeah, when you get home from the hospital and you have an actual baby to look after.'

'No, I'm not scared about that, Emma. I'm looking forward to that part – to me and Matt having our own little family.'

I suddenly feel a bit emotional, and I stuff some muffin into my mouth to distract myself as tears prick my eyes. Sophie's life is moving on, and I know that we will always be best friends, but once the baby arrives her priorities will change. That's absolutely the right thing – I just worry that we'll stop having so much in common. It's selfish, I know. But I'm not ready to start having children. I don't know if I ever will be.

Sophie reads my mind. 'You'll always be an important part of my life, of our lives, Emma.' I smile. She knows me better than I know myself sometimes.

'I know that.' I croak, still full of emotion.

'Look, we were going to ask you together but…' Sophie takes hold of my hand. 'We'd be really pleased if you and Joe would be godparents to the baby.'

'Really?'

'Of course. I couldn't think of anyone I'd rather have.'

I'm extremely flattered and surprised. I'm not exactly the model for how to live your life. Let's face it, I've made a thousand mistakes along the way, mainly falling for the wrong guy and drinking my way through my troubles, and I'm one of the most ridiculous people I know. If some craziness can happen to me, then it will. But maybe that's a good thing. I can help Sophie's child avoid all of the hideous things that I have encountered. Maybe I'm godmother material after all.

Chapter Seven

The following week goes by in a blur, and before I know it, it's Friday night and I'm preparing to go to the airport to pick up my mum.

'Are you sure you don't want me to come with you?' Joe hovers in the kitchen doorway as I put on my coat.

I smile. 'No, honestly, it's fine. Plus my mother brings that much luggage that there may not be enough room in the car for three adults.'

Joe laughs. 'Okay. I'll prepare some dinner.'

'Don't worry about that.' I wave my hand dismissively. 'I'll call for a takeaway.'

Joe raises his eyebrows at me. 'Emma, your mother has flown halfway around the world. The least I can do is make something nice for dinner.'

'You're too sweet.' I kiss him affectionately. 'Thank you.'

'Hey, come here,' Joe says as I go to pull away. 'I'm not going to get much of a chance to do this over the next two days.' He brushes his thumb over my bottom lip before kissing me full on the lips, his tongue gently searching for mine. A familiar rush of adrenaline tingles down my spine.

I leave the flat a few moments later hot and flustered, and with thoughts I shouldn't have in my head just before seeing my mother.

The journey to the airport is hellish, as it seems like the entire city has descended on the ring road. I only just make it in time, and pull up at the pick-up and drop-off point just as my mother appears through the glass doors. She has some unfortunate airport worker in tow, pushing a trolley on which her luggage is mounted. I shake my head – she does this every time. At least tonight she's chosen a member of staff to be her concierge – last time it was just some random stranger!

'Hi, Mum.' I climb out of the car as she approaches.

'Emma, darling!' She embraces me. 'You look wonderful!'

'Thanks, Mum.'

'But a little tired, darling.' She cocks her head to one side and studies me.

'I'm fine thanks, Mum.' I bite my lip. 'Let's relieve this man of the burden of your luggage.' I smile at the pale young man hovering by the luggage trolley and he smiles back politely.

After some serious physical exertion, we finally manage to load Mum's two cases and her "carry-on" bag into the boot and back seat of my small hatchback, and we re-join the mass of traffic on the ring road. It at least appears to be moving – even if it's only at thirty miles per hour.

'So, how was…' I pause, realising I have no idea from where Mum is en route. 'Erm, your business trip?'

'France, darling?'

'What?'

'I've been to France.'

'Right, of course. So how was *France*?'

'Very busy.' Mum shakes her head. 'These Parisians have no time for anything – dashing here, dashing there, car horns constantly honking.'

So, pretty much like New York, I think, but I'm careful not to say it out loud.

'Well, you can have a nice couple of days relaxing here,' I say. 'Joe is cooking dinner as we speak, and I have wine chilling in the fridge.'

To be fair, I always have wine chilling in the fridge. Although my drinking days have definitely reduced since Joe and I started living together again, and now Sophie's pregnant, my wine consumption has positively halved.

'You're so lucky, Emma, having a man who knows his way around the kitchen.'

'I know,' I concede. 'I'm very lucky to have Joe, a man who knows his way around the kitchen – and the bedroom. My cheeks flush as I recall our kiss before I left the flat.

'Emma?'

'Sorry, Mum, what were you saying?'

Mum just shakes her head at me.

'So, how are things with you and Parker?' I find myself asking, then immediately regret my compulsion to make small talk. I remember Simon's words from last week. Maybe Mum is visiting because she's having "man trouble", and if she is, I'm not sure I want to know the details.

'Parker's fine, thanks,' Mum says. She looks out of the car window, dismissing the conversation. Well, she can't say I didn't try.

'Is Sophie doing well? How far along is she?' Mum glances over at me.

'She had a bad week of sickness, but she's back to her glowing self now, and doing really well. She had her first scan last week. It's crazy when you see a picture of an actual baby.'

'I remember my first scan with you.' Mum smiles. 'But it was different in those days. Not quite as much technology as there is now. Sophie must be really excited.'

'She is. They both are. Matt's a lovely guy. They're going to be great parents. Although I'm not sure that Sophie has totally taken on board exactly how disruptive babies can be to your life.'

Mum looks over at me with a slightly amused look on her face.

'I realise I'm no authority on this subject,' I say. Mum remains silent. 'But I've recently become aware of how much the twins have changed life for Simon. I never thought I'd see anything tame and domesticate him, but his priorities have changed.'

'How so?' Mum probes, although I'm pretty sure she knows the answer, given that she's also a parent, even if it was a long time ago that I was a baby.

I shrug. 'They're just struggling to find time to be a couple, you know, some quality time for the two of them alone.'

Mum glances out of the window again before saying, 'Relationships are a constant challenge, Emma, children or not. It's a difficult balance to achieve.'

I try not to stare at Mum as I need to keep my eyes on the road, even though we're only travelling at a maximum of twenty-five miles per hour.

'We all have too many things to juggle – careers, looking after our home, trying to have some personal time to….' She stops mid-sentence and turns her head towards me.

'Mum?'

'Yes, darling.' She smiles brightly, but she's not fooling me.

'Is there something you want to talk about?'

'Me? No, silly.' Mum shakes her head dismissively. 'I was just… generalising, that's all.'

'Right.' I nod. This isn't the right time to push the subject. Maybe when she's had some wine.

We finally get through the traffic and reach home. I turn into the car park behind the block of flats and pull up in my allocated space. We climb out and I open the boot to start retrieving the luggage.

'They're very heavy, Emma.' Mum states the obvious.

'I know.' I bite my lip. 'I remember that from when I had to load them in not an hour ago.'

Mum puts her hands on her hips. 'I'm simply saying that perhaps we need a hand, darling. You don't have a lift and you live on the second floor.'

I pause for a moment, the first piece of luggage balanced precariously on the edge of the car boot. 'Come on, Mum. We're strong, confident women. This is the twenty-first century – we don't need a man.'

Mum just raises her eyebrows at me as I slide the heavy suitcase to the ground, immediately regretting my previous statement.

'Need a hand with that?'

At the sound of Joe's voice behind me I'm so relieved. I dread to think what Mum has packed in her three cases, but given the weight of this one, I'm tempted to say her entire wardrobe and shoe collection, plus some exercise weights and a drum kit.

I turn to face Joe and discretely wipe my brow with the back of my hand. 'I'm fine with this, thanks.'

A smile tugs momentarily at the corners of Joe's mouth before he composes himself. 'It's okay, Emma. Hi, Rosalind.' He turns to Mum and she embraces him warmly.

'Hello, Joe. So lovely to see you.'

'Don't worry about the bags – I'll get those. You must be tired and ready for a glass of wine,' Joe says to Mum as I hover, still clutch-

45

ing the monstrous case. 'Emma, why don't you and your mum go upstairs and get a drink? I'll follow up with these.' He holds out his hand towards the suitcase I'm holding and I reluctantly hand it over, feeling somehow that I've fallen at the first hurdle in my attempt at "independent woman" status.

'Sure.' I smile. 'Let's go up to the flat, Mum.'

Mum collects her handbag from the car seat and we walk up to my second-floor flat. Halfway up the second flight of stairs I have to silently concede that I would have suffered a severe injury had I actually attempted to lug three heavy bags up here. Maybe twenty-first century women do need a man...for some things anyway. Or maybe my mother could start to travel a little lighter?

As we enter the flat we're met by amazing aromas of garlic and rosemary.

'Mmm, what's for dinner?' Mum asks, wandering through to the kitchen.

I follow, muttering, 'Food that I didn't cook.'

Mum turns and smiles. 'You have plenty of other talents, Emma.'

'I know.' I nod – for one, I always have wine. 'Sauvignon?' I ask, taking a chilled bottle from the fridge.

'Sounds great.'

We catch up on how Joe and I are doing (fine, ticking along nicely, thank you), how Simon and James are coping with the twins (very well under the circumstances, if with the odd hiccup), and how Sophie and Matt are looking forward to the birth of their first child (I think Sophie's looking forward to it much more now she's past the stage of spending the evening with her head over the toilet bowl, throwing up).

The conversation stays firmly on me and my life; we don't venture onto the subject of Mum's personal life – or Parker.

'This is absolutely delicious, Joe.' Mum scoops up a forkful of roast lamb and rosemary potatoes. 'Where did you learn to cook like this?'

Joe blushes slightly. 'My mum is a great cook, and so was my grandmother.' He smiles. 'They both had a lot of influence in my life.'

Mum nods. 'I wasn't the best cook in the world, was I, Emma?'

'I wouldn't say that.' I shake my head. I remember family mealtimes as a child and we were never short of food.

'But baking...now, that's my speciality.' Mum grins.

'Really?'

Joe looks surprised, and I can understand why. The Rosalind Storey of today bears little resemblance to the mother I grew up with as a child. As we speak, my mum is dressed from head to toe in Donna Karan, and that's her looking casual. (I had no idea it was Donna Karan until Mum told me. I like nice things, but can't tell Gucci from Ralph Lauren, despite several years of Simon trying to teach me.)

'It's true.' I swallow the last of my mouth-watering dinner. 'Mum won the local summer cake-baking competition three times in a row,' I say proudly.

'Four,' Mum corrects, and I hide a smile. Despite everything she has achieved, and whatever complicated job she does for a living, she still remembers something as trivial as that from eighteen years ago.

'So, how's work?' Joe asks.

At this point I get lost in the conversation. The mere mention of the Dow Jones and the FTSE 100 confuses me, so I leave the table to make coffees. I'm just faffing around with my coffee-pod machine when Joe appears at my side with the plates.

'Why don't you take the drinks through to the lounge and I'll stack the dishwasher?' He kisses me on the cheek as Mum wanders out of the kitchen.

'No, you cooked dinner. The least I can do is clear the pots.' I take one finished coffee from under the machine and add another pod.

'Emma, you hardly get to see your mum. Go.' He smiles.

'Okay.' I collect the two coffees and head through to the lounge. 'What do you fancy doing tomorrow, Mum?' I ask as I hand her a mug.

'I don't mind, darling.' Mum takes a sip of her drink. 'Why don't we have a lazy morning and I'll make us pancakes for breakfast?'

'That sounds great.'

'Then we can go for a late lunch and have a few drinks in the afternoon. Maybe we try some cocktails.'

I have to nudge myself to remember this is my mother talking and not Jenny or Simon. Cocktails on a Saturday afternoon? I guess my mum is more "New York" than I thought.

Chapter Eight

'What's that amazing smell?' Joe mumbles into my hair as he snuggles closer to me.

'I have no idea.' I say, my voice muffled by the pillow. 'Hang on.' I push myself up onto my forearms. 'Mum said she would make pancakes for breakfast – and that smells like pancakes.'

'We'd better get up then.' Joe rolls over.

'What time is it?'

'Eight thirty.'

'Urgh. It's a little early for a Saturday morning.'

'No, it's not, Emma. It's just that you usually don't see eight thirty on a weekend unless provoked.' Joe tickles the curve of my back and I pull the quilt back over my head.

'Like now, you mean?' I mumble from under the covers.

'I don't call someone making pancakes for breakfast while you loll about in bed provoking.'

Hmm.

'Okay, you're right. I'm getting up.' I fling the quilt off me and pull myself up to a seated position. 'And I smell coffee, proper coffee.'

I pull on my fluffy dressing gown and pad through to the kitchen. It's no surprise that I find Mum already showered and dressed and looking immaculate, as she piles freshly made pancakes onto a serving plate. It resembles a scene from a *Good Housekeeping* article.

'Morning, darling.' Mum hands over a steaming mug of coffee. 'Sit down and I'll bring the pancakes over. Where's Joe?'

I shuffle over to the table, taking a sip of coffee. 'He's just getting dressed,' I say.

'Do you have maple syrup?' Mum asks, opening cupboard doors and inspecting the contents.

I'm about to say, 'I doubt it,' when she suddenly declares, 'Here it is,' and produces a small bottle of syrup. Quite how and why that item has made it into my cupboard is a mystery to me.

Mum places the heaving plate of pancakes down on the table in front of me and my stomach grumbles dutifully.

'Mum, I really appreciate this, but you didn't have to –'

'Emma, I'm your mother and I don't get many opportunities to take care of you, so I want to do this while I'm here.'

'Okay.' I smile. 'Thank you.'

'Wow, they smell amazing.'

Joe appears in the kitchen, showered and dressed. Instinctively I pat down my hair, which I can feel curling up as we speak, as if in protest at the abnormally perfect people I'm surrounded by. How some people can jump out of bed and look their best only five minutes later is difficult for me to understand. My own beauty regime requires much more time and effort to eradicate the puffy bags under my eyes, add some much-needed colour to my cheeks and control my wayward hair with a number of appliances until it finally admits defeat.

I help myself to two pancakes and smother them in maple syrup.

'What are you two ladies going to do with yourselves today?' Joe asks between mouthfuls of pancake.

'Some shopping and a late lunch – nothing too strenuous,' I say.

'Well, I'm at football practice later with Matt, so why don't I drop you off and pick you up? That way you can relax and have a glass or two of wine without worrying about driving home.'

I smile. Joe must be a mind reader.

'That's very kind of you, Joe,' Mum says. 'Maybe we'll have those cocktails, Emma.'

'Sounds good to me, Mum.'

'Why don't you see if Sophie wants to join us for lunch?' Mum offers.

'I'll text her,' I say as I help myself to another pancake.

Once I've consumed far too many pancakes I head to the shower, texting Sophie on the way. By the time I've washed my hair and wandered back through to the bedroom Sophie has texted back:

I'd love to meet you for lunch. Where? What time? X

If we're having lunch in town then there's only one place at which my mother will want to eat. I text back:

Michael's at one thirty x

It's Mum's favourite restaurant. I'll remind her to call and book a table before we head out.

It's an eventful fight between me and my hair this morning, but thankfully it gives up in round three and I pull it into submission with my new hair straighteners, which seem to possess industrial strength. I open the wardrobe and stare at my clothes, flicking between them. I'm trying to make more of an effort in my spare time and refrain from simply throwing on skinny jeans and a t-shirt. I'm, instead, wearing more dresses and skirts in an attempt to be, well, more feminine (Sophie's words, not mine). A few months ago, after three weekends in a row of seeing me in the same t-shirt and jeans, Sophie staged an intervention and dragged me clothes shopping and she then proceeded to "cleanse" my wardrobe of anything that she deemed was "too old", "too worn" or "too boring". Honestly sometimes Sophie can be so bossy. Joe just laughed when I told him, which didn't help the situation at all. I pull a flared grey skirt and a peach vest top from the rack of clothes. That's a compromise as far as I'm concerned.

I swish on some face powder, a neutral eyeshadow, mascara and blusher, and grab my handbag. As I approach the living room I see Joe and Mum sitting on the sofa watching some property development programme and chatting away like two old friends, and I can't help but smile. I'm lucky that Joe gets on so well with Mum, but then he's always made an effort with her, right from day one. I was nervous about them meeting for the first time; my mother can be quite a character. I needn't have worried. Mum adored Joe from the off, but I'm yet to find anyone who doesn't – myself included. In fact, when I think back now, I see that I fell in love with Joe the moment I met him. Any man who could ask me out on a date after I'd sent him flying from his bike (despite his claiming it was his own fault for riding straight into my car) really is a keeper.

I'm grinning as I head into the room. 'Are you ready to go?'

'Sure.' Mum stands up. 'I'll just get my handbag.'

'What are you smiling at?' Joe asks as he pulls me close.

'Nothing.' I shake my head. 'Have I told you how much I love you?'

'Mmm? Not nearly enough.' Joe kisses me.

'Maybe I'll have to show you later,' I whisper.

Mum's voice from the hallway interrupts the moment. 'Emma? Are you coming?'

'On second thoughts, I take that back.' I pull away from Joe shaking my head, amused. 'I'll show you how much I love you tomorrow night, when my mother is safely on a plane to New York.'

Mum and I have a couple of hours to shop together before we meet Sophie for lunch. I'm amazed that in that short period of time Mum purchases enough items to warrant a bank loan, yet this doesn't seem to concern her. How much money she earns, I have no idea, but I can safely say it's more than my own monthly pay cheque.

'Aren't there enough shops in Manhattan?'

'Of course, Emma. They're different, that's all.'

'I see,' I say, although I'm not convinced. Mum just has a shopping addiction, which seems to get worse when she's around me. Soon she'll be forcing me to choose a new outfit too in an attempt to justify her own purchases.

'Now, we just need to find you something,' she says, opening the door of the most expensive department store in the city.

'I'm fine, Mum. I don't need any new clothes.'

Mum strides purposefully into the shop. 'Rubbish, Emma. A girl can never have too many outfits.'

'I love fashion, really I do; I just don't always feel comfortable wearing the latest trend. I'm not "cool" in any way, shape, or form and simply feel like a fraud parading about in cool clothes.' I say, begrudgingly following her through the door. The cloying smell of a hundred expensive perfumes greets me like a slap in the face as we make our way through the makeup counters to ladies' fashion.

Half an hour later, I find myself in possession of a new pair of skinny jeans. Even though I'm supposed to be trying to wear more dresses and skirts, somehow I feel the need for comfort. They're designer, though, so surely that counts.

'What about this, Emma?' Mum holds up a pale-pink dress, sleeveless with a fitted waist and scoop neckline. It's classy and smart, and so not something that I would ever pick for myself.

I feel the incredibly soft material. 'It's lovely, Mum, but I'm not sure where I would wear it.'

Mum holds the dress up against me. 'Oh, I don't know. How about a certain baby's christening?'

Hmm.

'Okay, maybe I'll try it on.'

A few moments later, I stand admiring myself in the mirror. It's as though this dress was made for me. It fits perfectly and I look... like a grown-up. This, I decide, is how I am going to present myself from now on. Sophie may have been onto something with this dress/skirt thing, but I think it's equally important to make sure you pick the right dress. And this is it. I need to find more like this and it only costs...I flip over the tag. Jesus! Two hundred and twenty five pounds! I must get out of this dress immediately – and very carefully – and then we need to leave this department store before I accidentally bankrupt myself and Joe, all in the name of a new wardrobe and a bit of class.

'So?' Mum raises her eyebrows at me as I come out of the changing rooms dressed in my own clothes, with the dress draped over my arm.

'It's stunning, Mum,' I say, returning the dress to the rack. 'But a bit out of my price range. Okay, massively out of my price range.'

'Emma, you need to have a few signature pieces,' Mum says in a voice of authority as she picks the dress back up. 'Now, did it look nice?'

'Yes,' I mumble.

'And did it fit?'

'Yes.'

'Then I think you should take it – my treat for letting me stay with you and Joe at such short notice.'

'No, Mum, I can't let you keep buying me things. I'm thirty-four years old.'

Mum swishes her hand dismissively at me. 'So that's decided

then. You'll take it.'

Sometimes I don't know whether to hug my mum or scream at her. It's a fine line.

'Thanks, Mum. That's very kind. I'll get lunch then,' I say, feeling slightly belittled but also excited about my lovely new dress.

We head out of the department store a few minutes later, me swinging two bags holding my dress and jeans, and make our way to Michael's to meet Sophie for lunch.

The owner greets us both with elaborate air kisses, despite the fact that we're not exactly regulars here, and he ushers us over to a booth in the window. We unload the bags onto one side and I slide in next to Mum.

'Ah, here's Sophie,' I say as Sophie appears, waving from across the room.

'Hi.' I hug her gently, careful not to squash her barely visible baby bump.

'Rosalind – you look amazing!' Sophie exclaims as my mum embraces her.

'You're very sweet,' Mum says gracefully. 'It's the vitamins.' She nods, and I giggle. It's a wonder Mum isn't rattling all day with the amount of pills she takes in the name of youth. 'Let's order some food and then we can have a proper catch-up.'

We all look down at the menus. I'm spoilt for choice; everything sounds amazing.

'Shall we go for the sharing platters?' Mum suggests.

Sophie closes her menu. 'That sounds good.'

Mum does a funny little flick with her hand in the air and I nearly die of embarrassment as the waiter hurries over, notepad at the ready.

'A sharing platter for three, please,' Mum says, 'and a bottle of the New Zealand Sauvignon.' She clasps her menu shut.

'And a sparkling water,' Sophie adds.

'Sorry, Sophie.' Mum shakes her head. 'I wasn't thinking. Shall we cancel the wine?'

'Don't be silly.' Sophie smiles. 'I don't mind you drinking in front of me. I miss wine, I can't deny that, but it's a small price to pay.'

'Yeah, I'm not sure it would be quite so easy for me to get on board with that,' I say. 'Nine months is a long time.'

'I've come to terms with the fact that it will be a lot longer than nine months, Emma.'

'What do you mean?'

Mum laughs. 'She means that after the baby arrives, drinking wine will be the last thing on her mind.'

I glance at Sophie and we share a knowing smile as we silently acknowledge that drinking wine definitely won't be the last thing on Sophie's mind, even if it's the last thing she'll do.

'I'll be a cheap date afterwards too.' Sophie chuckles. 'It'll be Emma carrying me to bed for a change.'

Mum gives me a questioning look and Sophie blushes crimson.

'That never happened,' I say, shaking my head, but a smile tugs at the corners of Mum's mouth. 'Okay, maybe it did once.' I avert my eyes from Mum's gaze.

The waiter reappears and pours wine in mine and Mum's glasses, before placing a large bottle of sparkling water and a glass of ice in front of Sophie. I have to admire her will power. Although, I contemplate, maybe if you're pregnant, you don't need will power at all.

'How are the baby plans coming along, Sophie?' Mum sips her wine. 'Have you got the nursery sorted yet?'

'We're getting there.'

'If that means you're waiting for a man to start doing things then take my advice and don't. Just get on with it yourself.'

I tut at Mum's brazen attitude. 'What does that mean, Mum? Matt's really helping out with all the baby stuff.'

'I'm sure he is, darling, but men sometimes don't take a hint, Emma.'

'You're right.' Sophie interjects, and I raise my eyebrows at her. 'Matt's great,' she states, 'but I want the nursery painting and he's really busy, that's all. Plus there's furniture that needs assembling and that's really not my forte.'

I laugh. 'Mine either, or I'd be the first to offer to help.'

'I know that.' Sophie smiles at me. 'And I'm not complaining about Matt. I want to help him out by getting it done, that's all.'

'I know exactly what you mean.' Mum nods. 'It was the same for me when I was expecting Emma.'

'Really?' I take a sip of my wine and look at Mum.

'Don't look so surprised, Emma. Your father is a good man and has many talents, but being organised isn't one of them.'

Hmm.

'He was so excited about your arrival. He just had no concept of being prepared.'

'Being prepared? Don't you have an estimated arrival date?' I ask, realising too late that I sound like I'm talking about a delivery from Amazon. Sophie giggles.

'Yes, darling, but nature isn't a computerised timetable. Things can change, babies can arrive early.'

'Exactly.' Sophie states. 'And given that it's my first, I just want to make sure we have everything in place.'

'I understand.' Mum nods knowingly. 'Get a man in, Sophie.'

'But won't I hurt Matt's feelings by doing that?' Sophie looks troubled. 'Because that's the last thing I want to do.'

'His pride might be dented for a minute,' Mum says, 'but that will soon fade into the distance and be replaced by relief that he hasn't actually got to do all that DIY himself.'

I shake my head in amusement at Mum's words of wisdom. Just then the food platters arrive: two large boards piled high with bruschetta, olives, numerous cheeses, plus chargrilled veg and chicken skewers. We all tuck in, quiet in our own thoughts. I wonder what Joe would be like in the run-up to the arrival of *our* baby (if we ever have one). I understand Sophie just wanting to get things sorted, and I know Matt's a busy guy, but I can't help but think that getting it done for him might somehow be trampling on his masculinity.

Thankfully Sophie changes the subject.

'Do you miss the UK at all now?' Sophie asks Mum.

'Yes and no.' Mum pops an olive into her mouth. 'The day-to-day stuff, not so much. It's been such a long time since I moved to New York that it seems like a different life.'

I feel a small lump in my throat. It was a different life. Mum and Dad separated when I was only sixteen, and amicable as it was for them, the family unit I had known my whole life was suddenly destroyed. Mum moved to New York a few years later and transformed herself into the high flyer I know today. I'm proud of her for making a success of her life in New York, but also sad sometimes that she's so far away.

'I miss Emma, though.' Mum squeezes my hand.

'Mum...' I blink back threatening tears.

'Oh, I know, darling. You're all grown up now and have your own life, but I miss that fact that I can't just pop around any time I like for a cuppa.'

Popping around any time she likes for a cuppa? Yep, that could be dangerous!

'So how are the revamped dress designs coming along?' Sophie asks, breaking the emotional bubble that we've found ourselves caught in.

'Oh, don't ask!'

'How far along have you got with the changes?'

'Um, Sophie, this is me. How far along do you think I've got?'

'You haven't started?'

'Exactly.'

'What's this dress design?' Mum interrupts.

'Oh, nothing.' I wave my hand dismissively. 'It's just a few dresses I was asked to design at work. A one-off thing to coincide with the Prince and Duchess visiting the city.'

'That's great, darling. Why didn't you tell me? You must show me your designs when we get home.'

'What do you need to change?' Sophie asks.

'In all honesty I don't know, which is why I'm dawdling. Marissa Bamford likes the designs, but she wants more "va-va-voom".' I shrug.

'Right.' Sophie frowns.

'Don't worry, darling. We'll figure it out.' Mum smiles. 'I'm sure your dresses are lovely and it's just a few little tweaks that's required.'

Hmm. I'm not convinced. I'm pretty sure there's no pleasing Marissa, several years of working for her and trying and failing have proved that, but I'll give it my best shot. That's all I can do – maybe with a little help from Mum.

'Have you had a good pregnancy so far, Sophie?' Mum asks as the waiter clears our plates.

'Apart from the morning sickness, that came in the evenings instead, a few weeks ago.'

'You must be excited about the arrival of the baby?'

Sophie grins. 'We both are. We can't wait.'

'Is it your mum's first grandchild?' Mum says, and I cringe inwardly. Here we go, the guilt trip.

'No, my sister has children.'

'Oh, that's nice.' Mum nods.

'I know, I know.' I drink the last of my wine. 'I'm letting you down by not giving you grandchildren.'

'Emma,' Mum says as I huff in my seat.

Sophie looks slightly uncomfortable and I immediately regret snapping, but it's not fair to put someone under pressure to do something just for your own desires, when they're not sure they want to do it at all.

'Emma,' Mum says again as if trying to sooth a disruptive child. 'I know I joke about wanting grandchildren before I'm too old –'

'Joke?'

'Yes, darling, joke. I know it's a big decision whether or not to have children.'

I raise my eyebrows at her but decide to remain silent.

She continues: 'And if you and Joe decide that it's not right for you, then that's okay. I simply want to make sure that you've thought your options through thoroughly, that's all, so you don't wake up in ten years' time and regret your decision.'

'In all honesty, Mum,' I say, 'no-one has a crystal ball. I, we, can only make the decision based on how we feel at this moment in our lives.'

'That's true, darling, and I want you to be happy. That's all that matters to me, children or no children.'

Oh. Why hasn't Mum made that clear before? I thought she desperately wanted to be a grandmother.

'And Emma makes a great godparent to Simon and James's twins,'

Sophie adds, and I smile. 'And she'll make a great godmother to my baby too, I'm sure of that.'

'Of course she will.' Mum squeezes my hand.

'And you're okay either way?' I ask.

'Of course,' Mum says. 'But I'm not the one you need to convince.' She nods at me knowingly.

Oh no, she's right. Getting my mother to accept that I might not have children is one thing, getting my stepmother, Margaret, to get on board with that is another. If she says, 'You'll miss the boat,' one more time at me over dinner, I'll throttle her and suffocate her with her homemade Swiss roll. (Just kidding! I love Margaret, mostly. I'll just take Joe, who's much more diplomatic than I am when it comes to these conversations.)

We enjoy a dessert of strawberry cheesecake and a round of coffees (decaf for Sophie, naturally), and then Mum and I hug Sophie goodbye. She heads off and we lug our shopping bags up the road to a new cocktail bar that's advertising two-for-one cocktails between four and five p.m. – somehow we've made it to four p.m. already.

As we head into the bar, there are already a few customer sitting sipping colourful drinks, which looks promising. We order two Cosmopolitans and take a seat in a booth towards the back of the room. Gentle blues music, a singer with honeyed tones, plays in the background, and I sit back and realise that I could get used to this place. I'll have to bring Jenny here one night – she'd love it.

I take a sip of my drink. Wow – that's strong. I'd better watch myself or I'll end up completely sloshed and it'll be Mum, not Sophie, who's putting me to bed. I still can't believe she said that over lunch. Honestly it happened one time when I couldn't quite function enough to put on my pyjamas and climb into bed. And it was ages ago anyway.

Okay, that's a lie. It was four months ago, and I was so drunk that Sophie found me star-fished on the bathroom floor. I have no idea how she manoeuvred me into the spare room, or got my clothes off and my pyjamas on. I struggle enough changing a shop manikin – it must have been like heaving a dead body around for her. But we promised never to speak of that night. I said my apologies and I meant them. I blame Sophie anyway – it was her stupid idea to drink margaritas. She knows full well that I can't handle tequila! And we promised to keep it from Joe. What he doesn't know can't hurt him. Or rather, it's much better for me and our relationship if he doesn't know about every time I act like an idiot.

Given that we shared a bottle of wine at lunch and we're now drinking extremely potent cocktails, I feel that Mum may be tipsy enough for me to raise the subject of Parker again with her.

'So what's Parker up to while you're away?' I sip my drink nonchalantly.

'Why the sudden interest in Parker?' Mum tries to be equally as nonchalant. I guess we're both as bad as each other.

'I'm not suddenly interested in Parker, Mum, I'm interested in you.'

'What are you getting at, Emma?'

I shrug, realising I'm going to have to drag this conversation out of her. 'I mean, you and Parker were getting on so well. When you came to stay with me at Christmas last year you seemed…happy.'

'And?'

We seem to have done a role reversal now, and Mum has become the flippant teenager.

'And now every time I mention his name you get snappy.'

'I don't.'

'Case in point, Mum.'

She looks at me disapprovingly.

'I just want you to be happy, Mum, that's all.'

She presses her lips into a line and I can't read her expression. I decide to give her a moment and take a drink of my rocket-fuel Cosmopolitan.

Mum exhales loudly. 'He wants us to move in together.'

I'm not surprised by this; if anything, I had expected this sooner.

'And that's bad because…?'

Mum shrugs heavily and bites her lip, just like I do when I'm troubled by something.

'You like him, don't you?' I ask.

'Of course.' Mum sips her drink.

'Do you love him?'

'Love is a very complicated thing, Emma.'

'That's not what I asked, Mum.'

She drinks the last of her cocktail, so I do the same, still keeping my eyes on her expression, but I can't gauge a thing.

'It's complicated,' Mum states, waving over at the bargirl and signalling for two more cocktails.

I'd better get this out of her pretty quickly if she's going to keep drinking at this pace. If not, it could get very messy!

'How is it complicated?' I ask. 'If you love him, and he seems to love you, then what's the problem?'

A young waitress appears between us. 'Two Cosmopolitans?' She places two bright-pink cocktails down on the table.

'Thank you.' I smile at her and she heads back to the bar.

'I've been on my own for a long time, Emma, too long maybe, to make it work living with someone else. It's eighteen years since I separated from your father. I'm stuck in my ways, I like my own space, and I'm not sure I'm ready to give all of that up.'

Oh. I guess I hadn't really thought about it like that.

'Everything I have in New York is mine. It was a huge thing for me to leave the UK, to leave you, and start a new life with nothing familiar, no-one I knew; it was scary.'

Wow. I've never heard Mum talk like this. I can't imagine her being scared of anything, but she did move halfway around the world on her own. That's big, in fact that's huge, and I never really give her enough credit for doing that and for making such a success of herself.

'I never considered it like that, Mum. I suppose I just thought you were heading off to this glamourous lifestyle in New York and that it was all fabulous and amazing. I didn't think about how scary that would have been for you.'

'I made that life for myself, Emma, with hard work and some sacrifices along the way. But I love my life and I love my apartment.'

'And does Parker want you to move into his place?'

'No. He wants us to get a new apartment together.'

'Do you think you *could* live with him?'

Mum pauses for a moment. 'I think I'd like to try. But what if it doesn't work out?'

'Then it doesn't work out.'

Mum looks at me and half-smiles.

'Tell Parker you want him to move into your apartment,' I continue.

'That's not very fair, is it?'

'Aren't you the one who's always telling me that relationships are about compromise? Tell him everything that you've just told me – about how important your apartment is to you and what it signifies. If he loves you and he wants you two to live together then he should be prepared to try.'

Mum takes a drink of her cosmopolitan and laughs. 'When did you become so wise, Emma?'

'Honestly, Mum, I've learned the hard way by making stupid mistake after stupid mistake. If you love Parker then talk to him. I think that's the most important thing I've learned over the last two years. If I'd been strong enough to swallow my pride and talk to Joe sooner then we might not have lost all those months last year when we broke up. If I'd just told him how much I love him, but that I was finding the whole wedding scenario too much, then we might not have broken up at all.'

Mum nods. 'I know you're right. I guess I've known things were moving forward for some time now and I've been expecting this type of conversation. I just haven't done that well in planning what I need to say.'

As we finish our cocktails I can't help but wonder at how everyone has something going on in their lives, no matter what the situation. Take Sophie with the baby coming and trying to manage Matt's feelings, and then Simon and James, who adore the twins but are struggling to balance being parents with finding time to be a couple. Then there's Mum, who I always thought knew all the answers, but now I realise she's just as vulnerable as the rest of us when it comes to relationships. She has the same fears and apprehensions that we all do. It seems to me that there are challenges all around, and I for one am very grateful not to be right at the heart of one.

My relationship with Joe is solid, and apart from trying to decide whether we want children amid all of the babies around us, we're just ticking along nicely.

Although actually that's quite a challenge, and one with no easy answer. Damn it.

My mobile phone vibrates in my pocket and I pull it out and glance at the screen. It's a text from Joe:

Hi. Just finished football training. Are you ready for a lift home? X

I text back: *Hi, yes. We'll be outside the new cocktail bar on St George's Way. How long? X*

Ten minutes x

'That's Joe,' I say to Mum. 'He'll be here to pick us up in ten minutes.'

As we stand up to leave I feel slightly tipsier than I thought I was, and we wobble slightly as we make our way outside. The sun is blinding as we step out onto the street, and somehow I manage to trip over my shopping bags and narrowly miss falling flat on the ground as Mum grabs my arm. It's at exactly this moment that Joe pulls up to the kerb. He steps out the car with an amused smile on his face.

'It looks worse than it is, Joe,' Mum says. 'Emma just fell over her shopping bag. We've only had one or two drinks.'

I pull myself upright and smile sheepishly at Joe, thinking that Mum would have been so much more convincing if she hadn't been leaning on a lamppost.

As we make the short journey home, I decide it's best to remain silent. I don't think Joe's mad at us for being drunk, but it was probably a little unexpected. He's never seen Mum even slightly tipsy. To be fair, I've only seen her drunk on the odd occasion. The last time was the day before Christmas Eve, when she and Parker came to stay: they drank most of the contents of a bottle of sherry and copious amounts of wine, and were giggling like teenagers when I got home and found them.

I smile at that thought. They were happy, Mum and Parker; you could see it in their body language. Moving in together is the natural next step in their relationship. I hope they work things out when

Mum gets back to New York. I glance over my shoulder at Mum in the back seat. She's tapping furiously on the screen of her phone, and I can only hope that she isn't drunk-texting Parker, something she will regret in the morning (we've all been there!).

Once we've arrived home, Mum announces that she's going for a soak in the bath.

'Then we'll order a takeaway,' I call after her as she heads into the bathroom. Despite the huge lunch we ate, I think it would be a good idea to have something to soak up the cosmopolitans from that last bar. In fact, I'd better keep checking on Mum. I don't want her falling into a drunken doze and drowning in the bath.

'So, that was an interesting shopping trip,' Joe says as we walk into the kitchen.

I pause in front of my coffee machine. Was that a question or a statement?

'Um, well, sorry,' I say, fiddling with a latte coffee pod.

'Give that here.' Joe laughs as he takes the pod from my hand and inserts it into the machine. 'Is everything okay with your mum?'

'Of course. Why do you ask?' I try for nonchalant as the coffee machine springs to life and starts gurgling.

Joe raises his eyebrows at me and I contemplate the scene that greeted him: Mum holding on to a lamppost for support and me sprawled over my shopping bags.

'She just needed to talk,' I say. 'Girl things.'

'I see.' Joe hands me my coffee and inserts another pod for himself. 'Man trouble?'

'Not trouble exactly.' I take a slurp of my coffee. 'Just some things Mum needed to discuss. Well, maybe not "needed" to, more like was persuaded to by me for her own benefit.'

Joe laughs. 'I'm guessing that's why cocktails were required?'

I nod. 'Absolutely. I had tried to coerce her into a conversation while she was sober, but she was having none of it.'

'Well, it's good that you and your mum can talk about these things. Although…' Joe takes a drink of his coffee.

'Don't worry,' I say, smiling, 'I don't divulge anything detailed about us to Mum.'

'Good to know,' Joe says, placing his mug on the kitchen side and pulling me in close.

It's not a lie. Okay, so maybe it's a little white one. Over the last few years, I have discussed my relationship with Joe with Mum, but only when we were going through some difficult stuff and I needed some advice. Now I come to think of it, the circumstances were very similar, just reversed. I usually needed some prodding from Mum to start talking about things then.

'So how long do you think your mum will be in the bath?' Joe kisses me deeply and a tingle shoots down my spine, sending me slightly off balance in my tipsy state.

'No.' I shake my head playfully. 'I've told you before. There can be none of that while my mother is staying under my roof.'

'Come on, Emma.' Joe nibbles at my earlobe. 'We'll be quiet.'

I'm tempted, very tempted, but I couldn't look Mum in the face knowing I had been having sex not two rooms away from her while she took a bath, completely unsuspecting.

'Joe, no. We can't.' I try to wriggle from his grasp, but he pulls me in tighter.

'I can be quick,' Joe teases.

I shake my head. 'I know you – and you can't.'

Joe cocks his head to one side. 'That's supposed to be a good thing, Emma.'

'Mum leaves tomorrow afternoon, then I'm all yours.'

'Mmm, promises, promises.' Joe releases me. 'I suppose we'd better order some food then.' He grins.

'I'll grab the Chinese menu.'

I finish my coffee and order a selection of food to be delivered, then we head to the lounge. I think the strong coffee has sobered me up, as I'm feeling perfectly fine as I snuggle next to Joe on the sofa.

A few minutes later, Mum pops her head around the door and comes into the room, dressed in some silky grey jogging bottoms and a matching long-sleeved top. She looks completely refreshed.

'I could have stayed in that bath for another hour.' She smiles as she sits down on the armchair opposite me.

Joe raises his eyebrows suggestively at me and I hide my smile.

'I'm all packed, so I just need to be at the airport at two o'clock tomorrow afternoon,' Mum says, relaxing back in the chair.

'No problem, Rosalind. We'll both take you to see you off.'

'Thank you.' Mum pauses. 'And I apologise, Joe, for maybe having a few too many cosmopolitans this afternoon.'

'Don't worry,' Joe says. 'I know how persuasive Emma can be.'

'Oi!' I jab him none too gently in the ribs.

Mum laughs. 'I do enjoy our time together, darling,' she says.

'Me too, Mum.'

The intercom buzzes, announcing the arrival of food, and I stand up to let the delivery guy into the building. A few minutes later, I find myself eating seaweed for the first time – under protest, I must add. Apparently it's "very good" for me, which it may be, but the texture makes me feel like I'm a horse in a stable chewing hay. I alternate the seaweed with mouthfuls of sweet-and-sour chicken, to make it palatable.

Shortly after we finish our food, we call it a night. As Joe and I lie together in bed, I suddenly feel an overwhelming sense of happiness. I've had a great weekend with Mum, my best friend is happily pregnant and I'm cuddled up in bed with the one I love. Life's pretty good.

'Hey, what are you thinking?' Joe wraps his arm around me and nuzzles my neck.

'I'm just thinking, that's all,' I say into my pillow.

'Thinking what?'

'That life's good, and I love you,' I say, as my heavy eyelids close and I drift off into a deep sleep.

I wake feeling bright and, thankfully, no worse for wear from the wine and cocktails I consumed with Mum yesterday. I guess the Chinese food did its job.

I roll over and kiss Joe on the mouth. 'Do you want coffee?'

'Mmm, sure. I'll be up in a minute.'

I slide out from under the warm covers and pull on my dressing gown. Padding barefoot through to the kitchen, I find Mum already sitting on a stool at the small table, sipping a glass of fruit juice.

'Morning,' I say as I fish two coffee pods out of the box in the cupboard and switch on the coffee machine. 'Do you want coffee?'

Mum smiles. 'No, darling, I'm fine with my juice, thanks.'

I inset a pod into the coffee machine and press the button for my drink. 'It was fun yesterday, Mum.' I glance over at her.

'It was, Emma, and thank you for…for helping me put things into perspective about Parker.'

'No problem.' I lean on the kitchen side, watching my coffee being prepared. 'Have you decided what you're going to do?'

Mum nods gently. 'I'm going to talk to him about moving into my apartment.' She shrugs. 'I'll see what he says and go from there.'

I take my coffee from the machine and start the process again for Joe. 'I think you'll be pleasantly surprised.'

'I hope so.' Mum smiles as she drinks the last of her juice.

I take my coffee and join her at the table. 'So, what do you want to do for breakfast?'

'Let's have pancakes,' Mum declares, then adds hesitantly, 'I assume you have the ingredients?'

'Of course she does.' Joe's voice is confident behind me. 'Emma lives with me. We even have maple syrup.'

I turn to face Joe and smile knowingly. If the food shopping were left to me, it would consist of wine and cheese. 'Your coffee's on the machine,' I tell him.

Filled with far too many pancakes, we head to the airport just after lunchtime. It's a surprisingly warm day, and as I open the window as we drive it feels like summer has come early.

We arrive at the airport and, as usual, it's a mix: crazy hustle and bustle but also people wandering out of the Arrivals doors still dazed and chilled from their holiday. We pull up at the drop-off section of the car park.

'Are you sure you don't want us to come in with you, Mum?'

'Of course not, darling. I'm perfectly fine. You and Joe get off home and enjoy your afternoon.'

We climb out of the car and Joe dutifully drags Mum's heavy bags from the boot of the car.

I hug Mum tightly. 'Let me know what happens with you and Parker,' I say.

'Of course, Emma. I'll be in touch.'

'Have a safe flight, Rosalind.' Joe loads Mum's bags onto a trolley for her.

'Thank you, Joe, and thanks for understanding that Emma and I need girl time when I visit.' She winks.

Joe kisses Mum on the cheek. 'Not a problem.'

'I'll see you soon, Mum,' I say.

She takes hold of the trolley and, despite its weight, easily manoeuvres it towards the departures terminal.

'Take care, Emma. I love you.' Mum waves goodbye before she disappears through the revolving glass door.

'Are you okay?' Joe asks as we climb back into the car.

'Yeah.' I pull my seatbelt on. 'I just always feel a little sad when we say goodbye, as I don't know exactly when I'll see her again.'

'I get that,' Joe says as we pull away from the airport.

The drive home is short and I'm lost in thoughts of Mum and Parker. I guess I always thought relationships got easier as you got older, not that you'd be faced with the same issues in your fifties as in your twenties and thirties. But I suppose the dynamics of relationships don't change with age; you're just older.

We pull up at the flat, and the minute we get inside Joe's lips are on mine, kissing me passionately. He catches me a little off guard, but as his tongue brushes against mine I respond instantly, kissing him back.

'Hey, what's all this?' I ask, breathless, as I pull away from Joe's embrace.

He shrugs, smiling cheekily. 'You said you were all mine once your mother had gone back home.'

I bite my lip, grinning at Joe's comment. 'She's barely left.'

'So? I've been thinking about this moment since I pulled up yesterday to find you falling over your shopping bags on the pavement.'

'Really?' I can't hide my surprise. 'How and why you find my ridiculous behaviour attractive I don't know.'

'You're complex, Emma.' Joe slips his hands down the front of my jeans, causing my breath to catch in my throat. 'That's what makes you so intriguing.'

Intriguing? I'll take that. It's better than ridiculous.

'Let's go to the bedroom, so I can make love to you,' Joe whispers in my ear.

I love it when he's assertive. I take Joe's hand and lead him through to the bedroom. We each undress in seconds and I slide onto the bed, lying down as Joe lies beside me. He takes my face in his hands and kisses me as he moves his body over mine. I can feel him hard against me.

I instantly feel that drugged effect of adrenaline. The chemistry between us is instant and unexplainable. I lie back further into the pillows and close my eyes as I feel Joe's lips on my thighs. His mouth brushes against the soft skin on the inside of my thigh, causing me to bite my lip with desire. His teeth graze my lower stomach, before his tongue traces the line from my navel to my chest. I can already feel a tingling sensation throughout my whole body. By the time I feel him slide inside me, I'm lost in a sensual daze that's addictively overwhelming, and I lose control of myself and everything around me.

Later that evening, I find myself in familiar surroundings as Simon and I meet at Sophie's for tea and chocolate biscuits (our substitute for what used to be wine and tortilla chips). Matt and Joe have gone to play pool, or snooker, or some sort of boring sport, so we are left to gossip freely.

'So how come we're honoured with your presence this evening, Simon?' Sophie asks as she opens the family-size packet of chocolate digestives and places them on the coffee table.

Simon flops down on the sofa. 'A rare evening without James and the boys. They're stopping over at James's mum's house, and James has a work thing tonight, so I'm free as a bird.'

I smile and take one of the chocolate biscuits. 'It's been a while since it was just the three of us.'

'My thought exactly,' Simon states. 'I mean, I could have spent this evening sitting in a bubble bath with my anti-aging face mask on, drinking prosecco, but instead I thought I'd spend it with my two best girlfriends.'

Sophie looks at Simon in amusement. 'You don't actually do that, do you, Si?'

'What?'

'Face masks and prosecco in the bath?'

Simon glances at me, and with some difficulty I keep my expression blank. Then he returns his gaze to Sophie. 'Of course not,' he lies.

'I'll put the kettle on and make the tea,' I say, stuffing the chocolate digestive into my mouth and heading through to the kitchen.

Once we're all armed with a mug of tea and further biscuits, the real conversation starts.

'Can I ask you something?' I say sheepishly to Simon.

'Of course, Em. What's up?'

'Do, um, men get more turned on if there are, um, other people around?'

I hear the plop and splash of a biscuit dropping from Sophie's hand into her mug of tea as she stares at me with a weird expression.

'I'm not sure I get what you mean?' Simon says, perfectly calmly. 'Are you suggesting that Joe has suddenly turned into an exhibitionist? I'm pretty sure that sex in public is still illegal, Emma.'

'You haven't had sex in public, have you?' Sophie exclaims before I can respond to Simon.

'Of course not! Who do you think I am?'

'Well, I just…' Sophie looks perplexed.

'I wasn't talking about having sex in front of people.' Honestly! I do wonder about Simon sometimes, and what he got up to in his dating heyday, prior to James. I'm thankful I don't know the full answer to that.

Simon shrugs. 'Well, that's what you implied.'

'No, it wasn't.'

'Look, never mind all that,' Sophie interjects. 'What did you actually mean?'

I exhale. 'It just seems that every time my mother visits, Joe suddenly can't wait to get me into bed.'

'Really?' Sophie looks at me wide-eyed.

'Yeah, but there's no way in hell I would ever do anything re-motely sexual with my mum staying in the room across the hall.'

'You're not sixteen anymore, Em.' Simon takes another biscuit from the plate.

'I still think that's a line you shouldn't cross, whoever's parent is present.'

'Maybe it's the fear of getting caught – an adrenaline kick, that's all,' Sophie suggests.

'Just be thankful he can't keep his hands off you, honey.' Simon winks and I can't help but giggle. 'I mean, James and I barely have time for –'

'Simon!' I hold up my hand to silence him.

He shakes his head at me. 'What? I thought we were sharing?'

'No, I was sharing and asking your opinion. I don't need to hear the intimate details of your sex life with James.'

'Huh. You'd be lucky. There's hardly any time for action nowa-days, now we have the boys, and if there is, we're both too knack-ered to try it on.'

'Oh, Si.' I squeeze his hand.

He shrugs. 'I'm not complaining exactly. Life changes. I'm just saying be thankful for your carefree, "we can have sex any time we want" lifestyle.'

'He's right.' Sophie downs the last of her mug of tea.

'What are you talking about?' I say. 'You're pregnant. That means you had sex.'

'Exactly. I *had* sex.'

'And now you don't?' I ask cautiously.

'No. Matt won't come near me like that. He thinks he might dam-age the baby somehow.'

'And will he? I mean, can you have sex when you're pregnant?'

Sophie just shakes her head at me like I'm an idiot.

'What? I don't know these things,' I huff.

'Well, just because you're pregnant, doesn't mean you stop having feelings. If anything, your hormones are all over the place and more sensitive than normal.'

'Yeah, but to be fair, hun, Matt probably didn't think it was a good idea to seduce you while you were green around the gills and looking like a crazy woman.'

'Simon!' Sophie looks furiously at Simon, pursing her lips. 'I had a short period of morning sickness, which, I will admit, was not confined to the morning and perhaps did not leave me looking or feeling my best.'

'Soph darling, you had a virtual sign around your neck stating "Enter with caution".' Simon chuckles. 'It's no wonder Matt's treading carefully.'

Sophie folds her arms defensively.

'Okay, I think that's enough sharing,' I say. 'I'm sorry I started this conversation.'

'So am I,' says Simon. 'Here Soph and I are, starved of sexual activity, and you're complaining that your man's trying to bed you at every opportunity.'

I think about this for a moment. Perhaps Simon's right. I should be glad that Joe so obviously still wants me in that way. Maybe I'm the only one who's hung up on when and where.

'Anyway,' says Simon, handing me his empty mug, 'enough of the tea. Don't we have anything stronger?'

'There's some vodka and soda in the cupboard.' Sophie says.

A few minutes later, Sophie and I are sipping another cup of tea while Simon drinks a double vodka and soda. The atmosphere in the room seems to be a little calmer.

'Maybe you should talk to him.' I say.

'Who?' Sophie looks at me.

'Matt, silly. Tell him you still...you know...'

Simon nods at us knowingly. '...Are a woman who has needs.'

Sophie and I giggle at Simon's words.

'He's right, Sophie,' I tell her.

'I know. I guess this whole pregnancy thing is new for us both.'

'And you need to talk to James too,' I say, nodding at Simon.

'Yes, Emmie.' Simon scowls playfully at me.

'There are other ways that you and James can be intimate with each other if you're struggling for time and energy.'

'Name some,' Simon teases.

'Come on, Simon. You know what I mean. Relationships don't have to consist purely of sex.'

'Says the girl who's having it all the time.' Simon cocks his head at me.

'Okay. I'm not talking to you about this anymore.' I sit back on the sofa and tuck my legs underneath me, nursing my cup of tea. 'You're impossible.'

'Oh, don't take offence, Em. I'm just playing. And you're right: I should make more of an effort to just be physically close to James.'

'Wow!' Sophie grins. 'Listen to us. We really are all grown up. Who'd have thought we'd reach a point in our lives where Simon agreed that cuddling is just as important as sex?'

'Very funny,' Simon says, taking a gulp of his vodka. 'When your baby arrives, you'll know exactly what I mean.'

We're silent then for a moment, all contemplating our own relationship status, I suppose, and realising that whatever the situation, physical and emotional closeness are equally important. Life changes and provides challenges, but the core relationship requirements don't change.

When I get home later that evening, I find Joe already in bed, reading something on his tablet.

'Hi. How were Sophie and Simon?' he asks as I enter the bedroom.

I think about the odd conversation about sex that dominated our evening and decide not to divulge any of that, simply saying, 'Yeah, fine, it was good to catch up with them both.'

I undress and climb into bed. 'What are you looking at?' I ask, snuggling up to Joe.

'Nothing important.' He switches off the tablet and places it on the bedside table, before turning out the light and pulling me closer to him. 'Goodnight, Emma.'

'Goodnight.'

As I lie there, warm and safe, with Joe's arm wrapped protectively around me, I'm one hundred per cent sure that my words to Simon earlier were right. Yes, sex is important in a relationship, but the warmth of a lover's touch and the security that being wrapped in their arms provides are unmistakably important too, and perhaps we should all appreciate that more.

Chapter Nine

I'm so excited this morning; I can't believe that Lola is coming back to work at the shop. The three of us had such a good time when we worked together before. Not that Jenny and I don't enjoy our time together; it's just that it's been blighted by the ridiculous and unpredictable Julia Bamford appearing unannounced in a virtual puff of smoke and barking orders at us all day. We're never relaxed, just constantly functioning on our frayed nerves. But all of that is about to change, as Julia will become a permanent fixture in the London shop with her dear aunt, Cruella de Vil, also known as Marissa Bamford.

I pull up in the car park, and head straight to the coffee shop to collect skinny lattes for a celebration of Lola's return from the opposite side of the world. (I'm still amazed that she went backpacking around Australia and survived. I'd have been eaten by some human-sized spider, or been lost forever in the wilderness of the outback, or have created fear and confusion in the locals after three days without my hair straighteners.) We will, of course, celebrate in the more traditional style of alcohol and gossip on Saturday night, but for now good old-fashioned caffeine will have to do.

A few minutes later, I'm wobbling along unsteadily, carrying a flimsy cup-holder made of cardboard, which is clearly the wrong material to support large, heavy cups of liquid, while trying not to dowse myself in the very substance. I reach the back door of the shop, but between the three lattes and my handbag I fail to have a spare hand to actually open the flipping door, so I have to resort to shouting Jenny's name.

As the door is pulled open, I'm greeted by a skinny, suntanned figure that I barely recognise.

My mouth flaps open unattractively. 'Lola?'

'Emma!' Lola squeals, pulling me into a hug, nearly upending the lattes I've so carefully negotiated to this point. 'It's so good to see you.'

'You too, Lola.' I stand back in amazement. Lola was always skinny and pretty, but now she's glowing, literally glowing, with sun-kissed, highlighted hair and not a sign of stress anywhere on her face. 'You look amazing,' I say in awe as we enter the shop.

Jenny appears. 'I know, I'm green with envy too. If that isn't reason enough to pack a pair of clean knickers and head straight to the airport, I don't know what is.' Jenny takes a takeaway coffee cup from me without even enquiring what might be inside and takes a swig.

Lola grins. 'We've got so much to catch up on.'

And she's right. The last twelve months have been an interesting ride.

So the day is filled with story after story, interspersed by gasps and interruptions of 'No!', 'Really?' and 'I can't believe that', as I proceed to tell Lola about how I called off my wedding to Joe, moved out, kind of dated a student from college, was stalked by my ex-boyfriend Chris and then finally found happiness again last Christmas when Joe and I were reunited. As I hear myself telling the tale, I can't help but liken it to a storyline in a ridiculous soap opera. I never actually thought about it before as a whole, I just kind of went from one incident to another without linking them all, but in reality I see now that a lot of crazy stuff has happened in the last few years – and I appear to be the common denominator. Hmm. At least it has a happy ending.

Jenny delights Lola as she regales her with snapshots of her frequently changing love life, and I can't help but smile. I'm so glad that's not me now – dating is exhausting! Although Jenny seems pretty keen on her current man, Scott, and they've been dating for a few months.

Lola, as it turns out, had the most amazing time backpacking in Australia.

'I met a guy.' Lola blushes, which must mean it's serious, as she was never shy about previous guys.

'Ooh, do tell.' Jenny gives Lola a nudge.

'He's called Hugo.'

'Is this the guy we've seen snaps of on your social media?' I ask, vaguely remembering some good-looking guy appearing in most of the photographs Lola posted over the last six months.

She smiles instantly. 'Yeah, that's him.'

'So how did you two meet?' Jenny probes.

'He was one of the guides on a tour. We got talking in one of the bars the tour stopped on and...' Lola shrugs.

It's my turn to prod now. 'And?'

'And he kind of hung around. He was staying not far from me at that time.'

'Was it serious?' Jenny asks.

'Yeah.' Lola grins.

'You really liked him, didn't you?'

'I do. I really like him.'

'Hang on a minute,' I interrupt. 'You said "do", not "did".'

Lola glances at Jenny, then back at me. 'He came back with me.'

'What?' Jenny's surprise is evident.

'So he's here?' I ask. 'In England?'

Lola nods. 'In South Yorkshire as we speak.'

'How?' Jenny's still in shock.

'He applied for a travel visa for six months. He's been to England before, so it wasn't a problem and it got authorised pretty quickly.'

'Wow.' Jenny shakes her head. 'He must be quite a guy.'

'He is,' Lola gushes. 'He's the perfect guy.'

'Well,' I say 'Then the most important question is, when do we get to meet him?'

'Soon.' Lola smiles. 'We're taking some time to adjust to England after Australia.'

Jenny laughs. 'I'll bet. A massive reduction in temperature will do that for you.'

'Not just that,' Lola says. 'Australia has beautiful beaches, and I was on holiday so I didn't have to worry what I was doing from one day to the next. It really was amazing.'

'Aren't there huge spiders, though?' I enquire, cringing at the thought. I think my worst nightmare would be facing a big, hairy spider the size of my hand and having nowhere to run. I'm not sure any golden beach, or even the Sydney Opera House, would be worth that fate.

Lola laughs. 'I didn't see any.'

'That doesn't mean there weren't any,' I state. 'There could have been hundreds of the things following your every move.'

Jenny rolls her eyes. 'Always the pessimist, Emma.'

'What can I say? I've learned from past experience that if something crap can happen to me, such as being attacked by a deadly spider, then it usually will.'

Jenny nods. 'Unfortunately, that's true.'

We all giggle, each of us probably remembering a different scrape that I got myself into over the last few years.

'So when do we really celebrate Lola's return?' Jenny asks as we lock up the shop later that day.

'Saturday night? Tequila!' Lola grins.

Oh no! Lola and Jenny's drinking habits were legendary and I struggled to keep up with them at the best of times, but tequila? There has never been, and never will be, a good enough reason to drink that poisonous liquid. It's vile, and putrid, and I will not be drawn into doing shots of such potent alcohol. I've made that mistake before and paid the very high price.

Saturday night arrives all too quickly.

'It's my round,' Lola shouts over the beat of a tune I don't even recognise. How long is it since I was last dancing in a nightclub?

It's one o'clock in the morning and I'm in a new club just off the high street that opened last month. Apparently it's the only place to be. It's high class, bang on trend – and way out of my league. Old-school nineties' dance tunes are usually my thing, but I find myself shaking my hips to the repetitive beat of what sounds like an over-excited drummer. The rest of the drunken crowd seem to be loving it, so I play along. To be fair, the amount of vodka and Diet Coke that I've consumed over the last few hours has added to my rhythm, and I think at this point I could pretty much dance to silence.

Lola heads off to the bar, while Jenny and I remain bopping on the dancefloor. A few moments later, Lola returns and waves us over to a tall table and stools. As we sashay over I see the three shot glasses lined up alongside a saltshaker and lemon wedges and my heart sinks.

I have a very vivid flashback of the last time I downed tequila shots with Jenny and Lola. It was the evening that I met Connor, a.k.a. Johnny – or rather, Connor sought me out. I was drunk and vulnerable, and I ended up back at his apartment and in his bed. That would have been bad enough, but I found out only days later that he was actually dating my best friend, Sophie. A whole catastrophe of events followed, which led to the near destruction of mine and Sophie's friendship, and actually the very near destruction of me in a car chase and accident. Although it's irrational and I know that many elements impacted on that whole situation, I can't help but feel that the starting point of that horrible episode was a shot or three of tequila.

'Come on.' Lola waves her shot glass around, barely keeping the vile liquid in the tiny glass. 'Bottoms up!'

I cringe, begrudgingly, pick up my own shot glass and stare at it with trepidation.

It's only tequila, I reassure myself. Nothing bad is going to happen tonight if I drink just this one shot (except that I might throw up).

Lola sprinkles grains of salt onto the back of my hand. I exhale, lick the salt, pull a face at the disgusting taste, then raise my glass. 'Cheers.'

We all clink glasses, and I down the shot in one. My stomach flips dangerously as I bite into a lemon wedge – and the rest, as they say, is history. Well, three more shots at least.

As Jenny begins to entertain us with tales of her latest date with Scott, the accountant, I can't help but become fixated on a sun-tanned Adonis who's appeared in my eye line across the other side of the dance floor. He strolls confidently across the room, his strong physique clearly visible beneath his jeans and shirt, a large smile on his golden face.

Oh my.

Oh…wait…

He's heading over here, right towards us.

No...really?

Mr Adonis sidles up to Lola and casually drapes his arm around her shoulder, and then I see it, the resemblance to the guy in the photos on Lola's social media profile. The suntanned god is Hugo, the travel guide she met while on her Australian travels and seems completely taken with. Mind you, I think I'd be flattered too if a guy flew halfway around the world to spend time with me.

'This is Hugo,' Lola gushes, as Hugo smiles at me and Jenny, and I swallow my embarrassment at having checked him out from across the room. The photos really didn't do him justice at all.

'Nice to meet you, ladies.' Hugo's accent is clearly Australian and sounds so out of place in Yorkshire, but he's so friendly that Jenny and I simultaneously return his smile.

Hugo, as it turns out, is the most charming man you could ever wish to meet (besides Joe, of course). His adoration of Lola is evident, and she practically swoons in his presence. They're very cute together, and clearly in love. I'm pleased for Lola; she's a really nice girl and she deserves a lovely man. It looks like Hugo is the whole package too. He tells us story after story of the experiences he and Lola had while together in Australia. He strokes Lola's hair intermittently as he talks, and Jenny and I are a captive audience. I think we're all swept off our feet a little by Hugo!

'Sorry, ladies.' He suddenly stops one of his tales. 'I've been prattling on for ages. Can I get you all a drink?'

'That's very kind of you,' I say. 'I'd love a vodka and Diet Coke, please.'

'Me too, thanks,' Jenny adds, and Hugo heads off to the bar.

'You didn't tell us how gorgeous your boyfriend is.' Jenny nudges Lola, but Lola just smiles coyly. 'And if he's half as good in the bedroom department as he looks then –'

'Jenny!' Lola blushes bright-red, and we all giggle.

When Hugo returns with the drinks a few moments later, I can't quite meet his eye with Jenny's comment still fresh in my mind.

'Shall we call it a night after this one?' Jenny takes a sip of her vodka and Coke.

'Yeah, I suppose we should,' I say, wobbling ever so slightly to my left – how much have I actually drunk tonight? The fact that I can't recall doesn't bode well.

Once we've finished our final drinks, Hugo dutifully escorts us all outside, making sure we (well, maybe just me) remain upright. He then insists on us all getting in the same taxi and dropping me off first, then Jenny, so he can make sure we get home safely.

How sweet. I like Hugo. He's definitely a keeper.

Chapter Ten

'How are you feeling this morning?'

I can hear Joe's voice through the thick white fog that's consumed my very being. I try to open my eyes and fail miserably. But as the aroma of freshly brewed coffee wafts temptingly in front of my nose, I force one eye to open.

'Good morning.' Joe is hovering next to me with a smug look on his face. 'How much did you have to drink last night?'

A smile tugs at the corners of his mouth and his cute dimples appear. But this morning I find them more annoying than cute, as I fear that he already knows the answer to his probing question and he's simply taunting me in my hungover state. Bloody tequila. I was perfectly fine until Lola made me drink that stuff.

'Not too much,' I lie, sliding myself up against the headboard into a semi-seated position.

'Right.' Joe nods, smirking.

I follow his gaze and glance down. Not only do I have my pyjama top on backwards, but it's also inside out with the label flapping in full tell-tale fashion right under my chin. I choose to ignore this.

I clear my throat. 'Is that coffee for me?' I try to smile, but weirdly this causes my whole head to hurt.

Joe hands the cup over, but as I stare down at the brown liquid I'm pretty sure that I don't actually want to put it anywhere near my stomach. In fact, I don't think I want to eat or drink anything ever again, as it feels like I might throw up just at the thought of food.

'So you're fine for today then?' Joe sits down on the bed next to me, and the movement of the mattress as he sits causes my stomach to turn unpleasantly. I swallow, hoping against hope that I'm not going to be sick right here in my bed in my inside-out, back-to-front pyjamas.

'I'm perfectly fine,' I state. 'I'm just a little tired, that's all.' I realise I lack conviction, given that I can't quite get myself into a fully upright position and the fumes emanating from me must be fifty per cent proof.

'Great.' Joe stands back up, causing the mattress to move again. I feel like I'm in a dinghy on the sea, and I hold my breath and grip the side of the mattress for support. 'You need to be ready in an hour,' he adds.

What?

'An hour?' I enquire calmly, while racking my brain for some recollection of what could possibly be happening in an hour that requires me to leave the sanctuary of my bed and force myself to be mobile.

'We're going to Sophie and Matt's for brunch.'

Shit!

'Of course.' I go to drink from the coffee mug, but instantly stop myself. 'I'll get in the shower in a minute.'

'Okay. I'll just pop out to the shop for some bits while you get yourself ready.'

Thankfully, Joe leaves the room then, and a few seconds later I hear the front door close too. I lie back down, pulling the pillow over my head and squashing it to my temples in a vain attempt to force the hideous pain from my head.

Five minutes later, after ricocheting off three walls and a door, I find myself in the shower, crying. Instead of melting away my headache, each drop of water simply seems to anger it further. As I lather my body in shower gel, I reprimand myself out loud.

'Emma, you are too old to be doing this. You are easily led and lack the mechanism that makes you stop and say, "I think I've had enough to drink."

'Why, Emma? Why do you do this to yourself? Now you have to attempt to function today, mixing with other human beings while trying to pretend that you're not massively hungover and wishing you were alone under the duvet, instead of forcing food down at brunch with friends.'

Right, I decide, this is the last time. I am not going to get stupidly drunk again, no matter who is holding the shot glasses, and I'm not, under any circumstances, going to drink that damned tequila ever again – ever!

By the time Joe returns, I'm dressed, wearing a little makeup and about as presentable as I'm going to get today. I'm perched on the edge of the sofa, feeling only mildly less queasy than when I first attempted to move this morning.

Joe pops his head around the living room door, and I force myself to stand up. He looks me up and down, his face expressionless, but I recognise the glint of amusement in his eyes.

'I think I'd better drive,' he says, and I don't doubt that for a minute. If I can negotiate my body into the car in this state, I'll be pleased; negotiating a moving vehicle is not an option. Plus I may be ever so slightly over the legal limit for driving.

We head out of the flat and down the stairs (I lag behind, clinging on to the handrail for support). As we reach the outside, the cool, crisp morning slaps me in the face and it's just what I need. I gulp at the air as we make our way to the car. I'm feeling marginally better as I slide into the passenger seat and clip on my seatbelt – that is, until we set off moving. I then spend the rest of the journey praying that the remaining alcohol from last night that's still sloshing around in my stomach stays there and doesn't end up in my lap.

'Hi.' Sophie welcomes us as we arrive at her and Matt's house a short but unpleasant journey later.

'Hey.' Joe kisses her on the cheek. 'Be gentle with Emma this morning; she's a little worse for wear.'

He steps past Sophie into their hallway and I swear he's chuckling under his breath. How rude that he should be enjoying my clear discomfort! I'm outraged. As a loving boyfriend he should be sympathetic to my unfortunate predicament.

'I am not,' I protest a little too sharply.

'No, of course not.' Sophie gives me a hug as I enter the house.

'Thank you, Sophie.'

'You look a *lot* worse for wear, Emma, not a little.' She raises her eyebrows at me. 'What the hell were you up to last night?'

Great. Thanks. With friends like this who needs enemies?

'I merely had a few drinks with Jenny and Lola to celebrate Lola's return,' I say.

Sophie smiles. 'A few drinks?'

'Of tequila,' Joe interjects before I can respond.

'I see.' Sophie nods as she ushers us through to the living room.

'Excuse me, I'm right here,' I state. 'I'm fine. I feel a bit tired, that's all.' (I repeat the mantra I said to Joe earlier.) 'And how do you know it was tequila?'

'Do you remember getting home last night?' Joe cocks his head to one side.

I bite my lip. Okay. This could be dangerous. I remember leaving the bar in an ever-so-slightly wobbly state with Lola's charming new boyfriend, Hugo, helping me into the taxi. Then it's a complete blank. I don't remember anything about the journey home, or getting into the flat – nothing until I woke up this morning feeling horrendous. I'm perhaps provoking a conversation I don't actually want to have.

Matt, who until now has very wisely remained out of sight, appears in the living room and hands me a glass of what looks like purple milkshake. 'If you're not feeling too great, Emma, then drink this. It will have you back to normal in no time.'

I take the glass from him and sniff it warily as my stomach swirls in protest. 'What's in it?' I pull a face.

'Nothing bad,' Matt says unconvincingly.

I glance around and see three faces watching me expectantly. No pressure then. I weigh up the options. Either I don't drink it and prove everyone right that I'm so hungover I feel like I might actually be dying, or I drink it and feel much better, as Matt has so kindly predicted. Actually, there's a third option: I drink it and throw up. I guess there's only one way to find out, and I'm not conceding my hangover status. I bring the glass to my lips and pause for a second before downing the thick, gloopy liquid in three gulps. My stomach rebels for a second and a wave of nausea follows, then nothing.

There's an expectant pause, as clearly everyone else also suspects that I might throw up.

I hand the glass back to Matt, feeling quite virtuous. 'Thank you.' There's a collective sigh of relief.

'Ready for brunch?' Matt asks.

I grin. 'I thought you'd never ask. I'm starving.'

Joe shakes his head at me, then says to Matt, 'I'll give you a hand in the kitchen.' He's clearly aware that the cooking will be done by Matt and not Sophie. Somehow both brothers have inherited fantastic cooking skills from their mother, while Sophie and I are limited in our culinary knowledge – or should that be lacking?

Joe and Matt leave the room as Sophie and I flop down on the sofa.

Sophie looks at me. 'Are you really okay?'

'Honestly? No, I feel like I've been run over by a bus and then they've reversed back over me just for good measure.'

'Oh dear.'

'I feel better now, though, than I did when I first woke up, and I don't know what was in that milkshake that Matt gave me but it seems to be doing the trick. I feel less like I might be sick at any minute.'

'I think it's best that you don't know what was in it. He's been known to consume stuff with raw eggs and –'

'Soph.' I hold my hand up. 'I love you, but stop talking now.' Raw eggs? Urgh! 'So how are you?'

'I'm good, feeling well. In fact, you look greener today than I ever did during my morning/evening/all-day sickness.'

'I beg to differ. Remember that night when you answered the door to me looking like Medusa, and we spent the evening with you with your head over the toilet bowl and me holding back your hair?'

'Oh, yeah. You are a good friend.'

'I know.'

'And the colour is starting to come back into your cheeks.'

'It's the bacon smell coming from the kitchen,' I say. 'It's bringing me back to life.'

'So was it worth it?'

'What?'

'Did you have a good night?'

'From what I can remember, yes. I need to never, ever drink tequila again, though.'

'I think I've heard that before.'

'I'm serious. I mustn't let myself be talked into downing shots of it.'

'No, only bad stuff can happen where tequila is involved. It impairs your vision and your morals.'

'Agreed. It was good to see Lola again, though. I'm really glad she's back working with us.'

'Has she enjoyed her time in Australia?'

'Very much. She's returned bronzed and glowing, and with a good-looking man on her arm.'

'Really?'

'Yep. Hugo is the perfect gentleman, along with being funny, extremely handsome and charming to boot.'

'Sounds too good to be true.'

'I would have agreed with you had I not met him in the flesh last night and seen him for myself. They're so in love; it's cute.'

'Yes, but can he cook Sunday brunch as well as Matt?' Sophie smiles.

'I doubt it. It smells fabulous.' My stomach grumbles and I take that to be a sign that it's decided to give me a pass back into the land of the living and is ready to refuel.

As if on cue, Matt calls from the kitchen, 'Food's ready.'

We make our way through to the kitchen and I realise I'm feeling much better. Raw eggs or not, whatever was in that potion of Matt's has worked.

The kitchen table is filled with scrambled eggs, pancakes, bacon, syrup, fruit and Greek yoghurt, and the smell of freshly brewed coffee lingers amid the sweet smells.

'This looks amazing, Matt,' I say as I sit down at the table. 'I really need to learn how to cook proper food.'

'Why? You live with my brother and he loves cooking.'

'That's true.'

'Thanks, Matt. Now Emma won't even so much as heat a pizza.' Joe laughs.

'I wouldn't want to take away your joy of feeding me.' I kiss Joe cheekily on the lips. 'I know how much you like taking care of me.'

'Good job really.' Sophie helps herself to two pancakes. 'Or Emma would survive purely on cupcakes, wine and skinny lattes.'

'And your problem is?' I take a scoop of fruit and yoghurt. 'That's a balanced diet.'

We spend the next few hours eating, chatting, and easing our way through the Sunday afternoon. Later, as Joe and I arrive home, I find myself feeling a little weary.

'I'm going to take a bath,' I say as I hang up my coat.

'Okay, I'll only be a minute,' Joe calls as I head into the bathroom.

I pause in the hallway 'You'll only be a minute?'

'Yeah. I thought I'd jump in too.'

'Um, okay.' I pad slowly into the bathroom. This is new. In all the time I've been seeing Joe, we've never had a bath together.

I start running the water and add a glug of bubble bath. Glancing in the mirror, I acknowledge that I've looked better, although the grey/green pallor from this morning has at least gone. I strip down to my underwear and almost instantly feel Joe wrap his arms around me from behind. He kisses my neck and pulls me in close, and I enjoy the feel of the warmth from his body.

He releases me and takes off his shirt and jeans, and as I watch him standing in just his boxer shorts I can't help but feel slightly aroused. He looks after himself and it shows in his toned body. Joe tests the water with his hand and then turns off the taps, before taking off his boxer shorts and stepping into the bath.

'Are you getting in?' he asks, remaining standing naked in the bath.

'Of course,' I say as I quickly pull off my own pants and bra, and I climb in. As I sit down in the warm, fragrant water, instantly I feel relaxed. Joe slides down behind me and wraps his legs over mine. I lay my head back onto his chest, close my eyes and just enjoy the feeling of the water lapping over my hair as it gently massages my head.

'I'm sorry I came home so drunk last night,' I say quietly.

'There's nothing to be sorry about.'

'I was quite ill this morning.'

'I figured that, Emma.'

'Sorry.'

'Stop saying sorry.'

'Aren't you going to say something like, "It was self-inflicted, so I have no sympathy"?'

'No, I'm your boyfriend, not your mother.'

'Oh.'

'I do worry about you, though, that you were that drunk. I don't want anything to happen to you.'

'I was with Jenny and Lola; they're good friends. They wouldn't let anything happen to me.'

'Not intentionally, I know, but if they were as drunk as you were then –'

'I think I just react badly to tequila,' I say, having no idea how drunk Jenny and Lola were at the end of the night. I was certainly more than merry.

Joe laughs. 'I think a lot of people react badly to tequila, Emma. I'm just saying –'

'I'm thirty-four and should know better?'

'Emma, I'm not telling you off. I'm just saying that I love you and I want you to be safe.'

'Okay. Thank you. I promise, for my own benefit – if only to avoid having such a bad hangover – I will not consume tequila again.'

'You were funny, though.'

'Funny?'

'Yeah, when you came home.'

'Oh.'

Funny how? I'm pretty sure I wasn't telling "knock, knock" jokes. In fact, I'd rather not know how "funny" I was in my drunken state, thank you very much.

'You know what, Joe? Given my slightly delicate state today, I think we should follow the rule: "If we don't talk about it, then it didn't happen." How about that?'

'Alright,' Joe concedes as he kisses my cheek. 'But I'm going to need a reward for my silence.'

'And what kind of reward would you like?' I say, leaning further back into Joe's warm, wet body.

'You. Just you,' he whispers in my ear as his hands slide further around my chest, cupping each of my breasts. I can feel him hard against me and feel the familiar tingle of excitement run through my body.

Joe scoops me up and the water sloshes over the side of the bath, but neither of us gives it a second thought. He carries me, still dripping, towards the spare room and lowers me down on the bed. I lie back, not caring that my hair and body are wet. I want Joe now, inside me, making love to me.

Joe kisses me hard on the mouth and I kiss him back. Then he plants little kisses down the side of my neck, making me gasp. His lips follow my breastbone, and then his mouth closes tightly over my right nipple as his hand strokes the top of my thigh. I feel like I'm going to explode inside. Joe has this effect on me every time we make love. It's an instant chemical reaction that hasn't faded despite the time we have spent together. I'm extremely grateful for the closeness that we share.

I grab a handful of Joe's hair as his tongue traces my inner thigh. He pulls himself up over me until we're face to face and our eyes meet. He smiles at me and traces my lips with his thumb, before leaning down and kissing me deeply and burying himself inside me, and we make love, still warm and wet from the bathwater.

Chapter Eleven

'Morning.' I open the back door of the shop the following Monday morning and find Jenny and Lola standing next to the kettle, making tea.

'Hi, Emma. How was the rest of your weekend?' Lola asks.

'Well, I've felt better.'

'Yeah.' Jenny rubs her temples. 'I think I'm still recovering from all that alcohol.'

'I'm glad it's not just me,' I say as I hang up my coat and handbag.

'I felt fine yesterday,' Lola says as she pours boiling water into three mugs before adding a splash of milk.

'Of course you did. You're twenty-four. You can still go out three nights in a row with it barely taking its toll.'

Lola laughs and hands me a mug.

'She's right.' Jenny nods, picking up her own mug of tea. 'At some point – and as-yet-unrecognisable one – you suddenly find yourself in your thirties, struggling to get over a hangover and unable to get into bed at night without an hour's preparation with beauty products to try to preserve your youth.'

Lola giggles. 'You make it sound like you're both past it. It can't be that bad.'

I take a drink of my tea and push the thought of my inside-out, back-to-front pyjamas from the forefront of my mind. 'You might not think there's much difference between your mid-twenties and your mid-thirties, Lola – because you're still in the first age section – but you'd be wrong. Jenny's right. I apply anti-wrinkle cream to my face, anti-cellulite cream to my thighs, and hand cream and hair oil. Joe's lucky that I don't just slip right out of bed with the amount of lotions and potions I apply from head to toe as part of my daily ritual.' I laugh. Okay, so maybe it's not every day; more like when I remember, or when I look in the mirror and don't like the vision staring back at me.

Jenny's laughing now too. 'When did maintenance become so hard?' She turns to Lola. 'What's your beauty regime?'

Lola looks almost embarrassed as she says, 'I use facial cleansing wipes and apply moisturiser.'

'That's it?' I ask.

'And I bet it's not even an anti-wrinkle moisturiser.' Jenny shakes her head.

'I'm twenty-four,' Lola protests.

'Exactly,' Jenny says with an air of authority, 'and if I can teach you only one thing, Lola, it will be that prevention is better than cure.'

Lola looks at us, amused.

'I'm speaking from experience,' Jenny continues. 'For example, prevention – i.e. not drinking copious amounts of alcohol on Saturday night – would have been much more preferable than grovelling to Scott yesterday when I didn't quite feel fresh enough to go out to the cinema and for dinner.'

'Oh dear.' I cringe, knowing I felt exactly the same way.

'I know. It's not great. He says I'm going to have to make it up to him.'

'Oh really, and how are you going to do that?' I smirk, and think of Joe's reward last night for keeping his silence – then blush as flashbacks of our lovemaking go through my mind.

'Clearly I can see what you're thinking.' Jenny purses her lips.

I raise my eyebrows. 'Come on, Jenny, don't tell me that thought hasn't crossed your mind, and isn't that exactly what he means?'

'That's not the point.' Jenny's blushing now too. 'You know what, Emma? I can remember the days when you were shy when it came to talking about sex, and now look at you, insinuating all sorts.'

Lola's watching our exchange with interest.

'I mean no harm, Jenny. You do whatever you need to do to make it up to Scott.' I grin. 'I'm just saying that with a night of passion, you won't go far wrong.'

'Honestly!' Jenny huffs, but she can't hide her smile.

'You know I'm right,' I say. 'And I've mellowed in my conversations about sex as it's usually all you talk about. I've become accustomed to it.'

'I do talk about other things.'

'You must really like Scott.'

'I do.' Jenny bites her lip.

'I've really missed you two,' Lola pipes up. 'It's only my second week back, but I'm so glad to be here.'

'Really? You don't miss the golden beaches and tropical climate of Australia?' I ask, jokingly.

'Well, yeah.' Lola nods. 'But I missed my friends.'

'We missed you too,' Jenny says. She glances at the clock on the wall. 'Unfortunately it's time to open the shop. Let's see what havoc we can cause today, though.' She smiles as she turns to head onto the shop floor to open up for the day.

Chapter Twelve

It's Wednesday evening and I'm at Sophie's again, grabbing a quick cup of tea on my way home.

'Why do you find it so amusing that I'm looking after the twins on Saturday?' I ask.

Truthfully I'm a little hurt by Sophie's reaction to this. After my conversation with Simon about how little time he and James have alone together, I, being the good friend that I am, offered to look after the boys. I was, however, a little surprised when Simon called yesterday to take me up on my offer. I'm happy to, don't get me wrong, but maybe a little unprepared.

'I'm sorry, Emma, I don't mean to offend you. It's just that, well...'

'Yes?'

'Is Joe going to be there?'

'No, it's just me. But I'm a grownup, an adult. I'm perfectly capable of looking after two small children for a few hours.'

'Of course you are.' Sophie nods, but I can't help but feel she's a little patronising in her tone, and I frown.

'I mean it, Emma. I'm sorry. I'm just surprised, that's all. I didn't think you, um...'

'Just because I don't have children of my own, doesn't mean that I hate children and I'm some sort of monster, or am incapable of keeping them alive.'

'I know that.'

'I'm going to be perfectly fine.'

'I know that too, and I don't think that you hate children.'

'Well, society seems to think so.'

'Have you been doing those quizzes in *Cosmo* again?' Sophie smiles at me.

'I'm being serious.'

'Society doesn't think you hate children, Emma, just because you don't have any of your own.'

SASHA LANE

'Yes, it does, and clearly people think that I wouldn't know what to do with a child anyway.'

'Okay, okay. I'm sorry if I hurt your feelings and made a joke out of you looking after Fitz and Theo.'

'That's alright,' I say, feigning a hurt look.

'Will you still look after my baby when it's born?'

'Jesus, Sophie, always looking out for yourself.' I smile, shaking my head. 'Don't be silly; you won't be able to get rid of me.'

'It is really kind of you to offer to look after the twins. Simon and James are great with them, but it must be hard getting two at once when you haven't got a clue what to do with a baby.'

'You mean they don't come with instruction booklets?' I ask, and Sophie laughs again.

She raises her eyebrows. 'Maybe you'll be able to teach me a thing or two.'

'I'm less scared given that they're not still tiny babies.'

'In what way?'

'Well, with a baby you have to watch its floppy head, and not let it roll off anything.'

'I see.' Sophie presses her lips together.

'At least a toddler can sit up on his own without having neck trauma.'

'That's true. Although if they're mobile, then that means you have to keep an eye on them every second or they'll be eating the batteries from the television remote control.'

'Oh, I don't know, Soph. What have I done? What if I cock this up and –'

'Emma, you will be fine. Fitz and Theo love you, and you love them. You won't let anything happen to them.'

'Will you come and help me?'

'I would, but Matt and I have arranged to go and see my mum.'

'Oh.' Suddenly I fear that I've made a huge mistake.

'You'll be great.' Sophie squeezes my hand and I exhale.

'You're right, and I need to be a grownup and show that I'm responsible and can look after children. It's only for a few hours. What's the worst that can happen?'

Actually let's not contemplate that.

Saturday's here before I know it: my day of responsibility, which I'm facing all alone given Joe already has plans for the day.

As I buzz Simon and James into the flat, my stomach does a little flip. I'm kind of excited about the prospect of spending the next few hours snuggled on the sofa with Theo and Fitz, who have to be the cutest toddlers going, and they always smell so comforting – that mixture of talc and complete newness that only babies can emit. I understand that my vision may be idealistic and that there will be some challenges during the next few hours, but how hard can it be? I mean, people have children all the time and they seem to cope. Then again...

'Hey, Emmie.' Simon appears at the top of the stairwell, looking like the picture-perfect doting dad, holding Theo confidently with one arm. (I only know it's Theo as his bib is proudly displaying his name. His hair has a darker tinge to it, so when they're together I can just about tell them apart; other than that, if the twins are separated, I struggle tell which is which.) On his other arm is a large material bag covered in giraffes and bulging at the seams.

'I always forget how much harder two flights of stairs are when you're carrying a toddler,' Simon says. But as he leans in and kisses me on the cheek, I don't even see a bead of sweat on his brow.

'Morning, Emma.' James appears behind Simon, carrying Fitz and looking equally the capable parent. This doesn't surprise me in the slightest, as James has always been the strong, confident type. But honestly, how two gay men have become a textbook guide to parenting after only six months is a complete mystery to me. Prior to the twins, Simon had never so much as held a baby, to the best of my knowledge.

'Hi, James.' I usher them both into the flat. 'Can I get you a cuppa before you go?' I ask, frowning, as I take in what looks like a tent hanging over James's shoulder.

'I'll put the kettle on,' Simon says as he unloads the giant giraffe bag.

I stare at it, dumbfounded – how much crap do these babies

come with? I thought I was the queen of large handbags containing life's necessities (okay, maybe not necessities, perhaps more like three months' worth of old receipts, lip-glosses that have seen better days and the remnants of last week's blueberry muffin), but this is really something else.

'Why don't you give James a hand with the playpen?' Simon says, and then heads off into the kitchen before I can protest.

'Playpen? Right.'

I turn to James, who's unloading the tent-like package. Oh, playpen. I see. Not a tent. That would have been very unusual, and totally unnecessary. James starts to pull the material structure from its bag while still clasping Fitz under one arm. I leap forward.

'Let me get that for you.'

'Thanks, Emma.'

I take hold of the bag and pull the metal-and-material contraption out and lay it on the floor. It looks like a prop from *Challenge Anneka* and I stare at it with trepidation. Um, right, okay. Crouching down, I pick up one of the metal poles and stretch out the material until it forms a floppy wall. That can't be right. This will never contain a boisterous toddler.

James coughs diplomatically behind me and I glance up at him. 'Do you want to have a cuddle with Fitz while I do that?' He smiles warmly.

I try to hide my relief. 'Sure.' I shrug dismissively. 'If Fitz wants a hug from his Auntie Emma then who am I to argue?'

I stand up and hold my arms out to take the bewildered Fitz, who stares at me intently. A wave of fear washes over me, but then he smiles a big, gummy smile and dribble oozes down his chin. 'Come here, Fitz.' I scoop him towards me, trying to ignore the fact that he smears dribble all over my shoulder as he rubs his face on my T-shirt.

Simon walks back into the room carrying Theo. He places him gently on the floor before going back to the kitchen to collect the three mugs of tea. It's like watching a relay race and I wonder how people with children ever get anything done if everything takes twice as long. I lower Fitz onto the floor next to Theo and take a mug of tea from Simon just as James finishes erecting the playpen.

'So, that's everything, I think.' Simon glances around the room.

I take a slurp of tea and take in the calmness of the room. Fitz and Theo are playing together on the floor with some soft building blocks.

Simon and James drink their tea in record time, and before I know it they're heading for the door.

'Thanks so much for doing this.' Simon kisses me on the cheek.

'Of course. No problem. Happy to help,' I say confidently.

'See you in a few hours,' James says as he leaves the lounge.

'No rush,' I say instinctively.

As I hear the front door close, I turn back around to face the twins and am met with two sets of huge blue eyes staring at me with wonder. I can honestly say I have never been so terrified.

Two hours later, I feel like I've aged twenty years. I've lost track of how many times I've wiped sweat from my brow onto the sleeve of my cardigan, and I'm trying and failing to block out the over-excited voice of some random large pig that has occupied the television screen since Simon and James left – though in all honesty, it's barely entertained Theo and Fitz. I really should just switch the television off, but somehow that seems like the least important thing to do, given that my living room is chaotic and…oh no, what's that smell?

I already know what that smell is; I'm just in denial as Theo crawls up to my feet, mewling.

'Hey, Theo.' I smile gently, picking him up, but as I do so the smell becomes overwhelming and I realise this needs urgent attention.

Okay. I need to change one baby's bottom. I can do this.

I clutch Theo with one arm as I fling the changing mat onto the floor. As I lay him down gently on his back, he smiles at me with a smug expression. I'm guessing he can sense that this is my first time changing a nappy and he's done an extra-special surprise for me.

Holding my breath, I count to three before undoing Theo's romper suit and removing his nappy.

Jesus Christ!

Even though I'm holding my breath, the fumes hit the back of my throat, causing my stomach to flip. What have they fed this baby?

How people do this all day, every day, without throwing up is a mystery to me.

I toss the dirty nappy into a plastic bag and reach for the baby wipes. But they're not where I left them, within easy reach of the changing mat. I look up, confused, and see Fitz giggling to himself as he rolls around on the floor, not two feet away from me, with what looks like the whole packet of wipes strewn all over the place around him.

Damn it.

I grab the remaining few wipes from the pack and finish dealing with Theo's nappy demands, all the time keeping one eye on Fitz to make sure he doesn't choke to death on multiple baby wipes.

I deposit Theo in the playpen and then scoop up Fitz up to join him while I attempt to clean up some of the carnage. That two little people can make so much mess amazes me. But maybe it's just me. I'm not used to having to keep control of two tiny humans. There's two of them and only one of me, and I don't have eyes in the back of my head.

It seems that all three of us have reached exhaustion point, as by the time I've tidied up the baby wipes and numerous colourful toys, both little angels have fallen into a murmuring sleep in their playpen. Initially I'm relieved. Not only are they both still and in one place, but I can now definitely switch off the weird big pig on the television screen.

Silence descends and I exhale deeply, just for a second, before panic resumes – I can't hear them breathing! I crouch at the side of the playpen, my head lolling over the side as my eyes flit from one baby to the other, until I can confirm that their chests are rising and falling and each one is still alive.

Phew.

Right then. I just need to keep them alive for another half an hour until Simon and James return. I contemplate going to make a cup of tea, but decide against it, and instead spend the next thirty-five minutes kneeling on the floor and staring into the playpen, contentedly watching little chests move gently up and down. I only wish I could say the same for my own. My heart is racing frantically from my escapade this afternoon, as though I've run a marathon... well, at least a half-marathon.

The intercom buzzes and I leap up – on numb, wobbly legs, after kneeling down for the last half an hour – and grab the intercom phone.

Simon's jovial voice is on the other end. 'Hey, Emma.'

'Shush!' I hiss down the receiver. 'You'll wake the twins,' I whisper.

'Ooh, sorry.' Simon giggles. 'Are the little darlings fast asleep?'

'They were.' I glance nervously over at the playpen, but it looks like Fitz and Theo are oblivious to anything going on in their surroundings at this point and they remain silent. I press the door release and a few moments later Simon and James appear in the doorway to the flat.

'Not bad.' Simon smirks, glancing over my shoulder.

'Not bad?' I stand indignantly, hands on hips.

'I expected the flat to be barely standing.' He giggles as James nudges him none too gently in the ribs. 'Just kidding, Em.'

'I should think so.'

I stand to one side to let them in, and we wander through to the living room, where we are greeted by relative calm. I feel a moment of smugness, while hoping that the twins are still breathing and no harm has come to them in the thirty seconds it has taken me to answer the door. Thank God nothing has. As soon as they hear Simon and James, both Theo and Fitz open their eyes and grin up at us from the depths of the playpen. They look so cute I could almost forget the stress of looking after them for the afternoon, and the carnage that they caused.

'I hope you two have had a good afternoon,' I say to Simon.

'We have.' Simon winks at James.

I hold my hand up. 'Let's leave that there. I don't need the details.' I shake my head, smiling.

I help to repack the huge volume of accessories that come with two toddlers – seriously, I thought my mother came with a lot of luggage when she visits, but this is taking things to a whole new level. I pick up a still-sleepy Fitz from the playpen as Simon lifts

Theo up and snuggles him to his chest. This leaves James to expertly disassemble the playpen and place it, seemingly with ease, back into its carrycase.

The three of us somehow manage to get two toddlers and numerous bags back down the two flights of stairs and loaded into James's car without disturbing either twin.

'Thank you so much for taking care of the boys for us.' James kisses me on the cheek. 'We really appreciate it.'

'Anytime,' I smile, and I mean it. It wasn't so bad. In fact, I think I actually enjoyed myself – for some of it anyway.

'Yeah, cheers, Em.' Simon gives me a hug. 'I know I've made some jokes, but I am grateful, and it looks like the twins really enjoyed themselves.'

I smile. 'Good.'

'Next time we'll let you do feeding time.' Simon grins.

I keep the smile frozen in place on my face as I envisage a scene that resembles feeding time in the monkey enclosure at the zoo.

'Get in the car, Si, and let Emma enjoy the rest of her evening in peace.' James climbs onto the driver's seat and Simon dutifully follows and gets into the passenger side. I wave them off as the car pulls away.

Once back in the flat, I head straight to the kitchen and pour myself a glass of Sauvignon Blanc. Taking a sip, I ponder what amazing little creatures children are, and also how much energy and patience you must have to have on a daily basis to be a parent. I have a newfound respect and admiration for anyone who takes on the responsibility of children. I only hope Sophie realises exactly what she has ahead of her.

An hour later, when Joe comes through the front door he finds me dozing on the sofa.

'Hey.' I sit up groggily.

'Hi. How did it go with the twins?' he asks, looking slightly alarmed at the sight of my empty wine glass.

'I kept them happy, clean and uninjured for a whole three and a half hours,' I say with some satisfaction. On my first attempt, I'd say that's something to be proud of.

'I'm glad it's been a good practice run.' Joe leans down and kisses me. 'Want a refill?' He heads out of the living room.

'Wait,' I call, slightly alarmed. 'Practice run?'

'Yeah.' Joe looks at me, amused 'For Sophie's little one when it arrives.'

Ah, of course. Not ours. I see. Right. I feel my heartrate slowing back to normal.

Chapter Thirteen

The following Monday, at work in the shop, I find myself slightly distracted by something purplish and green as Lola makes the morning teas.

'Hey.' I glance down at Lola's arm. 'That's a pretty big bruise you've got there.'

'Oh.' Lola pulls the turned-up sleeve of her cardigan back down over her forearm, appearing embarrassed. 'Hugo and I went roller-blading in the park on Saturday.'

'That sounds like fun,' I say, clearly meaning fun for other people – it would be my worst nightmare, and would of course end up in me making an impromptu visit to the local Accident and Emergency department with broken bones.

'Well, it would have been a lot more fun if I wasn't so clumsy and I didn't keep falling over.' Lola smiles sheepishly.

'Really? You don't come across as someone who would be bad at sports,' I say, surprised. I always presumed Lola was just brilliant at everything, as well as being young, skinny and one of the nicest people you could hope to meet.

She shrugs. 'I'm much better with both feet firmly on the ground.'

'Ah, I see your point. Me too. In fact, I'm much safer avoiding all sport and exercise. I'm allergic, you know.'

Lola giggles. 'I didn't know that. But yes, best to avoid all physical activity if that's the case. You don't want to have a bad reaction.'

'I always see those adverts for skiing resorts, gorgeous scenery covered in twinkling snow, and I wish I could ski.'

'Why don't you learn?'

'Because I'm clumsy enough without adding in long, slippery feet and icy mountains. That's just inviting trouble.'

Lola laughs. 'Can Joe ski?'

'Yeah. They went as kids, so both he and Matt are good skiers. He keeps threatening to take me.'

'You don't want to go?'

'More like I don't want to die. Although I am tempted by the thought of champagne in front of an open log fire in my ski lodge. It might be worth going just for that.'

'Experiencing the benefits of skiing without actually skiing?'

'Exactly.' I nod. 'So is Hugo quite sporty?'

'Oh, um, yes.'

I presumed he was. He certainly looked pretty fit when Jenny and I met him the other weekend at the bar.

'He's keen to try new things too. I think we're going kayaking soon.'

'Wow. Kayaking?' I had no idea there was anywhere around here where you could do such a thing. 'Just take extra care, okay? If you're not used to those types of activities, they can be very dangerous.'

Lola nods as we walk through to the shop floor.

'Hugo will look after you, though. He won't let anything happen to you. He seems like such a gentleman.'

The front door opens and a regular customer, Mrs Appleyard, strides in.

Lola's already walking towards her. 'Good morning, Mrs Appleyard. What can I help you with today?'

As I watch Lola help Mrs Appleyard with her usual professionalism, I can't help but notice that something about her demeanour has changed. I can't put my finger on it; it's just a feeling in the bottom of my stomach – something doesn't feel right. Lola's body language is different, almost like she's gone into her shell a little, and she looks more fragile somehow. I'll talk to Jenny, see if she's noticed anything, or if I'm just seeing something that's not there. Lola has been away for a whole year and only been back for a short time. Maybe I'm imagining things. I wander back through to the staff area, still preoccupied.

Any further thoughts of Lola are forced to the back of my mind a few seconds later when I hear the door jingle again, followed by the familiar sharp tone of Marissa Bamford.

'Good morning, Lola. Where's Emma?'

Oh no. That can't be good.

My eyes instinctively dart around the kitchenette, like an animal cornered in the wild by a predator. Of course there's nowhere to hide. Suddenly the door from the shop floor swings open, and there, somehow filling the doorway despite her petite size, stands Marissa Bamford.

'Ah, Emma. There you are.' She points a long, manicured fingernail in my direction.

'Um,' is all I can manage to say.

She flings two dress carriers at me and I take them from her warily.

'I thought you might like to see a couple of the finished articles,' Marissa says. 'Not bad at all, Emma.'

'Finished articles?'

'Two of the dresses you designed. For the royal visit.'

'Oh.' I'm both excited and nervous to see the dresses. These are my first designs made into actual items of clothing for people to wear – if you don't count the items I made for my fashion course. It's a little overwhelming actually and –

'Come on, Emma. I don't have all day.' Marissa sighs heavily.

Right.

I hang the dress carriers on the hook on the back of the door and, with my heart beating a little faster, I slowly pull down the zip to reveal the first dress. I stand back to take in the full effect.

'Well?' Marissa says, looking right at me.

'I like it. It's good.' I can't help a huge smile spreading across my face.

'It's very good, Emma,' Marissa opens the second dress carrier to reveal the other dress 'We've confirmed the order and the stock will be arriving this week. Well done.'

'Um, thank you.' I don't know what else to say. Receiving praise from Marissa Bamford is unusual territory.

'I'll leave this one here. It's one of the samples,' she continues. 'Perhaps you can put it on one of the manikins in the window to get some interest.'

'I'll get straight on it,' I say, meaning I'll get Lola to do it. I hate those manikins, and they seem to protest every time I try to change them, somehow becoming even more inflexible.

'Well, I must dash.'

Marissa swirls around and marches back out onto the shop floor, and I follow her. Lola glances across at me as she finishes serving Mrs Appleyard, and I smile to reassure her that the visit from Marissa Bamford is nothing to worry about.

'I'll be in touch later in the week,' Marissa announces as she reaches the door, then she turns and is gone before I can formulate any response.

I hold the door open as Mrs Appleyard leaves, and then an air of calmness descends over the shop.

'What was all that about?'

'The dress for the royal visit promotion thingy. It's ready,' I say, biting my lip.

Lola squeals. 'Really? Is that what she brought to show you?'

I nod. 'Yeah. It's hanging in the back room.'

'Well, don't just stand there, Emma. Come and show me.'

Lola skips off to the kitchenette and I follow, propping the door from the kitchen to the shop floor open so we can see if anyone comes in.

'It's beautiful,' Lola states. 'I love the fitted waist, and the colour is just perfect. You must be so proud of yourself.'

I stare at the pale silvery-grey dress and I do feel proud. It is lovely. The material they have gone with is exactly what I wanted: a demure colour, but with a hint of shimmer, just to add a bit of glamour.

'I do love it,' I say, feeling sheepish. I'm not used to being the centre of attention, and it's not something I have ever been, or ever will be, comfortable with. 'We need to get it on a manikin.'

'Your dress, your job,' Lola says, laughing.

'Lola?'

She sighs, cocking her head to one side. 'What on earth did you do while I was in Australia?'

'I made Jenny do it.'

'You're unbelievable.'

'Come on, Lola, you're so much better at it than I am, and you can do it in half the time,' I plead.

Lola raises her eyebrows. 'Flattery will get you nowhere.'

'Latte and a muffin?' I offer.

'Deal.' Lola takes the dress off the hook and walks back into the shop.

I head out of the back and walk to the coffee shop, feeling exhilarated. My first design for sale in the window of a shop. Perhaps this is the start of something. I make a silent promise to take out my sketchpad more and start scribbling some designs, just in case.

I can't wait to tell Joe about the dresses, but when I arrive home from work at six o'clock the flat is empty. I hang up my coat and head to the kitchen. I think a celebratory glass of wine is in order. Just as I reach the fridge, I hear the front door open, then the familiar sound of Joe's footsteps as he heads down the hallway towards the kitchen.

'Hey.' Joe smiles as he opens the kitchen door.

'Hi,' I say as I take a chilled bottle of Sauvignon Blanc from the fridge.

Joe raises his eyebrows. 'Bad day?' He gestures towards the bottle.

'On the contrary,' I say, unable to keep the excitement from my voice. 'Marissa Bamford came to the shop today with two of my dresses as a finished articles.'

'And?' Joe waves his hands, encouraging me to go on.

'And they looked brilliant.'

'Oh, Emma, come here.' Joe takes the bottle of wine from my hand and places it on the kitchen side, before he pulls me into an embrace and kisses me. 'I'm so proud of you,' he says, smiling, as he pulls away.

'I'm proud of me too,' I say sheepishly. I still can't believe I've designed something that's going to go on sale in a real shop.

'Right, come on. Get your coat.' Joe grabs me by the hand.

I laugh. 'You do realise that sounds like a corny chat-up line.'

'Okay, I'll rephrase that.' Joe shakes his head at me. 'Grab your coat. We're going out for champagne to celebrate.'

I don't need telling twice: I do as I'm told and grab my coat, and we make our way out.

'Sorry for making fun,' I say as I skip down the stairs like a giddy child.

'It's fine.'

'Where shall we go for champagne?'

'How about Ivy's?' Joe says as we walk outside and he takes my hand in his.

'I love Ivy's, but it's really expensive.'

'So? We're celebrating. It's not every day that you see a dress you designed in a shop window.'

'I guess.'

'There's no "guess" about it. We're going to Ivy's, and I don't care tonight how much it costs.'

'Okay,' I smile, and we stroll hand in hand through the park in the direction of the wine bar.

Ivy's is fairly quiet, which is to be expected mid-week, so we find a booth in the corner of the bar area. A waitress is quickly at the table and Joe orders some pink champagne – not his usual tipple, but my favourite in this bar. It's crisp and refreshing and highly addictive.

'So?' Joe says, snuggling up close to me. 'Are you okay?'

'I'm great.' I smile as the waitress returns with our bottle of champagne. She pours two flutes and then leaves.

'To you, Emma.' Joe raises his glass.

I clink my glass on his and take a sip, enjoying the sensation of the bubbles as they fizz on my tongue.

We return a couple of hours later, more than a little squiffy after a lovely evening just sitting and chatting, Joe and me in our own little bubble.

'We should do this more often,' Joe says as he leans on the wall outside our flat and I struggle to negotiate putting the key in the lock on the front door.

'What? Drink champagne? I'd love to, but I'm not sure our budget will allow for that on a regular basis.' I finally slip the key into the lock and open the door.

'No, I mean go out for impromptu drinks. I really enjoyed tonight, just the two of us. It was like old times.' Joe closes the door behind us as I try, with some difficulty, to stand on one leg and remove my shoes.

I pause, barefoot, in the hallway and look up at Joe. 'Have we become complacent?'

'Emma? No, I'm just saying we should take more time out together. I'm guilty of saying I'll cook rather than go out, but that's because I enjoy cooking.'

That's true; I never say I'll cook rather than go out to a restaurant.

'Do I take you for granted?' I bite my lip.

Joe shakes his head. 'Emma, stop it. Why do you always think the worst? I should have worded it differently. What I meant to say was, I've loved this evening and I'm going to take you out more often. That's all.'

'Oh.' I smile. 'Take me out? We have a joint bank account.'

'Now you're just being cheeky.' Joe steps forward and catches me off guard as he scoops me up in his arms.

'Joe!' I wail. 'Put me down.'

'Nope. You dismissed my attempt at a romantic gesture with sarcasm, so now I'm going to have to punish you.'

'Joe,' I giggle as he carries me through to the bedroom and places me down on the bed.

'Now, are you going to behave and not make fun?' Joe nuzzles my neck as he presses his body down on top of mine.

'Yes,' I mumble.

'Sorry, I didn't hear that clearly.' Joe unbuttons my jeans.

'Yes. I won't make fun anymore!' I laugh as Joe's fingers brush the lower part of my stomach as he pulls down my jeans, and then my heartbeat quickens.

Joe leans over me. 'Good. I'm glad that's sorted. Now the real fun can begin.'

He leans down and kisses me, full and hard, and my body instantly reacts: a tingle shoots down my spine. He simultaneously strokes the outside of my thigh with his hand while his tongue caresses mine.

He pulls away and then begins to trace the line from my chest to my navel, planting soft kisses on my skin. I arch my back to meet his lips, and as his mouth reaches my inner thigh, I gasp at his touch.

He leans up on his forearms and looks right at me. 'I love you, Emma.'

'I love you too,' I smile.

Joe quickly removes my knickers, and I lie back on the soft quilt and close my eyes. As Joe lies on top of me, I feel him push inside me and my body welcomes him. The mixture of the adrenaline now pumping around my body and the earlier champagne makes me feel positively light-headed, like I'm losing myself in another world. Our world, mine and Joe's. This is our bubble, and no matter how complacent we may or may not be in our day-to-day relationship, the love-making always feels like it did on our first time together.

Chapter Fourteen

I'm looking forward to catching up with Sophie tonight after a hectic day at work, although our time spent together has taken on a different form now that she's pregnant. Don't get me wrong, I'm not complaining. I guess it's just taken something like Sophie having a baby to make me realise that we're all growing up. Gone are the days of drinking cocktails until three a.m. (the other Saturday with Jenny and Lola was definitely the exception, not the norm). Who am I kidding? We tried to keep up the pretence of being young party animals, but those days were long gone well before Sophie's pregnancy. Even Simon's had to throw in the towel now that he and James are happily married with two young children. Weirdly it seems that it's Simon who is the one dragging James to look at home furnishings on a Saturday evening, rather than getting his glad-rags on and heading out to a new bar in town.

It's just me who's left with no husband or baby yet. Well, I do have a boyfriend, and I nearly had a husband. I was proposed to; I had the ring and everything. But then, stupidly, I called off my own wedding. That feels like a lifetime ago now, and almost like it happened to someone else. Joe and I haven't discussed the idea of getting married since we got back together. Maybe he's too scared to ask me for a second time, in case I flip out again. Or perhaps we're both of the opinion that you're either committed to a relationship or you're not, and marriage doesn't or shouldn't change that. I suppose for all intents and purposes I do have a husband, if not by official title.

I pull up at the kerb outside Sophie's house, climb out of the car and collect the bag from the passenger seat that contains the non-alcoholic wine. I've been reduced to drinking this due to my commitment to mine and Sophie's friendship – I didn't think it was fair for me to get sozzled on the real stuff while she drank what is effectively adult Ribena. Plus if I've learned anything from getting the worse for wear with Jenny and Lola the other weekend, it's that I'm getting less tolerant of alcohol as I get older, and the enjoyment of drinking that volume of alcohol is not worth the hideous hangover the following day.

'Soph?' I call as I knock. I'm met with silence. 'Sophie?' I call a little louder as I use my spare key to unlock the door and make my way towards the kitchen to unload the wine substitute and nibbles.

But as I pass the lounge, something catches my eye and stops me dead in my tracks. My chest constricts to the point that I can't breathe, and I think for a moment my heart has actually stopped beating.

Sophie is in a crumpled heap on the floor in front of the sofa.

'Sophie! Oh my God, Sophie!'

My handbag and the carrier bag slip from my hands, and the bottles of non-alcoholic wine clunk loudly on the wooden floor. I have no idea whether they've smashed; right now I really don't care. Somehow I catapult my body into motion and I'm at Sophie's side. Her face is warm and clammy as I gently shake her, but Sophie's eyes remain closed and she's unresponsive. I grab at her hand, pressing my index finger against the underside of her wrist, trying desperately to remember the first-aid course I did as a child at Girl Guides. I can feel a faint pulse. I lean over Sophie and press my ear over her mouth and I breathe a huge sigh of relief. She's breathing, thank God she's breathing.

I scramble across the living room floor towards my handbag and fumble through the vast amount of useless rubbish I carry around, in search of my mobile phone. My hands are shaking so violently that I drop the phone twice before managing to dial the emergency services. The phone is answered after just two rings and a calm voice permeates the chaos in my head.

'Which emergency service do you require?'

'Ambulance. Ambulance,' is all I can manage to say.

A few seconds pass before I hear a man's voice on the other end of the phone.

'You're through to South Yorkshire Ambulance Service. What's your emergency?'

'It's my friend. She's unconscious.'

'What's your friend's name?'

'Sophie. It's Sophie.'

'And what's happened to Sophie?'

'I don't know. I just got here and found her on the floor.'

'Is she breathing?'

'Yes. But you need to hurry. She's pregnant.'

'How far along is she?'

Um, erm…my mind goes blank. 'Just send an ambulance, please!'

I crouch down next to Sophie again. Her face is cooler now but still clammy.

'What is the address of the property?'

I give him Sophie's address and he reassures me that help is on the way.

I kneel down next to Sophie and take hold of her hand. 'Wake up, Sophie. Please wake up. I don't know what to do. I don't know how to help you,' I sob.

After what feels like an eternity, I hear the shriek of sirens in the distance, and almost instantly I see blue flashing lights through the living room window.

I hear the front door open and close.

Voices calling.

Then a male paramedic appears in the doorway and I gulp back tears of fear and relief as I stagger to my feet.

'Please help her. Please help her. She's pregnant,' I hear myself repeating over and over, but I have no control over my mouth and the voice coming from my body is almost unrecognisable.

Strong hands are placed on my shoulders and I'm ushered to one side and gently seated on the sofa by a woman, a second paramedic – I didn't even notice her enter the room.

I watch in fear as a plastic mask is placed over Sophie's mouth, as she's lifted on to a stretcher, and then as she's carried from the room. My heart thuds so hard that it hurts with each beat in my chest and the sound is deafening in my ears.

'Miss?…Miss?'

I snap back into the room to find the female paramedic is standing next to me.

'Would you like to come to the hospital with us in the ambulance?'

'Um, yes.' I force myself to a standing position on jelly legs and am thankful to be guided to the waiting ambulance by the strong arms of the paramedic.

Once on our journey to the hospital, the reality and seriousness of the situation hit me. I need to call Matt; he needs to know what's going on. But I can't just call him up and blurt this out over the phone. He's with Joe, though, so Joe will look after him and get him to the hospital. But they're out drinking, so they won't be able to drive.

I stare down at Sophie, who's still not opened her eyes, and my heart leaps into my mouth. I don't even know what to say to Matt, or Joe for that matter. How do you deliver news of this magnitude? You can't just call up, ask how they are and then say, 'You need to come to the hospital right now as Matt's pregnant girlfriend, my best friend, is unconscious, and I have no idea what's happened to her, and I can't help her!' I clutch Sophie's hand tightly and gasp for air.

As we drive at speed, lights flashing and sirens blaring, the female paramedic is talking constantly to Sophie, trying to rouse her, while performing a number of tests on her and then scribbling furiously on a form on a clipboard. Sophie's eyes remain closed, and she's unresponsive to everything.

We arrive at the hospital and what feels like pandemonium ensues. The doors of the ambulance are flung open and three doctors or nurses – I have no idea how to tell the difference at this point – appear and help to lower Sophie's stretcher, before wheeling her towards the large glass doors of the Accident and Emergency area of the hospital. Different commands are being made at the same time as blood pressure readings are stated in a monotone.

I stand to the side, blinking rapidly, unsure what the hell to do now. Then I follow the group of hospital staff and Sophie's stretcher – until I reach another set of glass doors and a hand grasps my shoulder and stops me in my tracks.

'I'm sorry, but you can't go in there.'

I stare hopelessly as Sophie is wheeled down the corridor and then she disappears from sight.

'But...' I turn around to find a small, blond lady in blue scrubs smiling kindly at me.

'It's hospital staff only after this point. You can wait in the relatives' waiting room to the right.' She gestures with her hand to a door next to a large vending machine. 'The machine coffee isn't great, but it's warm and wet.' She smiles again. 'I'm Anne. Are you a relative?'

'A friend. I'm Emma.'

'Okay, Emma. Do you think I could take some of your friend's details?'

'Right, um. Yes.' I nod at her, still in a compete daze.

I answer all the questions to the best of my ability. I have never known Sophie to be allergic to anything, or to have had any medical conditions, and I have no idea what her blood type is. I don't think I know my own, which seems hideous. How and why do we not know these things about ourselves and those closest to us? A voice somewhere at the back of my mind says, *Because we don't ever think that we need to know these things. We think we're invincible, and nothing will ever happen to us.*

'Here, let me get you a cup of coffee.'

Anne walks over to the vending machine and presses a few buttons. The beeps from the machine seem so acute and I hear the plastic cup click loudly into place before the coffee starts to filter through. My senses are in overdrive from the adrenaline that's still pumping round my body, and every simple sound is magnified.

'Is there anyone I can call?' Anne asks softly, handing me the steaming cup.

'Um, no, thanks. I'll make the calls, thank you.'

'Okay. Go and take a seat in the waiting room and I'll be back as soon as I have an update for you.'

I shuffle towards a big white door. 'Thank you,' I say, before opening the door and stepping inside.

I'm greeted by a cold, clinical white room. Grey Formica chairs line the sides of the room, and floral prints have been hung sporadically on the cool white walls in a lame attempt to give the room some feeling. I can't imagine anyone feeling any better about anything in this room. In fact, the lack of comfort provided by the impersonal surroundings could only make the situation seem bleaker. I take a sip of the red-hot liquid before discarding the plastic cup on a small coffee table – yuck!

I have a vivid flashback to when I myself was hospitalised, not so long ago, following the car crash involving Connor. I woke to find myself in a similar clinical white room, having been in a coma for several days. I reach up instinctively and touch the side of my head where at the time I'd had a huge swelling. There are no physical scars now, and the emotional ones have almost disappeared too, thanks to the love and support of Joe and my friends. Especially Sophie.

Poor Sophie.

I sniff back tears as I sit down on one of the grey chairs and take my phone from my pocket. Unconsciously I pick up the plastic cup and take another sip.

Urgh!

I push the cup to the other end of the table and hit number three on my speed-dial list.

Two seconds later, I hear Simon's ever-cheerful voice. 'Hiya, babe. How's things?'

'Oh, Simon.' I gulp as my stomach churns.

'Emma? What's wrong? What's happened?' I can hear the panic in Simon's voice.

I take a deep breath. 'It's Sophie. She's in hospital. I'm at the hospital,' I ramble.

'What? Are you okay? Is Sophie alright?'

'Oh, Simon. I'm scared.' I begin to sob noisily, my shoulders heaving as I hold my head in my hands. 'I found her on the floor. She won't wake up.'

Simon, who is usually the most emotional person in any situation, is surprisingly calm and collected. 'Okay, Em,' he says soothingly. 'Don't panic. Where's Matt? Is he with her?'

'No.' I sniff. 'He's out with Joe, and I can't just call him and tell him this over the –'

'Where are they, Emma? James and I will go and get them both and bring them to the hospital. James's mum can watch the boys.'

'They're at The Crown on Miller Street. I dropped Joe there about an hour ago.'

'Right. We're on our way. Stay calm, and we'll be with you soon, honey. Bye.'

'Wait, Simon.'

'Yep?'

'Thank you.'

'No worries, Em. It's what friends do.'

And with that he hangs up, and I yet again reach for the plastic cup of rancid liquid and take a gulp regardless.

I have no idea how much time passes, but it feels like an eternity before Anne, the lady who assisted me earlier, pops her head around the door of the waiting room. Somehow the room is still empty except for me. Unusual for an Accident and Emergency department, yet I'm quite relieved, as I'm not up to making small talk with complete strangers.

'Hi.' I stand up to greet her. 'How's Sophie?'

'She's doing much better. She's come round, but she's still a bit groggy.'

'And the baby? Is the baby alright?'

'They're just running some more tests, but initially everything looks absolutely fine. Her blood pressure had dropped, which is probably what caused her to pass out. The doctor will be able to tell you more.'

'Oh, thank God!' My knees weaken with the relief. 'Can I see her?'

'Shortly. The doctor will be in to let you know when. Is there anyone I can call for you?'

'No, her boyfriend is on his way, thanks.'

'Okay, then just sit tight and the doctor will be with you as soon as he can.'

'Thank you.'

I sit back down and tears of relief slide down my cheeks. Two minutes later, the door swings open and Matt, Joe, Simon and James pile in, all asking questions at the same time.

'Matt?' I grab his shaking hand and look up at his pale face. 'It's okay. Sophie's alright, and so is the baby.'

Matt's shoulders visibly drop three inches. 'Are you sure? Where is she?'

'The nurse just came in. The doctor will be in soon to let you know what's happening and then we can see her.'

Matt pulls me into a huge hug. 'Thank you, Emma. Thanks for getting her to hospital so quickly.'

'Of course.' I swallow down the waves of emotion that are threatening to overwhelm me.

'I should never have gone out. I knew she didn't look right,' Matt says, still gripping me tightly. 'But she insisted.'

'You mustn't blame yourself,' I say, knowing how strong-minded Sophie is. If she insists you go out, then you go!

As Matt releases me, Joe takes hold of my hand and kisses me on the lips. 'How are you doing?' He brushes my cheek with his thumb.

'I'm fine now I know she's awake and the baby isn't harmed.' I nod, pressing my lips together. 'I just want to see her to make sure.'

'Hey, sweetie.' Simon grabs my other hand.

'You're a good friend.' I kiss Simon on his cheek. 'Thank you for being so calm and for going straight to get Matt and Joe.'

Simon grins. 'One of my many skills.'

I manage a half-smile. We both know keeping calm in a time of crisis usually isn't Simon's strong point. In fact, I can count on two hands the number of times he's flapped around aimlessly, providing little or no practical help, when I've hit a catastrophe. He makes up for it, though, with his huge heart and never-waning emotional support. I guess we all have different strengths.

The five of us take a seat in a row on the stiff plastic chairs, a stunned silence now hanging heavily in the air.

Matt stands up abruptly. 'I'll get everyone a cup of tea while we wait,' he says.

'I'll help you.' Joe stands up too.

I think this is more to do with Matt's need to *do* something than anything else. I know that feeling. I hate that feeling. That helplessness that smothers you in situations like this. Everything else is irrelevant, other than trying to help, and it's at this point that we realise our most definitive limitations. In reality I had no idea what to do when I found Sophie, other than call for an ambulance. I don't think anything can prepare you for the sheer panic you feel when you see someone you love hurt.

As Matt and Joe leave the room, my mind wanders back over the last few weeks. Could I have seen this coming? I should have spent more time with Sophie. I should have called in to see her more. I'm her best friend and I feel responsible for her, even though I know I can't be there all the time.

'Stop that, Emma.' Simon slides his hand over mine.

'Stop what?' I say, but I can't meet his eyes, so I stare down at the pale-grey linoleum and blink back tears.

'I know you, Em. I know what's going through your mind right now,' Simon says softly.

The lump that's forming in my throat prevents me from saying anything.

'This isn't your fault.'

'Really?' I wipe a stray tear.

'Really.' Simon pushes a strand of hair away from my face and tucks it behind my ear.

'I just feel like I haven't paid enough attention to Sophie over the last few weeks, like I've been too self-involved. I've been absorbed by other stuff.'

'Emma,' Simon says in a fatherly tone, 'Matt lives with Sophie. He sees her every day. From what I can gather, there were no warning signs. If he couldn't see anything wrong, why on earth would you feel responsible?'

'She's my best friend, Simon.'

'I know.'

'As well as you,' I correct myself.

'I know that too.' Simon smiles. 'But sometimes shit happens, Emma, and it's no one's fault. It's just life, and there's little you can do about it, other than be there to pick up the pieces.'

I exhale heavily. 'I can do that.'

'Sophie is going to be okay,' James adds. 'We all just need to make sure we do a little bit to keep an eye on her and make sure she stays okay.'

'Agreed.' I nod.

Matt and Joe return carrying plastic cups and hand one to each of us. I look down at the pale-beige liquid and pause before making any attempt to drink it. Everyone else takes a sip, and immediately pulls a face. A giggle escapes from my mouth. Maybe its nerves, or shock, but whatever it is, I can't stop.

'I think we'll all need admitting to hospital if we drink this stuff.' Simon scowls down at his cup.

The door opens and the doctor comes into the room.

'Doctor.' Matt rushes towards him. 'Can I see her? Can I see Sophie?'

'Of course. She's tired and needs some rest, though, so you can have ten minutes or so and then I'll need you all to let her sleep.'

'Yeah, good luck getting Matt to leave her once he's in there,' Joe says quietly under his breath, and I nod in agreement, realising that the doctor may have a job on his hands getting any of us to leave tonight.

'What caused her to pass out?' I ask the doctor.

'Exhaustion. She's been overdoing things and her blood pressure is high. We'll need to keep Sophie in here for a couple of days, just to monitor the situation.'

'But the baby's alright?'

'Yes, Mum and baby are both alright, and will continue to be so long as Sophie takes things easy from now on.'

'Right.' We all seem to nod in unison.

'If you'd like to follow me then...'

The doctor leads us from the room, and we walk in a convoy down the pristine white corridor and around the corner to a room right at the end. We enter to find Sophie propped up against huge white pillows. She looks pale and tired, and my chest tightens. I'm not used to seeing Sophie looking vulnerable – she's the strong one. She's the one who's always there to protect me.

Matt rushes to her bedside and she grasps his hand as he smothers her in kisses.

'Don't scare me like that again.' He looks right at Sophie. 'I can't lose you. From now on, you don't lift a finger.'

'Matt, I'm alright, I –'

'I don't want to hear it, Sophie.' Matt's voice is unusually stern. 'From now on, I'm at your beck and call. It's my job to keep you and our baby safe, and that's what I'm going to do.'

I blink back tears as I step around to stand opposite Matt on the other side of the bed.

'Hey, Soph.' I clear my throat as I take hold of her hand.

'Emma.' Sophie's face crumples.

'Don't cry, don't cry.' I pull her into a gentle hug.

'I'm sorry you found me like that. You must have been really frightened.'

'Just a little.' I roll my eyes. 'Although on a positive note, I'm not as hideous as I thought I would be in an emergency.'

'The doctor says you did everything right.'

'Well, let's not test the theory again, shall we – no more passing out, please. Promise?'

'I promise.'

'Do you want me to call your mum and dad?' I ask.

'No.' Sophie shakes her head. 'They'll only worry unnecessarily. There's no need. Everything's fine.'

'Are you sure?' I glance over at Matt. 'I don't think it's unnecessary to worry when you've passed out and ended up in hospital, Soph. In fact, I think that's exactly the appropriate time to worry.'

'I'm sure.' She nods. 'I don't want them to know.'

Matt shakes his head slightly at me and I decide to leave that particular subject alone for the moment.

Everyone else then takes it in turns to kiss and hug Sophie, with Matt standing watch at her side. Then before we know it the doctor reappears.

'I'm going to need you all to leave now and let Sophie rest.'

'Sure, Doctor,' Joe says, and we all begin the process of hugging and kissing Sophie again, to say goodbye this time.

The doctor ushers all of us from the room, except Matt, who

doesn't move.

'Sorry, Mr Stark, you're going to have to –'

'I'm not going anywhere, Doctor,' Matt states firmly. 'I'll sleep on the floor if I have to, but this is my girlfriend and the mother of my child, so I'm staying put.'

The doctor pauses for a moment and we all hold our breath, knowing there's no way that Matt will concede on this point. Thankfully the doctor appears to sense that too, and he just nods his head and we all turn to leave.

'Thank you, Doctor.' Joe shakes the doctor's hand, and we head back towards the relatives' waiting room.

Without any of us saying a word, it's presumed that Joe and I are staying the night at the hospital too. That's what friends do for each other.

'They must have a canteen,' James says. 'I'll get us all some food then we'll leave you to it and we'll get back home to the boys.'

'I'll help,' Simon adds.

Joe takes my hand and we go into the waiting room as James and Simon head off to get the food.

'Hang on.' I turn and head back into the corridor. 'Simon?' I call after him and James. 'Get Starbucks from somewhere, please. The coffee in here tastes like death in a cup.'

Chapter Fifteen

Two days later, Sophie is allowed home, and as Matt sets off to collect her I busy myself tidying their already tidy house. I must dust the same surfaces three times before I finally decide to switch the kettle on and distract myself with a cup of tea. I feel nervous. I don't know why. It's great that Sophie has been given the all clear and she's being allowed home today. I wander through to the living room and glance cautiously at the floor in front of the sofa. The vision of her lying there is still fresh in my mind and I close my eyes, willing it to go away. She's fine; I know she's going to be fine going forward, both her and the baby.

I wonder what she'll have.

I wonder what they'll call him or her.

I hope it's something sensible. I hate those silly celebrities who call their kids "Apple" or "North". I appreciate it's nice to be different, but the poor kids don't stand a chance. From what I can remember of my school days, kids can be cruel to each other. They weren't always kind to Simon, just because he was different to what they all thought boys should be. Simon never cared too much what others thought, though. And I was always a little too geeky to be cool. I behaved, did my schoolwork and wanted to learn. Apparently that doesn't make you popular in school, but Sophie was always my friend. We were always together and very rarely exchanged cross words.

I guess I'm lucky in that respect. My friendship pool isn't large, but those who are in it are long-standing friends whom I'd trust with my life, literally. It's quality, not quantity, that counts when it comes to friends – having people you can trust and rely on and who you know will have your back no matter what. Equally it's important to have friends who will tell you the truth too, and I can honestly say that my friends are happy to do that, although Simon could do with learning to sugar-coat his opinion on occasion.

I head back through to the kitchen and switch the kettle on to boil for the third time already. This time I might actually remember to make a cup of tea.

The front door opens and I hear familiar voices.

'Matt, I'm fine. Will you stop fussing?' Clearly Sophie.

'The doctor said you need to take things easy.' Matt.

'I've literally just got out of the car and walked to the front door. That's it.' Sophie again. She sounds back to her normal self.

'I'm going to have to put my foot down, Soph, if you won't do as you're told.'

This is dangerous talk from Matt, so I decide to intervene.

'Hi, Sophie.' I walk through to the front door, where Matt's helping to extract Sophie from her coat. Somehow in the last twenty-four hours I'd forgotten how big her baby bump is getting. 'How are you feeling?'

'Hey, Emma.' Sophie hugs me. 'Thank you for being here.'

'You're welcome,' I say, hugging her back.

'You know I love you and everything?' Sophie says as I pull away from her. I'm not sure where this is going, so I simply raise my eyebrows questioningly. 'But if you're going to fuss over me as much as Matt is, I might have to kill you both.'

Ah. I see Sophie is definitely feeling much better.

'Can I make you a cup of tea before I'm evicted from your home?' I ask jokingly.

'That would be lovely, thanks.'

'Matt?'

'That'd be great, thanks, Emma.'

I head back through to the kitchen to make the drinks, and return to find Sophie with her feet up on the sofa while Matt pats down a cushion behind her shoulders. It looks like the bad patient is maybe conceding a bit.

Matt takes his mug of tea from me. 'I'll run you a warm bath,' he tells Sophie. He kisses her forehead and leaves the room.

I hand Sophie her mug of tea and then perch on the edge of the sofa at her feet. 'Is there anything else I can get you?'

She shakes her head. 'I'm good, thanks.'

We sit there quietly for a second.

'You shouldn't be so hard on him,' I say quietly.

'Who? Matt?'

'He loves you, and he just wants to take care of you.'

Sophie takes a drink of her tea. 'I know.'

'So you need to let him.'

'It's not that easy, Emma.'

'Why?'

Sophie exhales. 'I'm independent. I always have been. I can't sit about while he waits on me hand and foot.'

'That's exactly what you need to do.'

Sophie opens her mouth, but I continue before she can protest further.

'Not just for you, but for that little baby inside you. You need to keep them safe, and that means following doctor's orders and resting.'

Sophie huffs.

'Stop behaving like a teenager, Sophie. I'm being serious. Matt's scared, and you have to let him do this for his benefit as much as yours.'

Sophie bites her lip.

'You have no idea how scared I was too, finding you here on the floor.' I try to stop the emotion from showing in my voice. 'I thought...' I stop, not wanting to say out loud what I imagined when I found Sophie lying on the floor. 'I'm just saying, I know it's scary being the person who something's happened to, but it's also terrifying when you see it from this side too.' I wipe an unexpected tear from my cheek with the back of my hand.

Sophie reaches out and touches my hand. 'I hadn't really thought about it from your point of view, Emma.'

'Nor do I particularly want you to focus on that. I guess I just wanted to say that it's been a pretty scary time for us all, and without wanting to sound clichéd, it makes you realise what your priorities are – family, friends, your health. They're what's important in life. All the other stuff is trivial.'

'I was scared too.' Sophie's voice is tiny. 'I thought I'd lost the baby.' She sobs.

'Oh, Sophie.' I put down my mug of tea and relieve Sophie of hers, and I grasp her hand.

'I'm supposed to take care of this baby, nurture it and keep it safe, and…and…' Sophie's sobs get more intense. 'What if something had happened to the baby?'

'It didn't, Soph. The baby is perfectly fine. This wasn't your fault. You're not to blame in any way.'

'Aren't I?'

'No, absolutely not. I won't have you say that, Sophie. You've taken care of yourself from the second you found out you were pregnant. You've eaten the right foods, drunk the right liquids – even that disgusting ginger tea that smelled horrendous – all to make sure you're the healthiest you can be. But things happen…' Simon's words in the hospital waiting room are ringing in my ears. 'The human body is complex, and sometimes the only way it can make sure you're listening to it is to fire a warning shot. That's all this was. Just a reminder to take things easy going forward, until this little one' – I touch her baby bump softly – 'is ready to come into the world.'

Sophie nods, and we both sit there quietly drinking our tea.

I leave Sophie an hour later and head home, exhausted, both physically and mentally, from the events of the last few days. As I drive home, I contemplate what the outcome could have been. I shake my head, trying to dislodge those images from my mind. Sophie and the baby are both alright. Everything is fine. But life can seem like it's simply ticking along and we become complacent, forgetting how fragile life is. We should remember to take stock of what we have and be grateful for it. I'm lucky to be surrounded by good friends and a loving family.

I park the car and head wearily up the two flights of stairs to my flat. I find Joe sitting in bed with his laptop on his knees, wearing headphones.

'Hey.' Joe slides off the headphones. 'How's Sophie?'

'Trying to resist Matt's efforts to look after her.'

Joe shakes his head. 'Sounds about right. She must be feeling better.'

I head into the bathroom to remove my makeup and clean my teeth, before sliding into bed beside Joe.

'It's hard, you know,' I say, leaning up on my forearm and facing him.

'What's hard?' Joe frowns as he places the laptop and headphones on the bedside table next to him.

'Letting someone look after you. We're programmed now to be independent women and not rely on men.'

Joe tries, and fails, to hide his smile. 'Independent women?'

'Don't laugh. I'm being serious. It's not enough for a woman to just be a woman nowadays. We have to have a career, keep a tidy house, keep a man, and in some cases look after the children too.'

'Keep a man?' Joe laughs outright now.

'I'm just saying women have to be strong and do a lot, and because of that we don't like to ask for help or let someone take care of us.'

'I see.' Joe nods.

'I realise that I may not embody all of those things. You do, I concede, make sure that we always have food in the fridge, and in a lot of cases, food cooked and on the table at dinnertime.'

Joe chuckles.

'But Sophie is organised and methodical, and I can see why she may have resistance to letting her guard down and allowing Matt to look after her.'

'I do understand that,' Joe says.

'Well, you should think yourself lucky.'

'Really? Why's that?' Joe raises his eyebrows, clearly amused.

I smirk. 'Because I defy the "modern woman" persona and allow you to look after me.'

'Turn out the light, Emma.'

Joe laughs as he snuggles up to me, and I can't help but laugh too.

Chapter Sixteen

South Yorkshire has been whipped into a frenzy as the date for the visit of Prince William and Catherine, Duchess of Cambridge, approaches. Most women in a fifty-mile radius are undertaking a mammoth reinvention involving leg waxing, hair extensions and potential liposuction, in a vain attempt to achieve the svelte, natural look of the duchess. Sales of nude tights and pale-pink lip-gloss have increased massively, and nail salons are booked up for months with requests for French manicures. The whole region has got "Royal Fever", and the anticipation of catching a glimpse of – or shaking hands with – Catherine is tangible.

I find myself getting carried along with the excitement. There's a buzz in the shop as middle-class women flock there, looking for the perfect outfit in which to be photographed at the opportune moment they shake hands with royalty. Sales of the dresses and Jackets I designed hit a record high last week, and we're fast selling out in all three colours.

I don't think that *I* will be fortunate enough to meet Kate and William face to face, and let's be honest, that's a blessing for everyone. My inability to engage my brain before opening my mouth would surely peak under the pressure to impress. And what would I say to the future king of England and his lovely wife?

Jenny seems to have other plans though and meeting the Prince and Duchess is absolutely on her agenda.

'Hey, Emma. It's not long until they're here.' Jenny clasps her hands together gleefully. 'I wonder if they'll bring the children?'

'Probably,' I muse. 'Kate seems to have mastered the art of making public appearances while carrying a toddler without having a hair out of place. I can't imagine my own appearance being so graceful if I had a small human being or two to keep alive on a daily basis. I think having a shower and brushing my hair would prove too demanding, let alone applying makeup and looking stunning.

I fear I'd resemble Marilyn Manson rather than Marilyn Monroe.'

I think back to the day I looked after Theo and Fitz for Simon and James. In fact, I had the kids for only about four hours, rather than the whole day, yet the calmness in my apartment disintegrated more quickly than a balloon bursting, and by the time Simon returned to collect the duo I looked like I'd been dragged through a mangle....twice!

'They're putting on loads of stuff at the park on the day of the visit. Are you and Joe coming down?'

'Yes, definitely. It sounds like a fun day. I think we're taking a picnic and meeting Matt and Sophie too.'

'That sounds lovely.'

'Are you bringing Scott?'

Jenny shrugs. 'Maybe.'

'So we can finally meet him?'

'I guess so.'

'Well, that's good. If I didn't know you better, I'd think he was a figment of your imagination!'

'Charming!'

'What?' I laugh. 'You talk about him all the time, but we're yet to set eyes on him.'

'He's real, don't worry.'

'Well, I can't wait to meet him. You can join us for our picnic.'

'That's kind, thanks. What about Lola? Do you think she and Hugo will be there?'

'I don't know,' I say.

While it's just the two of us, I consider saying something to Jenny about seeing that bruise on Lola a few weeks ago and thinking that she doesn't seem herself at the moment. But perhaps I'm imagining things. I don't really know what I think; it's just a funny feeling in the pit of my stomach that won't go away. From the outside everything looks like it's perfect, and I want Lola to be happy; she deserves to be happy. I can't help feeling, though, that something isn't right beneath the surface. Lola has lost some of her sparkle, and although Hugo seems like a great guy, I can't help but feel that something's not right. I should ask Jenny what she thinks, but I don't want to open a can of worms. Once I've said something, there's no taking it back. I take a deep breath and open my mouth, but quickly close it again. Maybe that conversation is best left for another time.

Chapter Seventeen

The intercom buzzes loudly in the apartment, making both me and Joe jump as we snuggle on the sofa watching a new crime drama.

I glance at my watch. 'Are you expecting someone?'

'No.' Joe shakes his head. 'Isn't it a bit late for unannounced visitors?'

'It's just after nine, so I'd say yes.'

The buzzer persists.

'I'll go.' I stand up and head into the hallway.

'Hello?' I say apprehensively into the intercom.

'Emma?'

It takes me a second to realise that it's Simon.

'Si? I hardly recognised you. Are you okay?'

'Can I come up?'

'Of course.' I press the button to release the external door of the building.

'Everything okay?' Joe appears behind me.

I turn around to face him. 'It's Simon,' I say quietly. 'Something's wrong.'

Two minutes later, there's a knock at the door to the flat. I quickly open it and find Simon hovering in the hallway, shoulders hunched under his hooded jumper.

'Simon?' I reach a hand out to him. 'What on earth's the matter?'

He gulps before saying, 'I think James is cheating on me.'

'What? Come in, come in.' I usher him into the flat and close the door behind us.

Simon rubs at his eyes with the back of his hands and I'd swear he's been crying. This is not a good sign.

'Go through to the lounge. I'll put the kettle on.'

Simon shuffles in a defeated fashion through to the living room as I head into the kitchen. I fill the kettle with a heavy heart. I can't honestly believe that James is being unfaithful. He loves Simon.

'Hey.' Joe appears in the kitchen doorway with his jacket on. 'I'm going to head out for a bit.'

'You don't have to do that,' I whisper, so Simon can't hear us.

'It's fine, Emma. I'll nip to Ben's. I've just sent him a text and he's fine with me calling round.'

I bite my lip.

'Look, Emma...' Joe stands in front of me. 'I like Simon, you know that.'

I nod.

'But I heard what he said when he walked through the door. If he and James are having problems then he's going to want to talk to you about it, and he's going to be a lot more comfortable if I'm not here.'

'Are you sure?'

'Absolutely.' Joe kisses me on the lips. 'I'll be back in an hour or so.'

'Okay. Thank you.'

I watch Joe leave, before continuing to make the tea. I grab a packet of Simon's favourite chocolate biscuits from the cupboard and carry everything through to the lounge, where I find Simon pacing the floor and chewing on his fingernails. I place the mugs of tea and the biscuits on the coffee table and take a seat on the sofa.

'Simon, come and sit down, please.' I pat the sofa beside me. 'You're going to make me dizzy if you carry on like this.'

'I'm sorry, Em. I shouldn't have come here.'

'Simon, it's fine. I'm your best friend. If something's wrong then you most definitely should be here. Now sit down and tell me what's going on.'

Reluctantly Simon sits down beside me, still chomping on a fingernail, and I slide the packet of biscuits across the table in his direction, if only to stop a serious injury to his fingertips. He accepts the packet from me, opens it and takes a thoughtful bite of a double-chocolate-chip cream. I wait patiently for him to finish his biscuit and begin. I've learnt from plenty of discussions with Simon over the many years we've known each other not to push him, but to let him tell me the story in his own time.

'James and I had a huge row,' Simon blurts out, shaking his head sorrowfully.

'Tonight?'

'No. Last week.'

'Why didn't you come to me then?'

Simon's shoulders sag. 'I thought it would all blow over.'

'Oh, Simon.' I take a biscuit from the packet, realising that denial is usually the route I take when faced with confrontation.

'What was the fight about?'

'Us not spending enough time together.'

'Okay. How did the argument start?'

'I don't know really.' Simon sighs emphatically. 'One minute we were talking about choosing a nursery for the twins to start going to, and the next we were fighting about the fact that I don't do enough to help around the house and...' Simon shrugs.

'And do you?'

'What?'

'Do your fair share around the house?'

Simon thinks for a moment. 'Maybe not. Oh, I don't know, I was never very domesticated.'

This is true.

'And now I'm a husband and a father, and what if...'

'What if what?'

'What if I'm just not up to it, and James has figured that out already and he's gone and found someone else who is?'

'Okay.' I take another chocolate biscuit from the pack and hand them back to Simon, who does the same. 'Those are some pretty big leaps you're taking.' I take a sip of my tea. 'First of all, where are James and the boys now?'

'At his mum's for the night.'

'And you didn't want to go?'

Simon shakes his head. 'Not like this. Not with this hanging over me. I couldn't pretend everything was alright when I don't think it is.'

'What happened after the argument?' I ask.

'We huffed and puffed a bit, but then got on with bathing the boys and putting them to bed. Things were a bit tense that night, and if I'm honest, they have been since.'

'How have you come to the conclusion from one fight that James is cheating on you? That seems a bit extreme.'

'It's not just that.' Simon takes another biscuit, which makes me fear for what's to come. 'There's more.'

And that's what I feared. I figured there would be. Simon may be a drama queen, but even he wouldn't be this upset over one argument.

'Okay, walk me through it.'

'He keeps disappearing, and he's lied to me about where he's been. He told me he'd left one of Fitz's toys at his mum's and he was going to pick it up, but when I called him I could hear street noise in the background and –'

Simon stops abruptly.

I encourage him to continue. 'And, what did you do?'

'Oh, I'm so ashamed, Emma.' Simon holds his head in his hands.

'Simon?'

'I checked where he was on that "Find Your Friends" app thingy on my phone.'

I take a sharp intake of breath. I know this application on my smartphone well. Sophie and I both have it, but it's a mutual "only for use in an emergency" app for our safety.

'I know, I know. I'm a bad person and a terrible husband.'

'No, you're not; you're human, and humans behave irrationally sometimes.'

'That doesn't excuse it.'

'That aside,' I say, 'where did your phone tell you that James was?'

'On the high street in town, at McGinty's bar. He's seeing someone else, Emma, I know he is. He must have been meeting them there.'

'You don't know that. All you know is that James said he was going to be in one place and he ended up somewhere else. There has to be a simple explanation for that. I honestly don't believe that James would cheat on you, Si. James loves you.'

'What if James is sick of me being a crap husband and he's going to leave me? I couldn't stand it. He and the twins are everything to me.' Simon sobs quietly.

'Come here.' I wipe the tears from his cheeks like a mother might do to her small child, and then wrap my arms around him. Simon clings to me like his life depends on it.

'I love him, Em,' he mumbles into my shoulder.

'I know you do. We'll figure it out, I promise you.'

Simon pulls away. 'I love you too. You're a good friend.'

'It works both ways.' I smile gently at him.

'As much as I appreciate the tea and sympathy, do you have anything stronger to numb my pain?'

I laugh. 'Of course. Come into the kitchen and we'll see what's in the cupboard.'

A few minutes later, nursing vodka and Diet Cokes, we sit on the bar stools at the small table in my kitchen.

'So what do I do now?' Simon asks, before taking a gulp of his drink.

'You only have one option, Simon, and that's to ask him. You need to speak to James.'

'I can't. What would I say?'

'You say that you're concerned about the fact he's been disappearing a lot, particularly after you've had a fight.'

'I can't tell him that I used that app to find him with his mobile phone.'

'No, I agree that telling the person you've promised to love and cherish for the rest of your lives that you've been tracking him via GPS, like a UPS parcel, isn't the smartest thing to do to defuse the situation.'

'Well, when you put it like that, it sounds really bad,' Simon huffs.

I just raise my eyebrows at him.

'Oaky, it is bad. But I'm remorseful – surely that has to count for something?'

I laugh. 'Well argued.'

He chuckles.

'That's better. I hate to see you sad,' I say. 'I'm sure this is all a misunderstanding, and you and James will be absolutely fine.'

'I hope so.' Simon shrugs. 'Can I ask a favour, Emma?'

'Of course, anything.'

'Can I stay here tonight? I really don't want to be alone.'

'Sure. That's why we have the spare room.'

'I miss the days of us getting sloshed on gin in your old house and sharing a bed together.'

'Yeah? I don't. You snore and flap around like a seal in shallow water when you've had a drink.'

'I do not!' Simon protests.

I grin. 'You'll never know.'

'James would tell me if I did.'

I cock my head to one side. 'James is too polite.' I know this, and I know in my heart that I'm right about James and that there must be another explanation for his behaviour.

'You know, you're the only girl I've ever slept with.' Simon downs the remainder of his drink and holds out his glass, hinting at a refill.

I wander back over to the bottle of vodka on the kitchen side and make us fresh drinks. 'You could really confuse someone by saying that out loud outside of this room.' I pour a small measure of vodka into each glass and add ice and Diet Coke.

'What do you mean?'

'When you say "slept with" that actually is a literal description.'

'Well, of course it is. We've never had sex, Emma. I'm gay and you're straight. Anyone who knows us is well aware of that.'

'They might think I "turned" you.' I giggle, handing him one of the glasses of vodka and Coke.

'It doesn't work like that.' Simon shakes his head. 'You don't turn someone gay, darling, they just *are*.'

'I know that, Simon. I'm just kidding.'

'It's simple. As much as I love you, I don't find you or any woman sexually attractive. I only fancy men and want to sleep with them.'

'Hi, Joe.' I lean past Simon as Joe appears in the doorway. Clearly Simon and I were too involved in our conversation to hear him come back into the flat.

'Oh, hi, Joe.' Simon turns to face him with a slight colour to his cheeks.

'Am I interrupting something?' A smile tugs at the corners of Joe's mouth. He's well aware of Simon's extravagance and has never had a problem with that, or his sexuality.

'No, we're just having a drink and a chat, that's all. Simon's going to stay the night, if that's okay.'

'Not a problem,' Joe says.

'And just for clarification,' Simon adds, 'when I said that I only fancy men and want to sleep with them, I didn't mean you, honey.'

'Understood.' Joe's still trying not to smile.

'I mean, you're a good-looking guy, just not my type. I don't want you worrying if we bump into each other in the hallway in the middle of the night.'

'Good to know.' Joe nods at Simon as I cringe. Honestly Simon really should think before opening his mouth. Then again, who am I to talk? I'm the queen of saying ridiculous things at inappropriate moments.

Later that night, once I've tucked Simon up safely in my spare bed after a few more vodka and Diet Cokes, and reassured him again that he and James will work things out, I slide into my own bed beside Joe.

'All okay?' Joe asks as I turn out the bedside lamp and snuggle up to his warm body.

'Yeah. It will be, I'm sure. I don't know what's going on with James, but I'm pretty confident he's not cheating on Simon.'

'They seem like a solid couple,' Joe says, kissing my shoulder.

'They are. I saw Simon date a lot of men prior to James and he never came close to commitment with any of them. But James was different from the start.'

'In what way?'

'He's not Simon's usual type of guy.'

'Really? Well, apparently I'm not either.'

I giggle. 'Don't be offended.'

'Don't worry, I'm not. Simon's a lovely man and everything, but-'

'But you prefer women.'

'Absolutely, and one specific woman.'

I roll over and tuck myself into Joe's side and he wraps his arm around me.

'They'll work it out,' Joe says quietly.

'I know,' I say.

But as we lie there in the darkness and I hear Joe's breathing soften as he drifts off to sleep, my earlier confidence begins to waver, and I can't help but worry that something must be really wrong. James wouldn't risk what he and Simon have together, as well as the twins, for someone else, surely? But in the end, how well do we know what goes on in other people's relationships? I think back to my time with Chris; I thought everything was rosy and I was about to be proposed to, not dumped for a younger model. Sometimes we don't know what's going on right in front of our noses.

I wake up early to find myself alone in bed, and I frown as I glance at the alarm clock and see that it's only seven thirty a.m. I pull myself up to a seated position and pat down my hair, which feels like it's trying to escape its current home on my head. I take my dressing gown from the hook on the back of the bedroom door and wrap it around myself as I make my way through to the kitchen. I can hear voices and smell coffee as I approach the closed door.

'Morning, you two,' I say warily as I walk into the kitchen and see Joe and Simon sitting and chatting at the table.

'Morning, Em.' Simon grins, taking a swig from his cup.

'Hey.' Joe smiles. 'Do you want coffee?'

'Please,' I say as I slide onto the stool beside Simon. 'Don't you think you should be wearing...well, something?' I raise my eyebrows in Simon's direction, taking in the fact that he's chosen to sit at my kitchen table with my boyfriend in just his boxer shorts.

'What? Joe doesn't mind, do you?' Simon glances over at Joe as he pours my coffee.

Joe cocks his head to one side. 'If you're comfortable then I'm comfortable.'

'Please don't encourage him.' I shake my head. 'Simon, in future when you cross the boundary from my spare room, you need to be at least half-dressed, not nearly naked, okay?'

'You're such a spoil sport.' Simon wafts his hand at me. 'It's a good job I love you, though.'

'You seem much better this morning,' I say to Simon as Joe hands me a mug of coffee.

'I think our talk last night helped. And I had a good night's sleep, which hasn't happened since James and I argued. So now I feel ready to face the day and, more importantly, to face James and demand the truth.'

'That's good, Si. But try the gentle approach, rather than going at it with a sledgehammer.'

'Of course. You know me, Em.' Simon winks.

'Yes, exactly.' I sip my coffee and shake my head.

Chapter Eighteen

The conversation about Lola that I have been putting off having with Jenny seems more pressing than ever in the days that follow. When I arrive at work after finally getting Simon dressed and out of my flat, I notice that Lola is dressed oddly. She's wearing clothing that covers her arms and neck, in complete contrast to the fashion style she usually embraces. Lola's in her twenties and very fashion-conscious. Being conservative about her clothing goes against every element of her being. So to see her dressed in plain clothes that mask every inch of her body, with a high neckline and long sleeves, causes me concern.

On Thursday night, I drag Jenny to the bar across the road to finally discuss the situation with her. I know it's terrible to suggest that someone is abusing their partner, and I really want to be wrong about Hugo. Everything at face value when I'm in his company tells me that I'm wrong, but the churning feeling in the bottom of my stomach tells me that I'm not.

I take a gulp of my wine, unsure how to begin this conversation with Jenny.

She calls me out. 'What's wrong, Emma?'

Clearly I'm fooling no one. Still, I ask, 'What makes you think that something's wrong?'

'You've been acting skittish all afternoon. You couldn't wait to get Lola out of the shop tonight and off home, and since we've sat down you've opened your mouth to speak and then closed it again three times. You're starting to look like a demented goldfish.'

'Oh, it's like that, is it?' I huff.

Jenny laughs. 'Just spit it out.'

Okay. Here goes.

I take another sip of wine.

'Um, have you noticed that lately Lola seems to be…well…she's got –'

'She's covered in bruises,' Jenny says quietly.

It's clearly not my overactive imagination. Jenny has noticed it too.

'Well, yes.'

'And are you thinking...?'

'I'm thinking – oh God, I can't believe that I'm going to say this out loud...'

'That all these bruises aren't from the random sporting activities she'd have us believe that she and Hugo are partaking in every weekend.'

'Exactly.'

We both take a gulp of our wine.

'This is serious, Jenny. What we're saying here is that her good-looking, smart and charming boyfriend is actually –'

'Beating the crap out of her.' Jenny's fist tightens around the stem of her wine glass.

'I know. I mean, it's awful to think that, but what if it's true? What do we do about it?'

'We have to talk to her.'

'And say what? We can't accuse her perfect boyfriend of physically abusing her.'

'He does come across as too perfect,' Jenny states.

'No man is that perfect,' I agree.

'Really? I don't hear many complaints from you about Joe.'

'He has his flaws.'

'Enlighten me.'

'Well, he, um, he's too organised,' I say, swishing my hand defensively as Jenny shakes her head at me with a look of disbelief.

'Two more wines, please,' she calls over to the passing barmaid.

'I mean like *really* organised,' I emphasise.

'What's *really organised* mean to someone like you?'

Ignoring the "someone like you" comment, I continue: 'It means that, for example, he plans and orders food shopping weeks in advance.'

'Making sure that you always have food in your house is not a flaw, Emma.'

'It is when you live with me. I don't know what I want to be eating for dinner on Wednesday night three weeks from now.'

Jenny sighs heavily. 'I'm just going to ignore you.'

'Honestly!' I protest as the barmaid places two fresh glasses of wine in front of us.

'Back to the much more serious issue at hand.' Jenny takes a sip of wine.

'You're right. How do we approach this with Lola?'

'We need an intervention.'

'An intervention?'

'We need to get her out on a Saturday night, away from Hugo, and get some alcohol down her so she's more likely to talk.'

'And what? We just ask her outright?'

'Yes.'

'That won't be easy, given that she refuses to have more than one drink on a Saturday night now, so she's not hungover on a Sunday when Hugo wants her to go tree climbing, or whatever.'

'We need it to be for an "occasion", Jenny says.

'Such as? No one's birthday is coming up.'

'I'll think of something,' Jenny says with a determined look on her face. 'Can you do this Saturday?'

'Yeah, sure. Not a problem. We need to do this sooner rather than later. I'm really worried about her.'

'Me too.' Jenny sighs heavily.

We sit there in silence. I expect that, like me, Jenny is contemplating what might happen if we don't intervene. I'm still in shock that we're actually having this conversation. I mean, I know domestic violence happens; I just never thought it would happen to one of my friends. I realise that thought is ridiculous. The sad truth is: it can happen to anyone. There's no hard and fast rule about who finds themselves in that situation. We've all fallen for the wrong guy at some point in our lives. I guess some men hide their true self more than others. Violence and emotional abuse are – scarily – more prevalent than any of us knows.

'How do you think she'll react?' I ask quietly a few moments later.

'If it were me, and you were accusing Scott of hurting me, I'd be pretty angry.'

'Yeah, I would too if you accused Joe of that. I guess we need to be prepared for that. Lola might not want to hear what we're going to say to her.'

'We're so lucky.' Jenny fiddles with her wine glass. 'I can't imagine how scared Lola must be if she's in a violent relationship. I mean, that's the person who's supposed to love you and take care of you. You shouldn't be in fear of them. I don't know how you end up in that situation.' Jenny shakes her head.

'I'm guessing it's easier than you think. I don't suppose Hugo started out being violent, or Lola wouldn't have entertained the idea of dating him, let alone wanting him to come halfway around the world to be here with her.'

'You're right. She's smart and streetwise, so Hugo must have lulled her into a false sense of security so she trusted him.'

'And fell in love with him.'

'That's the really sad and frightening part.' Jenny exhales. 'How do you deal emotionally with the fact that the man you love has turned on you?'

I arrive home around eight thirty, which is a little later than I anticipated.

'I'm sorry, I'm sorry,' I call as I close the front door behind me. I instantly smell Chinese food and my stomach grumbles, reminding me that lunch was a lifetime ago and a liquid fix after work doesn't count as a snack. It's a good job I decided to get a taxi home, as I feel a little tipsy after a couple of glasses of wine.

I walk into the kitchen just as Joe's setting the table.

'Hi.' He smiles.

'Hi.' I chuck my handbag on the floor and give him a kiss. 'Things took a little longer to sort out than I thought.'

'Clearly.' Joe raises his eyebrows.

'Are you mad?'

'Of course not, Emma. I'm just intrigued as to what the big secret is that you and Jenny had to discuss tonight...over wine.'

'I only had two glasses,' I state quickly.

Joe laughs. 'Emma, I'm not judging you. What's wrong? Why are you so jumpy?'

That's a good question. This whole thing with Lola has thrown me a bit. I guess because the gorgeous Hugo appeared so loving and devoted to Lola, I find it hard to accept that he could be hurting her behind closed doors. How could someone behave so differently in private than they do in public? I suppose I also struggle with the fact that Lola, a smart, funny, and confident girl, has somehow got herself into a situation where she's being physically abused and is covering it up and lying to her friends to protect the exact person who's hurting her. I don't know why she'd want to protect Hugo.

'Emma?' Joe breaks my train of thought. 'Are you ready to eat? I cooked Chinese food – it's in the oven. I presumed you wouldn't have had anything substantial to eat.'

I swallow back tears that have appeared from nowhere. With this simple gesture, I realise how lucky I am. Joe doesn't care that I'm home later than expected; he cares that I'm okay. He knows me well enough to know that I wouldn't have eaten anything with my wine – other than, potentially, salted peanuts, and I was so distracted by my conversation with Jenny that I didn't even think to order them. He's made me dinner to make sure I have something proper to eat.

'Emma?' Joe brushes my cheek, gently wiping away a tear that's escaped. 'What's wrong?'

'I'm fine, I'm fine.' I take hold of his hand and give it a squeeze. 'Thank you for making me dinner.'

'Come on, Emma, that's not why you're tearful. My Chinese chicken might be amazing, but...'

I nod, composing myself. 'Let's sit down to eat and I'll tell you.'

A few minutes later, we sit at the kitchen table and tuck into our food. I hadn't realised how hungry I was. Mental note to self: must eat more nibbles when drinking wine.

'So?' Joe prompts as I chew slowly on my chicken, wondering whether I should divulge the details of my conversation with Jenny. At this point we don't know for definite that there's anything wrong with Lola. Although it's quite coincidental that both Jenny and I are of the opinion that Lola is being…it feels wrong to even say the word "abused", but that's what it is.

'Emma,' Joe says softly, 'please tell me what's worrying you. You know you can trust me with anything. I just want to help.'

'I know, and I love you for that.' I smile warmly.

Joe shrugs. 'So tell me what's bothering you.'

I take a deep breath.

'It's Lola,' I say, and then stop, not sure how exactly to put into words that I think her lovely new boyfriend is hitting her. I decide that the best way is to simply say: 'I – no, we, Jenny and I, we think that Lola's boyfriend is…hitting her.'

I see Joe's mouth form a thin line as he digests what I've just said.

'You think? I mean, what would make you both think that?'

I exhale. 'We see bruises on her on a regular basis. I mean, she tries to cover them up and she gives us reasons for why she has them, but –'

'But you don't believe her?'

I shake my head. 'Maybe I did at first. I had no reason not to. Hugo seemed like the perfect gentleman.'

Joe puts down his knife and fork with a clunk and he stares at his plate of half-eaten food. 'What does Lola say when you ask her about the bruises?'

'She says that Hugo is really sporty and that the bruises are from them doing crazy things at the weekend – that she's really clumsy and she falls over when they're doing all this stuff.'

'I see.' Joe's expression is now one of anger.

'Nobody's that clumsy,' I say. 'Not even me.'

'So what do we do now? Where can I find this guy?' Joe stands up and steps away from the table.

'Joe, what are you doing?' I jump up from the table too, shocked by his reaction. 'You can't just go around and, well, "find this guy".'

'Why not? He clearly needs someone to talk to him, and I think I might just be the guy for that. See how he likes picking on someone a little bigger than poor Lola.'

I realise that this is completely inappropriate under the circumstances, but I'm quite turned on by this "macho" Joe. He's usually so placid and laidback. I quite like the idea of him being a "knight in shining armour", for want of a better phrase. Although I don't actually want him to go and punch Hugo, the fact that he's prepared to do so makes me love him even more, if that's at all possible.

'Joe, we need to tread carefully with this. We can't just steam in there, accusing him of all sorts, and expect it not to end in complete carnage.'

'Why not?' Joe's tone is defiant.

'Because we don't know how Lola will react to us accusing her boyfriend of this.'

'Well, why wouldn't she want to tell you? Why would she still be with this bloke?'

'It's complicated. She might be embarrassed to admit that she's in that situation. She might feel like it's her fault, even though it isn't.'

'There is absolutely no excuse under any circumstances for laying your hands on a woman – ever,' Joe states firmly.

'I know, believe me I know that. But if he is abusing her physically then the chances are, he's abusing her emotionally as well. She's probably in a fragile state of mind, even if she's trying to pretend that everything is okay. She could also be completely aware of what's happening and just not know how on earth to get herself out of the situation.'

'You're right.' Joe sits back down at the table, a little calmer now. 'Sorry, it just gets me so mad to hear things like this. I can't stand men who hit women. They're the lowest of the low. I just want to help her.'

'Me too.' I sit back down too. 'Jenny and I have a plan. We're going to talk to her this weekend. We're going to take her out for drinks on Saturday night and, well, approach the subject.'

'And how exactly are you going to do that?' Joe asks.

'I don't know. Clearly less boldly than I've just been with you.' I half-smile.

'Sorry.' Joe cocks his head to one side.

'Don't be. I'm glad the thought of men hitting women disgusts you. It only reminds me again how much I love you and how lucky I am. You are what you seem to be on face value, every little bit.'

'I love you too, and if I'm honest, I'm a little worried about you getting in the middle of all this. After what happened with Sophie and Conner, I guess anything could happen.'

I swallow hard at the memory. Connor was Sophie's boyfriend prior to Matt. A loving, caring boyfriend as far as Sophie was concerned, but in reality he was a complete psychopath who'd targeted me prior to Sophie introducing us. Calling himself "Johnny", he'd charmed me, after a few too many vodkas, right into his bed, when I was in a vulnerable state, having just been dumped by Chris, and then he played me and Sophie off against each other. He made me out to be the bad guy, and Sophie, completely under his spell, took his word over mine. It destroyed our friendship for a time, and very nearly ended up with us both dead in an accident at the end of a terrible car chase. Prior to that situation, I would never have believed that Sophie would turn against me and believe the words of a new boyfriend over mine. But it happened, because Connor manipulated Sophie and isolated her, so she only listened to him.

'I suppose you never know how someone is going to react when you accuse their boyfriend of something horrible.' I bite my lip, hoping Lola's reaction won't be the same as Sophie's.

'Just approach the situation with caution. You might have been right earlier – Lola could defend this guy completely and turn on you and Jenny, and where will that leave her?'

I think for a moment. The last thing we want to do is to alienate Lola. But if Jenny and I don't speak out then things will at best stay the same, and at worst escalate into something much worse, with Lola in even more danger. Quite honestly, neither of these scenarios is acceptable.

Chapter Nineteen

For the rest of the week, Jenny and I play along as normal in the shop with Lola, not hinting at anything to do with the conversation we had in the wine bar. Jenny manages to get Lola to agree to come out for a few drinks on Saturday night, under the pretence of Jenny wanting to chat to us about some made-up situation with her and Scott. Well, it might not be totally made-up. Jenny has a habit of stressing about a relationship the minute a guy gets serious about her. It's like a reflex: she wants to turn and run the minute they hint at commitment.

When Saturday night arrives, I can't help but feel apprehensive, and as Joe drops me off outside the pub where we're meeting, my chest feels tight and I can hear my heart beating a little louder than normal.

Jenny's already there, waiting, as I walk through the door and head over to the bar area.

'What are you drinking?' she asks as I approach.

'Vodka and Diet Coke, please.' I feel like I need some of the hard stuff to calm my nerves.

Jenny orders the drinks, and once we've been served we head over to a tall, round table and wait in silence for Lola, both gulping at our drinks.

Jenny hugs Lola hello when she joins us a few minutes later in the bar. 'Wow, that dress is stunning.'

It is, it's stunning, a black-and-purple block-patterned dress that clings seductively in all the right places. I can't help but notice, though, that it has long sleeves – not the usual dress of choice for Saturday night drinking; maybe this is to cover something she doesn't want us to see. I can't remember the last time I saw Lola's bare arms.

'Hey, I got you a vodka and Coke.'

I hand the glass to Lola, and she smiles and takes a tiny sip, then places the glass on the table. At this rate our plan to get Lola tipsy enough to broach the subject of her constant bruises could take a while.

'So, how's your friend Sophie doing?' Lola asks. 'It can't be that long until the baby arrives.'

'She has a few months to go,' I say, taking a drink of my own vodka and Coke.

'Is it making you broody?' Lola asks.

I see Jenny glance at me with raised eyebrows. Lola hasn't been party to my conversations with Jenny about my inner battle over whether or not I want children. So I decide to play this cautiously and simply say, 'No, Joe and I aren't quite there yet. But I'm excited to be a godmother.'

Lola smiles. 'It's lovely that she's asked you.'

'Yeah, I'm not sure that I'm the best role model, but I'm going to give it my best shot.'

'Ignore her,' Jenny interrupts. 'She's going to be great.'

'Yeah, I can see that. You have that motherly concern about you.' Lola takes another tiny sip of her drink.

'Really?' I don't see maternal instinct in my skillset.

'Sure.' Lola smiles warmly at me, and I take this as an opportunity to probe her a little more about her own desires.

'Do you see yourself having children?' I ask.

Lola glances down, away from my gaze, for a second before answering, 'Yes, absolutely.'

'I guess it's about finding the right guy to have babies with. It needs to be someone you totally want to spend the rest of your life with. Someone you trust completely. Someone who will take care of you, no matter what.'

'I agree.' Lola nods.

Jenny steps in now. 'So do you think Hugo could be "the one"?'

'Um...' Lola blushes. 'I think it's a bit too early to determine that.'

'Do you love him?' I push.

'We're just enjoying our time together,' Lola answers, a little dismissively.

I should take this as a hint to back off, but I feel the need to persist with this line of questioning.

Lola changes the subject completely, though. 'Are you looking forward to the royal visit?'

'I'm really quite excited.' I drink the last of my vodka and Coke. 'I'm in complete awe of the duchess. She's so glamorous, yet modern, and she looks like she's completely got everything sorted in her life. She's so "together".'

'I know, and the prince is always so adoring. They look really happy,' Jenny adds.

'Speaking of happy, how are things with you and Scott?' Lola asks. 'What is it you want to talk to us about? Is everything okay with you two?'

Jenny shrugs. 'We're alright.'

'What does "we're alright" mean?' Lola looks from me to Jenny.

I speak before Jenny can: 'It means that Scott adores Jenny, and after lusting after him for months, she's now become a commitment phobe the minute he's got serious about her.'

'That's not fair.' Jenny stands with her hands on her hips, defiant.

I grin. 'Alright, I'll indulge you for a second. Why don't you enlighten me and tell us both how it really is then?'

Jenny bites her lip and scowls good-naturedly at me. 'Okay, so maybe it is a bit like that.'

Lola and I laugh in unison.

'You're unbelievable.' I shake my head at Jenny. 'Scott is a lovely guy, and he clearly likes you a lot – and you like him too; I know you do.'

'I know, I know!' Jenny protests. 'I'll get there, I will. I just need a little more time before I hang up my "singleton" title forever.'

'Come on, drink up, Lola.' I motion at her still half-full glass. 'I think we need a cocktail.'

Out on the street, we link arms and sashay up to the cocktail bar that Mum and I visited (and got slightly drunk at) not so long ago.

Three shockingly strong cosmopolitans later, we're snuggled in a plush booth, laughing raucously, as we tease Jenny over her inability to commit to a grownup relationship. She's spent the last few years complaining to anyone who'll listen that all men want is to take you out when it suits them, seduce you when it suits them and then leave you hanging, as they run a mile when you actually call them your boyfriend. Now she's done a complete role reversal and is keeping Scott at arm's length. I guess I can understand her being battle weary, but you just have to pick the good ones out from the not-so-good ones, like Joe, and like Scott.

Clearly we've got distracted by talk of Jenny and Scott, and I decide it's time to broach the subject of Lola's "situation" with her: she's a lot more relaxed than she was when she first arrived, and a lot more inebriated, thanks to the cocktails.

'So are you and Hugo doing any crazy sporting activity tomorrow?' I ask.

Jenny nods discreetly at me, hopefully realising that we need to get Lola talking again.

'Oh God, yes,' Lola says. 'I forgot myself. I'm not supposed to have too much to drink tonight, and I feel a bit wobbly already.'

'A bit wobbly? Those cosmopolitans are like pure alcohol.' Jenny grins. 'Speaking of which, shall we have another?' She waves at a waitress who's doing the rounds, collecting glasses.

'Absolutely,' I say, downing the dregs of my cosmo.

'No, no.' Lola pushes her still half-full glass away. 'I've had far too much to drink already.'

'Another round, please.' Jenny gestures at our empty glasses as the waitress approaches our booth.

'It's Saturday night.' Jenny nudges Lola playfully. 'Let your hair down and enjoy yourself. There's nothing spoiling, is there?'

'Yeah, and the three of us haven't been out in ages.'

'But I promised Hugo that I wouldn't be drunk when I came home.'

'Came home? I didn't realise you two were living together?'

I'm taken aback by this. Lola has completely omitted to mention this development in their relationship. Hugo had rented his own flat when he arrived in South Yorkshire, so as not to "rush" things apparently, which seemed sensible. Now I can feel my heartbeat quicken. This is worse than we thought.

Jenny looks equally alarmed. 'When did this happen?'

'Um…' Lola fumbles for words. 'Last month.' She shrugs dismissively.

I take a deep breath and exhale. 'Lola.' I pause and she looks at me. 'Is everything okay between you and Hugo?'

She instantly averts her eyes. 'Of course,' she snaps a little too quickly.

'Three cosmopolitans.'

None of us had noticed the waitress reappear, and we're all silent as she slides the drinks down in front of us. I swish my bank card against the hand-held machine, thankful that modern technology allows you to purchase most things with a simple swipe of your card in a second.

'We're worried about you, that's all,' Jenny says once the waitress is out of earshot.

'We?' Lola looks from Jenny to me with a slightly hostile expression.

I jump in. 'It's just that…' But then words fail me. I can't be as blunt with Lola as I was with Joe.

'Does Hugo get angry with you at all?' Jenny asks, clearly taking the "non-sugar-coated" option.

'Angry? Why would he get angry with me?'

Jenny backtracks. 'Well, maybe not angry with you, but does he have a bit of a temper?'

'No!' Lola snaps. 'Why are you asking me this? I don't understand what you're getting at.'

'You've had a lot of bruises recently.' Jenny swallows and looks wary, but she doesn't take her eyes off Lola. I watch Lola too and notice her body language has changed. It's almost like she's retracting into a shell.

'So what? I'm clumsy. I've told you that.' She glares at us both, her cheeks flushed. 'And you think I'm lying?'

I cringe. This is *so* not how I wanted this conversation to go. I can already feel the shift in loyalties. She's leaping to Hugo's defence.

'You think that Hugo is bruising me, that he's hurting me? Is that it?' Lola's practically shouting now, which is attracting worried glances from some of the other customers.

'Lola, calm down.' Jenny holds her hands up submissively.

'Why would you think that he would do that to me?' Lola challenges.

I try to defuse the situation. 'We just want to make sure that you're...happy.' I touch her arm in an affectionate way, but she flinches and whips her arm away from my hand.

'Of course I'm happy. I don't know what you're trying to imply.'

'We're not trying to –'

'Just because you both have ridiculous relationship issues, you presume everyone else must have too,' Lola snaps angrily.

'Lola, you're being unfair,' Jenny interjects.

'Unfair?' Lola gasps. 'You're practically accusing my boyfriend of hitting me, and you think *I'm* being unfair?'

Jenny and I just sit in silence, aware that we've poked the hornets' nest and now they're flying in our face, stinging us with every word. This is the outcome that neither of us wanted.

'I can't believe you two,' Lola continues as she shuffles out of the booth. Standing up, she flings her coat on and it swirls around her, taking on a life of its own.

Jenny tries to placate her. 'Lola, where are you going? Sit down, please.'

'No,' Lola snaps. 'I don't want to spend another minute here with you two. I thought you were my friends.'

'We are.' I stand up too.

'True friends wouldn't accuse my lovely boyfriend of something so heinous. You're bang out of order, and you don't know what you're talking about.'

'Lola...' I reach my hand out to her.

'Just leave me alone!' she shouts, before turning on her heel and marching out of the bar.

I start to go after her, but Jenny grabs my arm. 'Leave her.' She shakes her head. 'You'll only make things worse.'

'But...shouldn't we go after her?'

'She won't listen to either of us tonight, not like this.'

I stare down at the three untouched cosmopolitans and feel a wave of defeat wash over me, followed closely by fear. Have we just alienated Lola and sent her fleeing into the arms of the one person whom we didn't want to be in that position?

'So what now?' I ask Jenny.

'Now? We go home and we try again on Monday at work.'

I nod, feeling terrible, but there's nothing else to say. Tonight couldn't have gone any worse. I just hope that Jenny and I haven't completely destroyed our friendship with Lola.

We head outside and wave down a passing taxi. The night's still young for most of the city, but I can't wait to get home and into my dressing gown. An uneasy feeling hangs heavily in my heart as we make the short journey home, both of us quiet, lost in thought. I hope Lola is okay. I hope I'm wrong about all of this, and Jenny and I have just made a terrible mistake. That would be the best outcome from this. Yes, our friendship would be damaged, but I know it would recover in time. That's far preferable to the other outcome, where Jenny and I have it absolutely right and all we've done is push Lola closer to the one person we were trying to get her away from.

We arrive at Jenny's house first and we hug goodbye.

'I'll try texting Lola tomorrow,' I say as Jenny climbs out of the car.

She nods. 'Okay. Let me know if she replies.'

'Are you seeing Scott tomorrow?' I ask before Jenny closes the door.

She smiles. 'Yeah.'

'Then just think on,' I say. 'I'm not saying you should rush into moving in with him just because of what's going on with Lola. But maybe we should all take a step back and realise what a good man looks like when he's standing right in front of us.'

'Fair point.' She shakes her head at me, looking amused. 'Thanks, Emma. See you on Monday.'

She closes the car door and the taxi drives the few miles to my flat. I climb the two flights of stairs wearily. Tonight feels like it's taken its toll on me physically as well as emotionally.

I walk into the flat, kick my high heels off and head straight to the kitchen to switch the kettle on. Despite the vodka and Cokes, and the cosmopolitans, I feel completely sober now and in need of a cup of tea.

'Hey, how did it go tonight?' Joe walks through the kitchen door and I turn to face him.

'Not well,' I say as I drop a teabag into my mug. 'Do you want a tea?'

'Yes, please.' Joe takes hold of my hand. 'What happened?'

'She denied everything. She defended him. She accused Jenny and me of not being real friends, and then she stormed out of the bar.'

'Oh dear.' Joe pulls me into a hug and he kisses my hair. 'You had to try, and you always knew this could be her reaction.'

'I know.' I press myself closer into Joe's embrace.

'So you keep trying until she hears you.'

I nod into his chest.

Joe cups my chin and lifts my face up to meet his gaze. 'You're a good friend, Emma. Lola will realise that. She's just vulnerable at the moment, and scared.'

I look into Joe's warm eyes and wonder how I've ended up with a kind, loving partner and yet Lola, who's the nicest girl you could wish to meet, has ended up with someone who thinks it's okay to use her as a punch-bag.

'I love you,' I say, and I lean in and kiss Joe on the mouth. It starts off as a slow, gentle kiss, but then it intensifies, as Joe wraps his arms around me and his tongue caresses mine.

Tonight, more than ever, I need to feel close to Joe, need to feel his warm body next to mine. To feel safe and protected in his arms. I feel the familiar pull of him and the heat between us that never seems to fade. It's instant, and I can't explain it. Maybe if I could, it wouldn't be there.

Joe takes my hand and leads me through to the bedroom. He lifts my arms above my head and slowly removes my dress, his fingers grazing my bare skin making every nerve in my body stand to attention. He removes his jeans and T-shirt, barely taking his eyes off me, and then he kisses me again and lowers me down onto the bed.

Every movement is slow and sensual as Joe's mouth finds mine again and I reach my arms around his back and pull him tighter against me. I enjoy fast and frantic lovemaking, the "can't get each other's clothes off quickly enough" moments, but this is what really turns me on: slow and intense love-making, absorbing each and every moment, losing ourselves in each other. That's what I need tonight. I need to lose myself in Joe. To feel aroused and loved, and to know that I'm having the exact same effect on him. To know that as his mouth finds my breast and his tongue teases my nipples, he's as turned on as I am.

'I love you,' I murmur as I close my eyes, and then Joe pushes himself inside me and takes me to another place.

Chapter Twenty

The next morning I'm summoned for coffee and *pain au chocolat* with Simon at our usual coffee shop, and I can't help but fear the worst. I've barely heard from him in the last few days since he stayed over, which is unprecedented as he's usually texting me rubbish all the time. I hope I did enough to persuade him to speak to James about how he was feeling. Maybe I did, and maybe everything is alright. But as I walk to the coffee shop, a part of me can't shake the niggling worry that Simon will have approached the situation in his usual blunt, tell-it-like-it-is way, and all kinds of havoc could have ensued.

Oh, who am I kidding? Of course Simon will have approached this in his usual manner. But James knows Simon and his personality; he married him, for better or worse, and he knows the more important something is to Simon, the more candid he will be.

I needn't have worried. As I approach Simon in the coffee shop he jumps up from the large brown-leather sofa and squeezes me into a bear hug.

'Hey, Em. How's things?' he asks in his usual singsong voice.

'Never mind me.' I extract myself from his embrace. 'How are you? What's going on with you and James?'

'Oh.' Simon swishes his hand dismissively. 'I feel so silly, Emma.' His cheeks colour slightly, which is very rare. 'Sit down, and I'll tell you all about it.'

I fall onto the squishy sofa and rearrange the cushions so I'm actually in an upright position rather than lolling half-horizontally. Simon pushes a huge latte in my direction and a delicious- looking pastry, which after last night's vodka and cosmopolitans, I'm very grateful for. I take a sip of coffee followed by a huge bite of pain au chocolate and I sit back and wait for Simon's story to unfold.

'So after I stayed at yours – thank you for your hospitality by the way.'

'You're welcome.' I say through my mouthful of pastry 'although I'm not sure that Joe has fully recovered. It's not every day that he gets to have breakfast with a half naked man.'

'You're welcome too.' Simon pats my hand 'I'm just exposing him to new experiences.'

I wash the pastry down with a mouthful of latte and grin. 'By exposing yourself to him.'

'Oh, Emma, you make out like I came on to him.' Simon shakes his head. 'I was wearing boxer shorts.'

'Small, tight underpants.' I bite my lip, trying not to laugh.

'Enough of all that. Do you want to hear what happened between me and James or not?' Simon looks mildly annoyed.

'I'm sorry, I'm sorry. You're right.' I hold my hands up. 'Please, go on.'

'So, after I stayed at yours,' Simon repeats, and I press my lips together as he looks over at me, 'I decided you were right. I needed to speak to James and ask him what was going on.'

'Okay.' I nod, encouraging him to continue.

'Well, it turns out that I got it all wrong.'

'I see.'

'Don't look so smug, Emma. I know you didn't believe that James was cheating on me, and you were correct to trust your judgement.'

'That's good to know,' I say. 'So what *was* going on?'

'I told you we had a fight?'

'Yes.'

'I thought James was going to conclude from that disagreement that I'm a crap husband and father and he's better off elsewhere.'

'Simon...'

'But he didn't. He decided that we need a break, and to spend some quality time together. As much as we love the twins, Fitz and Theo are very demanding of our time, and James recognised that we haven't spent that much time together as a couple recently.'

I think back to the conversation I had with Simon the other month about them not spending enough time together. This resulted in me offering to babysit the twins, which I think went really well. We all survived, the flat wasn't in that much disarray and, well,

I really should offer to look after the boys more often.

I can still remember the look of sheer amusement on Simon's face when he and James left my flat after dropping the boys off, although I suspect that the lack of chaos he found me in when they picked the twins back up was completely unexpected. It was my first time being left alone with two small children. Two at once. Not one at a time, which might have been more manageable, given my complete inexperience. Although Simon pointed out that many new parents have no, or very little, experience looking after a child, and I have to agree with him. It's not like they arrive with an instruction manual and a twenty-four-hour emergency advice helpline. To be honest, I think the fact that I kept the boys alive and in one piece was a huge achievement.

'It's good practice for when you have your own,' Simon keeps telling me, but that thought still causes my stomach to churn slightly and sweat beads to line my forehead. I mean, keeping two children alive for four hours is one thing. Keeping them alive all day, every day for, well, at least eighteen years until they can become responsible for their own safety – that's another thing completely.

'So he's booked us on a mini city break.' Simon clasps his hands together, grinning, and I realise I may have missed a sentence or two of the tale. 'We're going to Paris for a long weekend at the end of next week.'

For a second I panic and wonder if the giant latte and chocolate pastry is merely a bribe to get me to look after the twins while they're in Paris. A few hours is one thing, but a long weekend? I think that's over and above my capabilities.

Simon seems to sense my fear and quickly lets me off the hook. 'James's mum is going to have the boys for us.'

'Oh, Simon, that sounds great. I'm so happy that you two have worked things out.'

'That's where he was.'

'Where?' I take a sip of my coffee, confused.

'When the stupid GPS thingy said he was in that bar in town, he was actually in the travel agent's next door, booking the trip.'

'Ah.'

'I know. I feel so silly now.'

'Did you tell him?'

'Tell him what?'

'That you tracked him like a UPS package.'

'No!' Simon thwacks my arm. 'Don't be stupid.'

'He figured it out on his own, didn't he?' I cock my head to one side and watch Simon's face.

I can see by his expression that he's toying with whether or not to admit the truth. He knows he can't lie to me, though. He never could, even when we were kids.

'How do you know these things, Em?' he huffs.

I just laugh. 'So everything's back on track?'

'Yes.' Simon nods emphatically. 'But I did have to promise to do the hoovering more.'

I chuckle.

'What?'

'Nothing.' I grin.

'Like you do the hoovering?'

'How rude! I, um...' I have to stop myself. 'I know where the Hoover lives in the flat.' It's Simon's turn to laugh at my expense. 'Shut up,' I tell him. 'I have other skills.'

'Yeah? You must be really good at *those*.'

'Simon!' I slap his arm, and now it's my turn to blush.

Chapter Twenty-One

The following morning at the shop, Jenny and I get an unexpected phone call from Marissa Bamford, advising us that Lola has called in sick with a bad case of the flu, and she won't be in work for the next few days. I had sent Lola two texts yesterday on my way home from meeting Simon, but neither were met with a response.

Jenny shakes her head at me and we both seem stuck for words.

'What do we do?' I ask tentatively.

Jenny sighs. 'I don't know.'

'What if he's done something worse to her? What if he's really hurt her?' A horrible panic washes over me. 'She was a bit tipsy when she left us, and she said she wasn't supposed to be drinking much. What if we've made everything a hundred times worse? What if we got her a bit drunk and then she went home angry and, well, he did something?'

'Oh God. This isn't how it was supposed to be at all. I had no idea that Lola had moved in with Hugo. I thought she'd be going back to her flat alone after we'd spoken to her.'

'I know, I know,' says Jenny. 'We misread the situation. I think it's more serious than we thought. She doesn't have flu.'

'So do we go round there?'

'We can't. What if he's home?'

'Hang on, maybe we're blowing this out of proportion. Maybe Lola's perfectly fine, and she just doesn't want to see *us* after Saturday night.'

'Hmm.' Jenny looks thoughtful. 'Maybe you're right. She might still be angry at us. We should try contacting her tomorrow. Give her some space for today.'

It ends up being a busy day in the shop for a Monday, which is good as it provides plenty of distraction for us both from the Lola situation.

I arrive home at five thirty to an empty flat. I'd forgotten Joe had an extra football practice tonight with Matt; he went straight from work. I really don't feel like being alone, but I decide to make the most of my evening of solitude and embark on a beauty regime. Well, I decide to scrub my body with the expensive-looking product Mum bought me last Christmas, shave my legs and put a face mask on. Let's face it, that's more of a beauty regime than my body usually gets on a regular basis. I curse myself for failing to keep the promise I made to myself after the announcement of the royal visit that I would endeavour to be more like the duchess, Catherine. In all honesty, that just means making the best of myself, as I realise that I'm in a completely different league to her and have no chance of competing. However, I did endeavour to at least keep on top of hair removal. I glance at my spikey legs. Hmm.

I pour myself a glass of wine and add a splash of soda water – it is only Monday, after all – and head into the bathroom.

Half an hour later, I return to the lounge looking like a creature from the Black Lagoon – the face mask is less than flattering. However, I'm hair-free in all the right places, and the skin on my body is so soft, I'm annoyed at myself for not using the product Mum bought me before now, having left it sitting on my bathroom shelf for the last six months. I sit down, wrapped in my fluffy white dressing gown, and decide to catch up on my magazine reading while the face mask works its magic and takes ten years off me, or whatever it's supposed to do.

Ten minutes later and my face has set into what feels like concrete strong enough to build a house. I'm just about to go back into the bathroom and attempt to chisel it off when the intercom by the front door buzzes.

Damn it. Who can this be on a Monday night?

I decide to ignore it. Unless it's a matter of life and death, there's no way I'm answering the door looking like an extra from a horror movie.

But the buzzing persists.

I huff loudly to myself and stomp over to the door.

'Hlo,' I mumble into the receiver – incoherently, as my mouth refuses to function now that the blue cement has set it in a permanent line.

'Emma?'

I hear the whisper at the other end and it takes me a second or two to recognise the voice. 'Lola?'

Her voice is barely audible. 'Is it okay if I come up?'

'Of course,' I say, feeling cracks beginning to form in my rock-solid face, and I press the external door release.

I hover, undecided, in the hallway, wondering if I have time to remove this stupid face mask before Lola reaches the flat. I decide not to, given it looks like removing it is going to be challenging.

I hear a soft rap on the door and hurry over to open it.

'Don't be scared,' I mumble as I open the door. I see Lola recoil slightly before composing herself. 'Come in.'

I step to one side and Lola eases past me into the flat. It takes me a moment to realise that despite the fact she's indoors, she hasn't removed her dark sunglasses, and she's clutching an unusually large handbag.

'Lola?'

We stand facing each other, and I'm a little cautious after how we left things on Saturday night.

'I'm sorry,' she says quietly. 'I didn't know where else to go.'

'What do you mean?' I ask, already dreading the answer that I fear is coming.

She says nothing, her hand hesitating near her face, and then she slowly slides the sunglasses down and I see it: the swollen eye socket, and the red-and-purple bruising that looks fresh and like it hasn't reached its peak yet.

'Jesus, Lola.'

The face mask cracks in a multitude of places, but I don't care. I'm shocked to see such brutality up close and personal. Lola looks like she's shrunk to half her size since I saw her only two days ago. The skinny jeans she's wearing seem to hang from her every bone, and I'm taken aback as I realise how thin she has become.

'Oh, Lola,' I gasp as the tears flow freely down my cheeks. I wasn't prepared at all to see this. 'What has he done to you?'

Lola's bottom lip quivers as she tries to speak, but no words come out.

'Come here.' I wrap my arms around her fragile frame and she clings on to me as though her life depends on it, and the reality is that it might just do. I hold her, telling her everything's going to be alright, as she sobs in my arms.

'I'm sorry,' she gulps, pulling away from me.

'What on earth do you have to be sorry for?' I ask.

'For Saturday night. I yelled at you and Jenny, and you were only trying to help me, to be good friends, but I threw that back in your face.'

'None of that matters, Lola. All Jenny and I care about is that you're okay, and you're clearly not, but we'll sort this out. Just give me a minute to get this thing off my face. Go in the kitchen – there's wine in the fridge. Pour yourself a large glass, and get me one too. I'll be back in a minute.'

I usher her into the kitchen and then nip into the bathroom and begin rubbing a wet facecloth on the rock-solid mask. Thankfully it comes off pretty quickly and, although with a slight blue tinge still, I make it back to the kitchen a few minutes later. Lola is nursing a glass of wine as she stares out of the window at the park below.

'Hey,' I say softly, so as not to make her jump. 'Sorry about that.'

She turns around to face me and my breath catches in my throat. The shock of seeing her bruised and swollen eye hasn't diminished; in fact, I think it looks worse as I see it under the glow of the kitchen spotlights.

'Don't focus on that,' Lola says, gently touching her eye socket with her fingertips. I think that's going to be easier said than done.

'Do you want to sit down?' I gesture towards the kitchen table, but Lola stays rooted to the spot and doesn't even answer me.

'Hugo doesn't know I'm here.' She shrugs and takes a gulp of wine and I notice her hands are shaking. Seeing her like this makes me feel sick to my stomach.

'Where does he think you are?' I ask.

She takes another sip of wine. 'He's out. I just packed a few things and ran.'

Oh no. This doesn't bode well.

'I'm guessing he'll be none too pleased to find you gone when he gets home?'

Lola shrugs again, but this time tears trickle slowly down her cheeks. 'What else can he do to me?'

I don't answer her. I have no answer to give.

'Why didn't you say something sooner, Lola?'

'How do you say that? How do you tell people that you've allowed someone to do this to you? That you've allowed someone who's supposed to love you to physically hurt you?'

'Whoa. Don't you dare blame yourself for any of this,' I say, a little firmer than I intended.

'Why not? I used to be a strong person, a confident person. Now look at me.'

'He did that to you, Lola. A man always has a choice, and there's never, ever a good reason to use violence. In fact, there's no excuse for violence in a relationship no matter who is dishing it out.'

'But –'

'No buts.'

She just looks at me and nods. 'I'm so sorry about all the things I said to you and Jenny on Saturday night.'

'Don't worry about that. It doesn't matter.'

'I know you were only trying to help me.'

'Maybe we could have approached the situation differently, Lola.'

'No, I reacted badly. I didn't know what to do. I knew you both knew what was happening then, but I wasn't prepared. I didn't know how to answer your questions. Do you think Jenny will forgive me?' Her bottom lip quivers.

'There's nothing to forgive.' I take a gulp from my own glass of wine before asking gently, 'But do you mind if I text her to let her know you're here and you're safe? She's worried about you too.'

'Yeah. That's fine. Tell her I'm sorry.'

I walk over to the other side of the kitchen where I discarded my phone on the worktop earlier. I pick it up and begin typing:

Lola has turned up here with a black eye. She's left Hugo. It's all a bit crazy, but she's okay. Wanted to let you know. I'll make sure she stays here tonight. xx

Immediately the phone beeps. Jenny's lightning-quick reflexes must be in overdrive. I look at the screen, where the text reads:

Oh my God! Are you sure she's okay? I'm at Scott's. Do you want me to come over? Xx

I text back:

Don't worry, Lola's okay. I'll update you tomorrow. Enjoy your evening with Scott. xx

I place the phone back down on the kitchen worktop and turn to face Lola. 'When was the first time it happened?'

She looks down at the floor.

'Lola, you don't have to tell me if you don't want to, but don't not tell me through any misguided loyalty to Hugo, or because you feel embarrassed that this has happened to you. You have nothing to feel embarrassed about.'

'What about shame?' she says quietly.

'Lola, I mean it. Don't you ever feel like you were in any way to blame for this, okay?'

She takes a sip of wine. 'It was not long after we got back from Australia.'

'What was?'

'The first time he...'

I swallow down the anger and sadness that's swelling inside me. Despite my speech about violence never being acceptable, I want to rip Hugo's head right off his shoulders for what he's done.

'He thought a guy had smiled at me in the queue at the cinema. I don't recall it happening; I certainly didn't think I'd smiled back at him. But Hugo grabbed my arm and he squeezed it so tightly. I asked him to stop and told him he was hurting me. He let go of my arm immediately and he looked shocked, like he couldn't believe what he had done.'

'And he said it wouldn't happen again?'

Lola nods slowly. 'A cliché, I know.'

'You wanted to believe him. I get that. But it wasn't the only time before tonight?'

'No. It happened again a week or so later. I'd gone to visit some friends and I was half an hour late getting to his flat. He was angry.

He said if I was going to be that late again meeting him then not to bother turning up.'

'That's extreme. It's not like you left him standing in a bar all night waiting for you.'

'I know, but it became the norm that I would just go straight to his flat from work and I wouldn't keep him waiting.'

'I see,' I say, but in reality I don't see at all how someone could want to manipulate another person like that, especially someone he was supposed to love.

'Anyway,' Lola continues after drinking the last of her glass of wine, 'I was spending so much time at his flat that when he suggested I move in, I couldn't really say no.'

'But you didn't want to?'

'No. I knew by then that it wasn't a one-off, his hurting me; it wasn't going to be the last time. I'd just got myself into a situation that I didn't know how to get out of.'

'Oh, Lola. I wish you'd come to me and Jenny. We would have helped you, you must have known that.'

'It had snowballed and gone too far. I didn't know where to start.'

'So what happened tonight?' I gesture at her eye.

She bites her lip. 'This wasn't tonight.'

My chest tightens. 'It was Saturday, wasn't it?'

She nods.

'Oh God, I'm sorry, Lola. Jenny and I made you drink cocktails when you'd already said you weren't supposed to be drinking much.'

'It's not your fault. I drank the cosmopolitans. Yes, I knew it could end up in Hugo being angry at me, but I carried on. I was being defiant. It felt like old times, and I'd missed that.'

'We've missed that too.' I squeeze her hand.

'I didn't think he'd go this far.' Lola shakes her head. 'I should have known, but I stupidly thought that he'd get angry and shout at me, that's all.'

I'm almost afraid to ask. 'What did he do?'

Lola takes a deep breath and exhales heavily. 'He was waiting for me the minute I stepped through the door. I hadn't even had a chance to take off my coat before he got hold of both my wrists, squeezing them tightly. I told him he was hurting me, but he didn't stop this time.'

She gulps for air, clearly struggling with her emotions, and I can feel my own heart hammering in my chest with a mixture of anger and fear.

'He knew I'd been drinking and…I don't really remember the first punch, I just remember feeling like the side of my face was going to explode.'

'You know you need to go to the police, Lola,' I say gently. 'It's not just about you, right here, right now.'

She nods. 'I know, but I'm not ready for that yet.'

'There's no rush.' I squeeze her hand. 'No one's going to make you do anything you don't want to do. But…'

'There could be other girls in the future if I don't.'

'I'm sorry, Lola. You shouldn't have to bear that responsibility; it's not fair.'

We stand there in silence, the weight of the situation hanging heavily in the air.

'He changed overnight,' Lola whispers. 'It was such a shock the first time he punched me that it took me a few seconds to realise what was happening.'

I swallow, wanting to be there for my friend but feeling uncomfortable, knowing the intimate details she's about to share will enrage me.

'It was totally unprovoked that first time. He hit me so hard. I couldn't defend myself.'

I feel my hands instinctively curl into fists as Lola talks – not because I'm violent myself, but because my whole being is repulsed by those who are.

'He hit me with the back of his hand so it wouldn't leave a mark, but the force of it knocked me to the floor.'

I lean forward and top up our wine glasses. I don't think it's appropriate for me to interrupt Lola by making any comment, so I just let her continue, let her tell her story. She picks up her wine glass with noticeably shaky hands and takes a large gulp. I do the same, waiting for her to speak again.

Lola bows her head. 'For a second I thought I was dreaming, that I was in some horrible nightmare and I'd wake up to find myself snuggled up in my bed, warm and safe.'

I blink back tears. This is heart-wrenchingly difficult to hear.

'But I wasn't dreaming, and it didn't stop at that one punch. He pulled my arm behind my back so roughly that I thought it might come out of its socket. I was terrified. All the time he never said a word, not one word. And when it was over and I was lying on the cold tiles on the kitchen floor, exhausted physically and mentally, he just lay beside me and stroked my hair, still not saying a word.'

'So what happened after that?' I ask gently.

'He pulled me up off the floor and walked me to the bedroom. He...' She exhales noisily. 'He undressed me and then himself, and we got into bed as though nothing had happened and it was just a normal night.'

I rub my temples, trying to comprehend how Hugo, the likeable, cute and funny Hugo, is actually a monster of the worst kind.

'I lay facing away from him. I was just numb, completely numb. But then he cuddled up against me and wrapped his arm over me tightly. He said he was sorry for what he'd done, but that he'd been overcome with feelings for me and jealous when he'd seen me talking and laughing with a guy in the supermarket. I don't even remember any guy. I have no recollection of what he was talking about.'

I can't help myself. 'Jesus, Lola. I'm so sorry that happened to you. Why didn't you just leave him then?'

'Because I was scared, more scared than I've ever felt in my whole life. It was the sudden change in Hugo that shocked me the most. From the moment I met him he'd been nothing but funny and chivalrous and loving, and then –' Lola gulps.

'Hey, hey.' I pull her into my arms. 'He's not going to hurt you again.'

'Not physically maybe.' She pulls away. 'But how do I trust another man after everything? I thought Hugo was perfect. He seemed perfect.'

'He showed you what he wanted you to see, Lola.'

'Maybe. But I didn't question anything. I took him at face value.'

'Oh, Lola.' A silent tear trickles down my cheek. Why didn't Jenny and I do something to intervene before now, before it got to this?

'The third time it happened, he hit me around the head a few times.' She shakes her head. 'I don't know how many. I crouched down, trying to deflect the blows.' She shrugs. 'But it didn't stop him. I lay there waiting for it to end. Then I just curled up on the floor of the hallway and he went to bed.' Lola's crying now too, and I wrap my arms around her and pull her close to me.

'He left you on the floor, beaten, and just went to bed?' I whisper, and she cries harder. 'You're safe now, Lola. I won't let him hurt you anymore, I promise.'

I hear the front door to the flat open and close, and then Joe's familiar footsteps approaching the kitchen.

'Emma?' he calls.

Lola goes into panic mode. 'Oh, Joe can't see me like this.'

'Lola, it's okay.'

But she turns away, looking out of the window again with her back to the room.

Joe appears in the doorway to the kitchen. 'Hey, there you are.' He smiles at me. 'Oh, hi, Lola. I didn't know you were here.'

I glance at Lola, then back at Joe, and I see him frown. I don't know what to do or say, so I just stand there in silence. Then I see Joe's eyes widen as Lola turns around to face him. For a second he looks completely shocked, and then he composes himself, but I notice his fists clench into tight balls.

'Lola's going to stay here tonight,' I say.

Lola looks at Joe and then fixes her gaze on the floor, avoiding eye contact with both of us. I know it must be so hard for her to show us what Hugo has done to her.

'Of course.' Joe nods. 'Lola can stay as long as she likes.'

I go over to the fridge and take out the open bottle of wine. 'Why don't you take the wine into the living room and pour us another glass.' I hand the bottle to Lola. 'I'll be in in a minute.'

She takes the bottle from me, picks up our glasses and leaves Joe and me in the kitchen.

'Have you called the police?' Joe asks.

'No. We've broached the subject, but she's not ready for that yet. She turned up about half an hour ago and the story has been slowly coming out. She's terrified, as you can imagine.'

'Well, no police might be a good thing. Where does this Hugo live?'

'Joe, you're not going anywhere near him.'

'This guy needs a serious talking to, Emma.'

'But you're not going to *talk* to him, are you?'

Joe presses his lips into a firm line.

'Joe, I get it. This guy makes me want to punch him in the face too. But that would make us just as bad as him. Violence isn't the answer.'

'I think it might be the only language this guy understands.'

I'm a little taken aback. My usually placid boyfriend is itching to punch Hugo's light out. And although his macho stance the other night was a turn-on, the reality is something totally different.

'I'm sorry, Emma. I hate men who hit women. It makes me really angry that they think it's okay.'

'I know, believe me I get it. I was pretty shocked when I saw Lola tonight, and anyone seeing that would want to even the score, so to speak. But what Lola needs, I think, is to feel safe and to be in a calm environment. So I'm going to let her be tonight, and tomorrow we'll talk about what happens next and if she wants to involve the police.'

Joe nods. 'You're right. You need to take care of Lola tonight. Have you had anything to eat?'

'No.'

'Then I'll make you some food.'

'Joe, you only walked through the door two minutes ago – you don't need to do that. I can order us a takeaway.'

'If I can't go and punch this guy, at least I can make you dinner. Then I feel like I'm doing something to help.'

'Have I told you how much I love you?' I step forward and kiss Joe on the lips.

'I know that, Emma.' He kisses me back. 'You don't have to tell me.'

While Joe makes us spaghetti Bolognese, I try to raise the subject of going to the police with Lola, but she seizes up and says she doesn't want to talk about things anymore tonight. I contemplate pushing her further, but decide to respect the fact that this is hugely emotional for her and she needs to deal with things and process what's happened in her own time. All I can do is be here as her friend.

So we spend the next hour or so eating pasta, drinking wine, making small talk and blatantly ignoring the fact that Lola has a black eye. After dinner, I run Lola a bath and tell her to take as much time as she wants. Joe and I are curled up in front of the television watching a documentary on armed police when the intercom buzzes loudly.

'I'll go.' I pull myself up from the sofa and walk to the intercom. Half of me already knows who this is going to be, but the other half of me is still in denial.

'Hello?' I say into the receiver.

'Is she with you?' says a singsong voice I don't even recognise.

'Is who?'

'Lola? Is she with you? It's Hugo.'

I'm so shocked by the tone of Hugo's voice that I stand open-mouthed, staring at the receiver in my hand.

Joe appears behind me. 'Who is it?'

'Lola doesn't want to see you, Hugo. You need to leave.'

'Now that's just silly, Emma. We had a fight and she fell and hit her head. I need to talk to her to make sure she's alright. She just overreacted, that's all.'

'What did she fall into?' I ask coldly. 'Your fist?'

There's a sharp intake of breath on the other end of the intercom. The sensible part of my brain is telling me not to provoke him. He's violent and unstable. But the adrenaline that's now pumping around my body is giving me bravado.

'I don't know what exaggeration Lola's been telling you, but it's simply a misunderstanding,' Hugo says.

'Really? I don't think she's misunderstood anything. I've seen her face, Hugo, and I've seen the constant bruises on her arms over the last few months. So I'm going to tell you again: you need to leave.'

Joe pushes past me – I hadn't noticed him putting on his coat and shoes – and he opens the front door.

'No – Joe!' I call after him as the door slams loudly behind him.

I go to follow him.

'Emma!'

Lola's voice stops me in my tracks. I turn around and there she is, standing outside the bathroom, her hair wavy from the bath, clutching a towel around her tiny frame. The purple bruise around her eye is more prominent now that she's not wearing any makeup to cover it.

'It's him, isn't it?' Her voice is bordering on hysterical. 'He's here for me, isn't he?'

I step away from the door and walk over to her. 'Don't worry Lola. You're safe here.' I hug her, and feel her body shaking. 'Let's get you into something warm. Here, put this on.'

I step into my bedroom, pull my huge, fluffy dressing gown from the hook on the door and wrap it around her shoulders. I walk her through to the lounge and we sit down in unison on the sofa.

I have no idea how long we wait. It feels like forever, but in reality it's probably only minutes until Joe returns to the flat. My heart is in my mouth as the front door opens. Joe comes into the lounge and Lola stares up at him, wide-eyed.

'Don't panic, Lola. Everything's okay. I don't think Hugo will be bothering you again.'

'Joe, what did you do?' I ask, my voice heavy.

'I'll go and collect the rest of your things tomorrow. You don't need to see him again.'

'Thank you,' Lola sobs.

'See.' I force a smile. 'I told you it would all be alright.'

Lola nods, wiping tears from her eyes.

'I'll make everyone a cup of tea,' Joe says and he walks out of the room. It's not lost on me that he didn't answer my question.

I tuck Lola up in the spare bed half an hour later, after a large brandy to calm her nerves and help her sleep. My body feels sluggish and tired from the adrenaline spike and crash earlier and I'm longing for my own bed. I go into the bathroom and wash my face. The events of tonight seem to have taken their toll and an ashen reflection greets me from the bathroom mirror. I slap on some face oil before my moisturiser and then slump off to bed.

A few moments later, Joe comes into the bedroom, climbs into bed beside me and snuggles into me as I lie facing away from him. I still haven't got to the bottom of Joe's confrontation with Hugo outside the flat; he avoided my questions while Lola was in our company.

'Goodnight, Emma. I love you,' he whispers into my ear.

'I love you too.'

We lie there quietly, our bodies entwined, and I contemplate asking Joe again what happened when he went outside to face Hugo. A few moments pass. It's no good. I need to know. I have to ask. I think sleep will evade me tonight unless I do.

'Joe?' I say into the darkness.

'Yes,' he mumbles.

'What happened tonight between you and Hugo? What did you say to him? What did you do?'

There's a long pause before Joe finally answers.

'Honestly, Emma, I think it's best that I don't answer that. All you need to know is that Hugo won't be a problem from now on.'

Joe pulls me tighter against him and I contemplate what he's just said. This is a man I thought I knew inside out. A man who could tell me anything. But maybe when faced with a situation like tonight a person is forced to behave in a way they otherwise wouldn't. In a way that I never imagined that they could. Is Joe right? Is it better that I don't know what went on tonight? Should I just be glad that Lola is safe and Hugo, it appears, won't be harming Lola anymore? Or do I need to know? Can I honestly accept Joe's response?

I was wrong. It would appear that sleep is going to evade me tonight regardless.

Chapter Twenty-Two

The following morning, I wake from a sleep deprived night of toss-ing and turning, with an uneasy feeling nestled in the bottom of my stomach, from both the events of last night and Joe's final words to me. I know we all want the strong, protective partner who makes us feel completely safe, but I guess we don't think too much about what the reality of that may mean, and what it might entail. It's still dark, and as I roll myself up to a seated position I glance down at Joe, still asleep and softly snoring, and my heart tightens. I love Joe so much. He's warm and kind and respectful of women. I can't imagine him threatening Hugo or getting physical in an aggressive way, and that's a good thing as Joe has never shown me that kind of behaviour but when push comes to shove, literally, he's prepared to do what it takes.

I slide off the bed and take my dressing gown from the hook on the back of the door as I creep out of the bedroom. I pull it tightly around me, enjoying the soft, warm feeling, as I pad softly through to the kitchen. I'm more in need than ever this morning of my strong coffee. I glance at the clock on the kitchen wall. It's six a.m.; not a time I usually see on any day of the week. I rub my temples as I switch on the machine and place a little foil pod in the top.

'Hi.'

The soft voice behind me makes me jump a mile and a little squeal comes out of my mouth.

'I'm sorry,' Lola says nervously.

'Don't be silly,' I say, going over to her. 'I just wasn't expecting anyone to be up; it's still really early.'

'I couldn't sleep.'

'I can understand that,' I say, thinking of my own night spent tossing and turning under the bedcovers. 'Would you like a coffee?'

'Yes, please.'

I hand Lola the finished coffee and put another pod in the machine. 'What happens now?' I ask. 'Are you going to press charges?'

Lola shakes her head vigorously. 'No. I just want to move on and get past this. I want to forget about Hugo, as much as I can do.' She sighs.

'Joe and I will support you going to the police, Lola, if that's what you're scared about.'

'No.' She shakes her head again. 'I know I probably should do that, to make sure it's documented, but I can't, I just can't do that right now.' Tears form in the corners of her eyes.

'You don't have to do anything that you don't want to do,' I say. 'And you can stay here for as long as you like.'

'Thank you Emma. You're a good friend. But you and Joe have done so much already. I'll call my sister, Michelle, today and go to stay with her. Do you think you and Jenny could cover for me at the shop for a few days?'

'Of course. Don't even think about that. Anyway – you have the flu, don't you?' I smile. 'Take as much time as you need. But while you're here you need to eat, so for the first time ever you're going to witness me making pancakes,' I say confidently.

'I hope not.' Joe's appeared in the kitchen doorway.

'Sorry, did we wake you?' Lola looks worried.

'No, I usually get up early.' Joe smiles warmly at Lola. That's true; he's always off to the gym or out on his bike at some unearthly hour. 'And there's a reason Emma hasn't made pancakes before. I don't want food poisoning, or the entire fire department put to work as the entire block of flats burns to the ground.' Joe raises his eyebrows at me and I contemplate challenging this statement, but retreat. He's right, I don't cook for a reason.

'I don't know,' I say cheekily, 'a bunch of firemen turning up might just make my morning.'

Joe chucks a tea towel at me and Lola giggles. I think that's the first time I've heard her laugh in weeks.

Joe treats us to a pile of pancakes with raspberries and maple syrup, and we finish every last bite. I'll go for a run later to burn off those calories, I think with some conviction, before acknowledging that there's a strong likelihood that won't happen.

Lola puts down her knife and fork on her empty plate. 'I'd better go and call my sister.'

'Sure,' I say. 'I'll make a cuppa for when you're done.'

Lola gets up from the kitchen table and leaves the room as Joe and I clear the plates.

'Is she going to the police?' Joe asks as I start stacking the plates in the dishwasher.

'No, she wants to put it behind her and move on.'

Joe nods. 'I'll get the rest of her stuff for her today and then take her to her sister's if that's where she wants to go.'

'No, Joe, I don't want you going anywhere near Hugo. He's going to be even more irate now Lola has left him and God knows what he could do to you.'

'I can handle myself, Emma.'

'I don't want it to come to that,' I say firmly.

'It won't. I promise.' Joe kisses me on the mouth.

'And how exactly will this go then? Are you going to turn up, knock on the door and ask nicely for Lola's belongings? Because I can't see Hugo getting on board with that and helping you pack them.'

'You might be surprised.' Joe shrugs.

'Joe.' I can feel the hairs on the back of my neck standing to attention. 'What happened with you and him last night?' I press.

Joe's saved from answering as Lola walks back into the kitchen. 'I called Michelle. I didn't tell her everything; that's not a conversation I want to have over the phone.'

'But she's okay with you going to stay at hers?' I ask.

'Yes, I told her Hugo and I had a fight and it's over and I need a few days to sort things out.'

'I'll go and get your things, Lola,' Joe says, 'and then I can take you to your sister's house.'

I bite my lip, not wanting to make a fuss in front of Lola.

'Are you sure, Joe? What if Hugo's there?' Lola says, concern in her voice.

'Just give me your key, tell me where everything is and don't worry about the rest.' Joe smiles as he passes Lola a notepad and pen.

She scribbles down a number of things. I glance at Joe but he's watching Lola, probably avoiding eye contact with me on purpose as he knows I'm not happy about this situation.

'These are the most important things.' Lola hands Joe the pad and then fishes in her pocket for her keyring. She unhooks a large key and hands it to him. 'Be careful,' she says, squeezing his hand as she passes Joe the key.

Joe walks over to me and kisses me on the cheek. 'I won't be long.'

I don't trust myself to speak, so I just nod, and as the front door to the flat closes behind him I pray silently that Hugo is nowhere near his flat this morning.

'Come on,' I say to Lola. 'Let's go through to the lounge and put something funny on the television; we need a distraction.'

This is more for my benefit than Lola's. I can't pace the floor and stare at the front door until Joe returns, but that's exactly what I feel like doing. I'm torn between emotions. On the one hand, I'm mad at him for putting himself in danger and risking getting hurt, but on the other, I feel extremely lucky to have someone who cares enough about someone else's misfortune to do that for them. It's two sides of a coin: being pig-headed and adamant he's doing something despite my objections, and being chivalrous and a hero. It's all very frustrating.

Joe walks back in around an hour later, looking completely calm and collected.

'Everything you wrote down is in the car,' he says to Lola.

'Was Hugo there?' Lola asks, biting her lip.

Joe shakes his head. 'No. He was nowhere to be seen.'

I study Joe's face and see nothing to suggest that was a lie, but nothing to confirm that he was telling the truth either.

'Let's have a cup of tea before you go,' I say to Lola as I stand up.

As I walk past Joe to leave the room, his hand brushes against mine and he squeezes my little finger. I turn to look at him and we lock eyes for a moment and Joe just nods. I squeeze his finger back and then pull my hand away and head to the kitchen to make the tea.

A short while later, Lola is ready to go. She rechecks her large handbag for the dozenth time.

'Don't worry. If you've left anything then I can bring it over,' I say as I help Lola into her coat.

'I can't thank you enough, you and Joe.' Lola smiles at me and then at Joe, who's waiting by the door.

'That's what friends are for.' I hug Lola. 'Just know that you can call any time of the day or night if you need anything.'

'I'll be okay. I need to get my head sorted and then I'll be back at work, I promise.'

'There's no rush. Jenny and I can cope. Take care of yourself and we'll see you soon.'

'Thanks again, Emma. You're a good friend.'

Joe kisses my cheek. 'I won't be long.'

'Take as long as Lola needs.'

I close the door softly behind them, then walk through to the kitchen. I make a coffee, then take my phone through to the lounge and call Jenny.

She answers after only one ring. 'Hi. How are you? How's Lola?'

'Hi. Lola's okay, I think.'

'Where is she now?'

'Joe's just taking her to her sister's.'

'Did she really have a black eye?'

'Yep. It was pretty shocking to see.'

'I'll bet.'

'She said she just packed some things and left. She knew the situation with her and Hugo was deteriorating quickly; she just didn't know how to get herself out of it.'

'How awful.'

'I know. I'm so glad she was brave enough to leave.'

'How do you think Hugo will have taken that?'

'I can tell you first hand he didn't take too kindly to it.'

'What do you mean? What happened?'

'He turned up at the flat demanding to see Lola.'

'No!'

'Joe dealt with him.'

'What does that mean?'

I decide to skip past that and just go on to explain that Hugo went away and Lola stayed the night.

'Joe collected her stuff this morning and he's taking her to her sister's house as we speak.'

'How was she?'

'Scared. But I think now that she's finally left him she'll be okay.'

'Just because she's left, doesn't mean Hugo will go away. I can't imagine that someone who has that much control over his girlfriend will just disappear.'

That thought had occurred to me too.

'Hopefully Lola never told Hugo where her sister lives,' I say, feeling uneasy.

'Well, whatever happens now, it's a hundred percent better than Lola living in fear with the enemy.'

'You're right.'

'I guess I'll see you in an hour.'

'Yeah. I won't be long.'

'Bye, Emma.'

I end the call with a heaviness in my heart. Jenny's right. The situation with Lola and Hugo may have evolved, not ended – only time will tell.

Joe arrives back home about half an hour later. I'm hovering by the door with my coat on, as I need to get to work. Although I'm sure Jenny won't mind, under the circumstances, if I'm a little late. I still feel a strange tension as soon as he walks through the door.

'Everything okay?' I ask.

'Yes. Lola's sister was shocked, of course, but Lola's safe.'

I nod. 'That's good, for the moment.'

'What do you mean?'

'Well, Hugo might not just go away simply because Lola has left him.'

Joe shakes his head. 'He won't be a problem.'

'You keep saying that.'

'Because he won't.' Joe walks past me towards the kitchen and I grab his arm.

'I have to go to work,' I say.

'Then I'll see you tonight.'

When I arrive at work, Jenny is already there.

'Hi,' she says, filling the kettle. 'Have you heard anything else from Lola?'

'No. Not since Joe dropped her off at her sister's. I thought I'd give her some space, but maybe go visit her tomorrow after work if you want to come too?'

Jenny switches the kettle on. 'Sounds good. I'd like to see her.'

'How was your evening with Scott?'

'It was okay.' Jenny spoons coffee into two mugs. 'But I was massively distracted by Lola.'

'I know, it's been pretty intense over the last few days. Perhaps we should try to lighten the mood a bit today to distract us, seeing as Lola is safe at her sister's now, and we'll check on her tomorrow.'

I arrive home that evening to find Joe already home. I'm still feeling uneasy about how we left things this morning.

'I'm sorry, Joe,' I say as I find him in the lounge. He looks up at me. 'I have to ask. Hugo. Did you...?'

Joe raises his eyebrows questioningly. 'Did I what, Emma? Did I hit him? Threaten him with violence?' His tone is sharp.

I press my lips together.

'No, Emma, I didn't. That's not who I am. You should know that by now.'

'I do know that.'

'Really? Then why won't you just trust me?'

'I do trust you,' I protest.

'Well, you've had a funny way of showing it over the last twenty-four hours. Lola is safe. Hugo won't bother her going forward. That's the best outcome you could hope for under the circumstances.'

Joe stands up and walks past me into the kitchen, and I stay rooted to the spot as I hear the fridge door open and close, followed by the sound of a beer being opened.

Deciding to let us both have a moment to calm our thoughts, I head to the bathroom to run a bubble bath and take stock.

I slide into the warm bubbles and lay my head back, closing my eyes. Why are men so damned frustrating? What's with all the secrecy? Is it a macho thing, needing to take control of a situation? It's not like I keep things from Joe.

Okay, that's not entirely true.

I didn't tell him about Connor taunting me over Sophie when we first started dating. That's different, though. I'd only just met Joe then and I didn't want to scare him away.

I wasn't honest with him when I was drowning under the pressure of planning our wedding while starting an evening course for my qualification in fashion.

Right. I sit up, opening my eyes, and – ignoring the water sloshing freely over the side of the bath – I climb out and wrap a towel around me.

I march out of the bathroom and into the kitchen, where I find Joe leaning on the kitchen worktop, drinking his beer. He looks up at me as I stand, admittedly dripping water onto the kitchen floor, clutching the towel around me.

'I was wrong, okay? I thought you might have got physical with Hugo, but I should have known better. I should have trusted you. I do trust you. I'm sorry.'

Joe takes a sip of his beer. 'I'm sorry too. This whole situation has freaked me out. I've just been feeling very protective. I wanted to make Lola safe, but also you.'

'I was never in any danger.'

'Emma, Hugo is a six-foot man who's clearly fit and strong. You're five feet two and weigh nine stone.'

'Eight and three quarters, if you don't mind,' I correct Joe. He rolls his eyes at me. 'I see your point,' I say.

'There's no way I wanted you coming face to face with him, given the violence he's inflicted on Lola.'

'He wouldn't have done anything to me. He was denying touching Lola, so if he'd laid a finger on me, it would only have confirmed what he'd done.'

'I wasn't going to take that chance.'

'I can look after myself, you know.'

Joe smiles softly. 'I know, Emma. But it's my job to keep you safe.'

Hmm. As much as I like to feel that I'm a strong, independent woman, it also feels kind of nice to have a loving boyfriend keeping me from harm.

'I'm going to get dressed,' I say, as I'm shivering from standing half-naked in the kitchen. The tension from earlier seems to have passed now we've both said our piece.

'I simply told him he was on a temporary visa,' Joe says as I turn to walk out of the room. I stop and face him. 'And I would make sure he was deported if he contacted Lola again.'

'How could you do that?'

'If it's reported to the police and he's convicted then his visa would be revoked.'

'But Lola might not go to the police.'

'He doesn't know that. He thinks she will. Plus, they don't need her to testify to convict him. I told him we have photo evidence of Lola's injuries.'

'I see.'

'He's a bully, Emma. All you need to do is put him in a situation he can't bully himself out of. Hugo might think he can overpower Lola, but now I'm involved and so are you, and he can't escape that.'

I nod and smile, relieved. My worries about Joe were completely unfounded. I knew deep inside that he wasn't a man who would use violence, either actual or threatened. He's smart and methodical. It hadn't even occurred to me to think about Hugo's visa. I guess the threat of deportation is enough to make anyone think. At least I hope it's enough to ensure that Hugo doesn't bother Lola ever again.

Chapter Twenty-Three

Jenny hands me a mug of coffee as I hang up my coat the following morning at work.

'Are we still going to see Lola later?'

'I'll text her to see how she is.'

'Okay. So have you started planning the baby shower?'

'Baby shower?'

'For your friend Sophie.'

'Hmm.' I nod – unconvincingly, apparently, as Jenny sighs and rolls her eyes at me.

'You're going to be the baby's godmother, right?'

'Yes.'

'Then you're responsible for throwing the baby shower.'

'Baby shower?' I shrug dismissively.

I've heard of these things, of course, but I've somehow managed to never be party to such an occasion. Until now none of my close friends have ventured down the path of motherhood, meaning my knowledge of such an event is, well, sparse.

'Sometimes you can be so inept, Emma.' Jenny places her mug of coffee down on the worktop and starts tapping away on her mobile phone.

'Since when did you become an expert in everything baby?' Honestly, sometimes Jenny acts like she's the font of all knowledge.

'Well, I have organised three baby showers in the last few years.'

'Three?'

'Yeah, for my two sisters and my friend Joanne.'

Oh yes, that's right. I have a vague recollection of Jenny rambling on about Moses baskets and sterilising kits, but I always zoned out of those conversations. Perhaps I should have paid more attention, realised that at some point someone in my life would have a child and I would need to know about such things. A sudden panic washes over me. Sophie will be expecting me to throw her a baby shower.

I'm her best friend and I have no idea what I'm doing.

'Help me, Jenny.' I grab hold of her arm. 'You have to help me.'

Jenny just smiles dismissively. 'Don't worry, Emma, you're in good hands with me.'

I breathe a loud sigh of relief.

'Look, it's simple.' Jenny thrusts her mobile phone in front of me and I'm greeted by a baby-care website. I scroll down the webpage and image after image appears of useful baby items that any new mother must need.

'Just create a list,' says Jenny, 'email it to all her friends that you're inviting, and ask them to confirm with you what they want to buy so Sophie only gets one of each item.'

That seems straightforward enough. Create list, email, tick off items. I can do that surely.

'Okay, you're right, Jenny. Thank you. I'll get on with sorting this tonight,' I say, feigning confidence. I have no idea whom to invite really – maybe Sophie's mum and sister? Some of her friends from work? Do I invite Simon, or are men of any description and sexuality barred from these events?

I will just google "baby showers" when I get home. I'm sure there's plenty of advice on numerous websites that will help me, and Sophie will never know that I was completely bewildered by the prospect of organising her baby shower.

Once we've locked up for the day, Jenny and I jump in my car. I texted Lola earlier, and she quickly replied, saying that she'd love to see us.

At the address Lola has given me, a petite brunette answers the door. She's the spitting image of Lola, and instantly I realise that this is Michelle.

'Hi,' I say softly. 'How are you doing?'

'Honestly? I'm not sure,' Michelle says. 'But please come in. Can I get either of you a drink?'

'No, we're fine, thanks,' Jenny answers. 'How's Lola?'

'Doing better, I think.' Michelle glances over her shoulder, then ushers us through to the living room, where Lola is perched on the sofa.

'Hey, don't get up,' I say to Lola as Jenny and I enter the room.

'Hi.' She smiles at us as we both take a seat.

'How are you?' Jenny asks.

'I'm so sorry for last Saturday night...' Lola begins, but Jenny holds up her hand to stop Lola.

'I won't hear of it. You have nothing to apologise for. I'm just glad you're okay.'

'I think I will be, and I'm going to go to the police and press charges.'

'Really?'

'Yeah.' Lola looks down at her feet. 'I think it's the right thing to do.'

I take hold of her hand. 'We'll be here for you, every step of the way.'

'Thank you.'

'Look, why don't you take a bit of personal time? Sort things out. Go through the procedure you need to with the police. Get back on track,' Jenny says, and I have to agree.

'I can't. I've not been back that long.'

'We'll sort it with Marissa Bamford,' I say.

'Are you sure?'

'Absolutely,' Jenny agrees.

Jenny and I leave Michelle's house half an hour later and head back to where Jenny's parked her car. We're both quiet on the drive.

'It's a shock, isn't it?' I say to Jenny as I pull up alongside her Fiesta.

'I wasn't expecting...' She trails off.

'The massive bruise on her face.'

'Yeah.'

'I know. It's hard to take. But Lola's in a much better place now, and we're all here to support her through this.'

'You're right.' Jenny nods at me solemnly.

'That's all we can do,' I say.

'See you tomorrow,' Jenny says as she climbs slowly out of my car.

'Don't forget the baby shower,' she calls before closing the car door.

As soon as I arrive home, I pour myself a glass of wine and log on to my laptop. I click into Google and type in "baby shower". About a million items appear on the list. Great – on a positive note I have endless information to assist me in planning this shower, but on the downside, it's going to take me three weeks to wade through all this. I scroll down page after page, sigh loudly, take a gulp of wine, then click into one of the websites.

I'm still staring at the screen when Joe arrives home about half an hour later.

'What are you up to?' Joe leans in and kisses me, before stealing a sip of my wine. I'm so relieved that things between us have returned to normal.

'I'm looking for ideas to use in planning a baby shower for Sophie.' I bite my lip as I focus on something unrecognisable on the screen.

'Ah, I see.' Joe grabs a glass and the bottle of wine from the fridge and then sits down next to me at the kitchen table. 'And what's that exactly?' he asks, pointing at the screen.

'It's, um, well…oh, how am I supposed to know?' I click into the item description. 'It's a breast pump. That's what it is.'

'Okay, I didn't need to know that.' Joe smiles and I just raise my eyebrows at him. 'Are you supposed to buy practical things like that as gifts?'

'As opposed to?'

'Nice, cute, cuddly baby things.'

Right.

'Joe, the fact that I'm googling "baby showers" should give you some indication of my knowledge of the subject matter at hand,' I say, exasperated, reaching for my own wine glass.

'I think you're overthinking things, Emma.'

'In what way?'

'Well, my understanding of Sophie is that not only is she slightly a control freak –'

'Hugely,' I correct.

'Okay, hugely a control freak, but she also doesn't like being the centre of attention.'

'Oh, you're right. She hasn't let people sing "Happy Birthday" to her since we were six years old.'

'So maybe you run the idea of a baby shower past her and see what she says?'

'You know what, Joe? You're right,' I say, closing the laptop. 'Sophie is someone who organises things with military precision. If she wants a baby shower then I'd like to get her input, so I don't make a total cock-up of it from the start.'

Joe smiles. 'Good plan. Now, what shall we have for tea?'

The following morning, Jenny and I reconvene in the staff room before the shop opens.

'So, good luck with speaking to Marissa Bamford about Lola,' she says, switching on the kettle.

'Oh no you don't. You know you're her favourite.'

Jenny shakes her head. 'She loves you. You just designed a fabulous range of dresses for her.'

'This is ridiculous!'

Jenny shrugs. 'Rock, paper, scissors?'

I huff. 'Every time.'

Chapter Twenty-Four

I glance at my watch. I'm running five minutes early, for a change, for coffee with Sophie (decaf for her, of course). We decided to meet on Saturday morning, just like we used to before...well, before life got too busy. Just as I turn the corner onto the high street, my phone rings in my bag. I reach for it, wondering if it's Sophie, cancelling after all, but as I glance at the screen I see it's Mum calling.

'Hi, Mum,' I answer the phone.

'Hello, darling. Why do you sound out of breath?'

'Um.' I hadn't realised I was. I've only walked for ten minutes at a steady pace. 'I'm rushing,' I lie. 'I'm meeting Sophie and I'm late.'

'Oh, don't worry, Emma, I won't keep you long.'

Mum's voice doesn't sound quite right.

'Mum, is everything okay?' I ask hesitantly, remembering our conversation when she came to stay not so long ago, about how Parker wanted them to move in together but she wasn't sure she wanted to leave her own apartment and commit to that.

'Oh, yes, everything's fine. More than fine.'

'That's good,' I say, but somehow I fear what's coming next. I push the door to the coffee shop open and wander inside, inhaling the amazing smell of ground coffee and warm pastries.

'It's, well...oh, I don't know how to say this, darling.'

I glance around. Sophie isn't here yet, so I take a seat at a corner table.

'Say what, Mum? What's going on?'

I glance over at the door, watching out for Sophie.

'Parker and I are getting married.'

Sophie walks through the door, and I swish my hand in a random movement meant to be a wave as I gulp for air. If I'm not mistaken, my mother just told me that at the age of fifty-eight she's going to get married again.

'Emma?' I can hear Mum's voice but I'm still adjusting to this knowledge. 'Emma?'

'Um, yes. Oh, um, wow,' is all I can manage to say.

Sophie stops at the counter and looks over at me. I have no idea what expression is plastered on my face, but it looks like it's causing Sophie to be concerned.

'Is everything alright?' she mouths.

'Get cake,' I mouth back.

'What?' Sophie shakes her head with a confused look on her face.

'Get cake!' I yell across the coffee shop, much to the surprise of the many customers enjoying their peaceful morning coffee.

'Emma?' Mum says for the third time.

'Yes?'

'Are you okay?'

'Yes. I'm fine.' My voice has gone a few octaves higher. 'Absolutely fine. I just thought for a moment there that you said you were getting married to Parker.'

'I did say that,' Mum says.

I repeat: 'To Parker.'

'Yes, to Parker.'

'Oh.' I put my head in my hands and press my forehead against my palms.

'I took your advice and spoke to him about us moving in together.'

'I see,' I squeak.

'And he said, if I wasn't comfortable with moving in together then would I prefer to get married?'

'That doesn't sound very romantic,' I say, then immediately cover my mouth with my hand. That sounded really bitchy. It was just a reflex. I didn't mean it.

'Well, it might not have been very romantic, Emma,' Mum continues, 'if he hadn't already anticipated the conversation and come prepared with a ring.'

'I see,' I say again, realising I sound completely unhinged at the moment.

'You are happy for me, aren't you?'

I take a deep breath and compose myself. 'Of course I am, Mum.

I'm very happy for you. It just took me a bit by surprise, that's all.'

'I'm sorry, Emma. I wish we didn't have to do things like this over the phone. I would have much preferred to have told you this face to face.'

I take a deep breath and exhale. 'I know, Mum. It's fine, honestly, and I'm very pleased for you, and Parker. He's a nice man.' I sound robotic.

'He is,' Mum says softly. 'Anyway, I'll let you go if you're meeting Sophie.'

'Thanks, Mum, and congratulations.'

'Thank you, Emma. I'll call you later in the week.'

'Bye.' I hang up the phone just as Sophie approaches the table.

'Oh God, I'm sorry. I should have carried the tray – you're pregnant.'

'Don't be silly.' Sophie shakes her head at me. 'I can carry two coffees and some cake.'

She slides a large slice of chocolate fudge cake in front of me and hands me a fork as I sigh with relief.

'What on earth is wrong?' Sophie asks, sitting down opposite me and handing me a cappuccino.

I take a slurp before answering. 'My mother and Parker are getting married.' I scoop up a chunk of chocolate fudge cake with the fork and shove it into my mouth, enjoying the instant sweet, sugary hit.

'Wow! Married? That's great.'

I swallow my cake noisily.

'Isn't it?' Sophie looks at me apprehensively.

'Yes. I guess. I mean, of course it's great for her.'

'And you like Parker?'

'Yeah.' I shrug. 'I like Parker.'

'So what's the problem?'

Sophie eats a forkful of her own cake while I contemplate what has made me react like this. I should be happy for Mum. I am. I suppose it's just that Mum getting married again in her late fifties highlights that I'm thirty-four and not married, not planning a wedding, not even engaged. I was, I was doing all of those things, until I made a huge mess of everything – as usual.

'I guess it took me by surprise, that's all,' I say, scooping up some more chocolate cake.

'Why? Because it's your mum, or because you didn't think that she'd get married again?'

'My dad…I hadn't even thought about him. I'm sure he'll be absolutely fine about this, though. He hasn't been married to my mum for sixteen years, and he's since married Margaret.'

So back to just me having an unusual reaction to this news.

'That doesn't really answer my question, Emma.'

'I know, but I'm not sure what the answer is. Maybe it's the fact that she's fifty-eight and getting married again.' I shrug. 'I'm thirty-four and I…well, I presumed I'd be married with kids by now, and I couldn't be further from that point.'

'That's not exactly true, is it? You and Joe are in a solid, loving relationship. Being married doesn't make that. You're either committed to a relationship or not.'

I smile. 'When did you become so wise?'

'Look, I've spent some time thinking about this type of thing too, Emma. I'm pregnant but not married.'

'Oh. I know we've talked about this in the past but…does it bother you that you're having a baby and you're not married to Matt?'

Sophie takes a drink of her coffee. 'Not really, no. It seems to bother other people more than me.'

'What do you mean?'

'I mean that since I've been pregnant, people seem to think that it's fair game to ask me completely inappropriate questions and/or make openly rude statements.'

'Such as?' I'm intrigued by how someone could possible dare to be rude to Sophie. Certainly no one who knows her well would be so bold.

'Such as, "Aren't you getting married if you're having a baby?" And, "Was the baby unplanned?"'

'Well, it kind of was,' I say, trying to hide my smile.

'Not helping.' Sophie pouts at me across the table.

'Why do you care what people think about you? You're having a baby with the person you love, and you're both going to adore this baby. That's all that should matter.'

'Why do you care about not being married?'

Good point.

'I don't – at least I think I don't. It simply annoys me that we – and by "we" I mean women in their thirties – are made to feel that we've somehow failed if we aren't holding down a superstar career while preparing homemade food to serve our husband in our immaculate home, while we bring up two-point-four children.'

'I know, society does seem to want to force us into a version of life that's idealistic and unrealistic. There are only so many hours in a day, and women can't be four different versions of themselves. If on top of having a job a woman can find a man she wants to spend the rest of her life with, and he feels the same way about her, then that's an achievement, whether they're married or not. Children are a lifestyle choice each couple has to make, and that's nobody's business but theirs. And an immaculate home is nice to have, but in reality, as long as it's fairly clean and tidy, who cares? We're human beings, not robots.'

'Well said.' I grin, swallowing the last of my cake.

'So now we've put the world to rights, are you going to be okay about your mum getting married?'

Now the shock has worn off, I nod and say, 'I guess so.'

'I guess this means another trip to New York.'

'I guess so. I wonder where they'll get married.'

I pause. Where *will* they get married? Surely not a church? Can you do that when you've both been married before? Has Parker been married before? Why don't I know this information?

'Do you think it will be a huge occasion at The Plaza or something?' Sophie continues excitedly.

Honestly, you mention the word "wedding" and she immediately switches to giddy, over-excited mode. God help Matt if he ever asks Sophie to marry him – she might just implode! Actually, who am I kidding; Matt won't know a thing about it. It'll be me who has to weather that storm. She was bad enough when it was me planning a wedding, although that didn't go to either mine or Sophie's plan.

But here we are again. Wedding fever will soon consume us all, and we'll start contemplating our own lack of marriage vows. And why? Does it matter if you're married as long as you're happy? If you're both in your relationship for the long run, through thick and thin, in sickness and in poverty, then does it matter if you haven't declared that officially under oath?

Why is it that in your twenties marriage and babies are imminent possibilities, and you sail along not focusing on when you want them or whether you want them at all? Then suddenly you find yourself in your thirties surrounded by other people's weddings and babies, facing questions about the status of your own relationship and defending your current position (and by this I mean deflecting challenging questions from my mother and stepmother!) and constantly berating yourself for not conforming-and becoming "Mr & Mrs" with two kids and a dog?

'Emma?'

'Yes?' I look at Sophie.

'Are you alright?'

'Yes,' I say, wondering how long I was distracted by the ramblings in my head.

'You haven't heard a single word I've just said, have you?'

'Um...' Honestly I have no idea. Sophie could have shouted that Justin Timberlake just walked in for all I know.

'What's going on? You look like you're carrying the weight of the world on your shoulders.'

'Nothing, I'm fine,' I say. 'It's just...nothing. I was surprised by Mum's announcement. I'm guessing Parker has been married before, but I don't know – so in answer to your question, I doubt they would get married in a church. Mum's not really religious, and in New York you can get married pretty much anywhere. Didn't that woman on *Sex and the City* get married in a public garden?'

'Emma, that's television. It's not real.'

'Oh. So you can't get married in a garden?'

Sophie looks confused. 'I don't know.'

I wave my hand dismissively. 'I'll have to ask Mum.' I take a drink of my coffee. 'Anyway, enough of Mum and Parker. I've been meaning to ask you about baby showers.'

'What about them?'

'Do you want one?'

'Oh, no.' Sophie shakes her head. 'I hate being the centre of attention.'

Ah, Joe may have been right.

'But isn't it a great way to get loads of baby gifts?' I suggest.

'We have everything we need.'

In fairness, after the shopping trips Sophie has dragged me on, I can believe that. I think she's bought one of everything you could ever need for a baby, and then bought it again in another colour.

'So you wouldn't want a surprise baby shower or anything?' I ask cautiously.

'Emma, you haven't?!'

'No, don't worry. I haven't organised anything.'

'Okay, that's good.' Sophie smiles. 'But thank you for the thought.'

The thought? I was thinking more about the time I spent looking at weird things like breast pumps on the internet the other night. That's an hour of my life I won't get back.

A short while later, I hug Sophie goodbye – with some difficulty, as her bump is getting bigger by the day. Then I saunter home, my mind still in turmoil over Mum getting married. I walk through the front door and call out to Joe to let him know that I'm home, before I head through to the kitchen. I open the fridge door and hover my hand next to a bottle of chilled Sauvignon Blanc. Is it too early for wine? I glance at my watch. It's only twelve fifteen p.m.

'What are you doing loitering by the fridge?'

I jump guiltily at Joe's voice. 'Nothing,' I lie. 'I was just going to make a cup of tea.' I take hold of the carton of milk and make a show of presenting it to Joe like a prize on a TV show..

Joe tries to hide a smile. He clearly knows me too well. 'Then I'll have a tea too, if you're making one.'

'Of course,' I say, turning to fill the kettle and switch it on.

Joe watches me, saying nothing. He obviously wants to say something to me but isn't quite ready to, so I carry on the charade and make the cups of tea.

'How's Sophie?' Joe finally says.

'Doing well,' I reply, although I suspect he already know this as Sophie lives with his brother.

'And how are you?'

'Me?'

'Yes, you.'

'I'm fine,' I say, handing Joe a mug of tea.

'"Fine" in the intended meaning of the word?'

I bite my lip. 'Of course.'

'Only your mum called –'

'Oh.'

'Yeah. She was a bit worried about how you'd taken the news of her and Parker getting married.'

'Oh,' I repeat. I don't know what else to say.

Suddenly the apartment feels stifling on this warm summer's day.

'Shall we forget the tea and go and get ice creams at the park?' Joe suggests.

'That sounds good.'

One of the many benefits of living next to the city's park is that you can be surrounded by greenery and floral aromas within seconds of leaving your front door. As we walk through the large iron gates and head towards the ice cream vendor, I finally feel like I can breathe again. Joe takes hold of my hand and clasps it tightly. We order our ice creams – vanilla for Joe, mint-chocolate-chip for me – and once armed with cones filled with enough ice cream to feed a family of four, we stroll, still hand in hand, through the park towards the lake in the centre.

Joe clears his throat. 'We never really spoke about the fact that we didn't get married,' he says completely out of the blue.

My heart constricts and mint ice cream starts to churn in the pit of my stomach. 'I guess not,' I say quietly.

And the truth is, we haven't. I called off the wedding and we separated. I was so miserable for those months we were apart. Well, the truth is that I plunged into a drunken depression. I missed Joe so much, but I thought we had gone past the point of no return.

It was only under some romantic illusion on Christmas Eve that I realised I wouldn't be happy again without him and I needed to see if there was any hope of a reconciliation. As it turned out, when I landed unexpectedly on Joe's doorstep, I found he had been miserable without me too.

After that, we were both so relieved and so happy to be back together that neither of us brought up the subject of our called-off wedding. I guess neither of us wanted to rock the boat. So the fact that Joe asked me to marry him and I then called off the wedding has just kind of sat there, silently, to one side, not really causing an issue, but not going away either.

'So maybe we should talk about it now,' Joe says.

I carry on licking my ice cream. In my mind, I recognise that we do need to talk about this, that it was always going to rear its head at some point. But in my heart, I never want to have this conversation. I hate confrontation, I hate talking about my feelings – I always have done. I'm a "wipe your eyes and carry on" kind of girl, not someone who wants to delve into every emotion. Maybe that's my problem, though. If I'd talked about how I was feeling at the time, rather than burying my emotions, the situation might never have reached such a critical point, and our story would be different now.

'Does it concern you that I haven't asked you since we got back together?'

'To get married?'

'Yeah.'

I bite my lip.

'Emma?'

'It worries me that you don't want to ask me again in case I flip out.'

'Ah.' Joe stops and we stand facing each other. 'I do love you, Emma.'

My whole body feels tense. 'But?' I hold my breath. There's never been a "but" that anyone has ever wanted to hear.

Joe smiles. 'There's no "but", Emma. I just love you, and I want to spend the rest of my life with you. Will we get married at some point? Maybe. Does it change the way I feel about you that we're not?' He shakes his head. 'Definitely not.'

I feel my chest start to relax and my breathing return to normal.

'Are you just going to leave me hanging?' Joe squeezes my hand. 'I've just laid my feelings bare for you.'

I look up into his eyes and my chest tightens. I'm not great at telling someone that I love them; in fact, I'm really bad at telling people how I feel full stop. I love Joe, he knows that, but he needs to know that I feel the same as he does and that not being married doesn't bother me. A few years ago it might have, but now knowing that the man I love with all my heart loves me back and wants to share his life with me is enough; it's more than enough.

I squeeze Joe's hand and smile. 'We're enough. Just as we are.'

Joe smiles back, and we continue walking through the park, eating our ice creams in a very comfortable silence.

Chapter Twenty-Five

'I'd ask how it was, but I'm guessing from the stupidly large grin on your face that you and James had a great time in Paris,' I say, sliding into a booth in the local wine bar beside Simon the following week.

'Oh, it was amazing, Em,' Simon gushes, handing me a glass of I-don't-know-what. 'The Champs-Élysées, the Eiffel Tower, the sex.'

I take a gulp from the glass, hoping that there's vodka in there. Thankfully I'm not disappointed.

'Please tell me you didn't have sex in the Eiffel Tower, Simon!'

'Honestly, Emma.' Simon feigns a hurt look. 'We're not animals, you know.'

I raise my eyebrows and take another gulp from my glass of still-unidentified liquid.

'I'm going to ignore that look.' Simon sucks in his cheeks.

'Sorry, Simon, please continue,' I say, biting my lip and trying to compose myself. 'What's this I'm drinking, by the way?'

'A new cocktail we tried over there.' Simon takes a sip of his drink. 'Do you like it?'

'It's lovely.' I slurp some more.

'So, back to our trip,' Simon continues. 'It was like our love was reignited.'

'Oh no, we're back to the sex again, aren't we?' I shake my head.

'No, of course not.' Simon swats me like an annoying fly. 'Although it was amazing.' He winks.

'What?'

'The sex.'

'Okay. Enough already. For the rest of this conversation you are no longer allowed to say the word "sex".'

'Spoilsport.'

'Just tell me about the sights of Paris. The fashion – oh, the shoes and handbags.'

'We didn't go there simply to browse the designer shops.'

'Simon, I know you, and there's no way you went all the way to the fashion capital of the world and didn't peruse what was on offer.'

'We may have done a little shopping,' Simon concedes, trying to hide his smile.

'I won't ask, but I'm guessing the credit cards are bending under the weight.'

'It's not that bad.' Simon shakes his head. 'If it were left up to me then you know they'd have been maxed, but James is slightly more cautious than that.'

'He's like your alter-ego.'

Simon cocks his head to one side. 'My better half.'

'I would never say that.' I drink the last of my cocktail, feeling the warmth in my cheeks already. 'Maybe just your safety net.'

'He is that. And we had so much fun over the weekend. Does that make me sound awful? We did miss the boys, but it was nice to spend some time alone together.'

'Of course it doesn't make you sound awful.'

'We managed to fit loads in to the weekend, Em, but we'll have to go back as there's so much to see. We couldn't get through half of what we wanted to do.'

'Is that because you spent hours dragging James around the art galleries?'

Simon pouts. 'I don't *drag* James around art galleries. He willingly accompanies me.'

'Willingly?'

'Yes, Miss Pessimist,' he huffs. 'James pays some attention to my interests, unlike you, who only goes anywhere I want to go if there's cake or wine.'

I open my mouth to protest, but close it almost instantly as I acknowledge, regretfully, that Simon is correct. I could try to argue my point, but that would only lead to Simon listing the dates, times and venues at which this has occurred, which would serve neither of us well.

'It's romantic too,' Simon continues.

'What? Looking at art?'

Simon thwacks my arm. 'No, silly. Honestly, Emma.'

'What?'

'Paris!' He shakes his head. 'Paris is romantic.'

'Oh, I see.'

Simon fiddles with his empty glass. 'It probably sounds idealistic, but the atmosphere as you walk around feels different, and not just because you're on a mini-break. The whole place gives you a sense of excitement.' He shrugs. 'I can't really explain why, it's just there.'

I nurse my empty cocktail glass as I ponder Simon's words. Maybe we should all go on more weekends away, to have a bit more time out. Not from reality – I happen to like my reality – but to get away from the everyday stresses we get so caught up in. It's nice not to have an agenda for each day. To get up when the sun rises, not when your alarm clock shrilly awakens you.

'Emma?'

'Yes?' I glance over at Simon.

'You were away with the fairies.'

'Oh. Sorry.'

'That's okay. While you weren't paying attention, I took the liberty of ordering another cocktail.'

'Simon. No. I promised Joe I wouldn't come home drunk.'

'Just one more. Don't worry – you're not even tipsy. Joe knows you're with me and I'll make sure you get home safely. Anyway, you must be going "cold turkey" while Sophie's pregnant.'

'I'm afraid not,' I say, thinking of the numerous times that I've been for wine after work with Jenny, and how I got a little worse for wear when Mum came to stay. Perhaps I should have taken advantage of Sophie's pregnancy to cut back a bit more on my alcohol intake.

Ironically, at that moment the waitress appears at our table. 'Two more cocktails?' She slides two tall glasses of sparkling pink liquid in front of us.

Maybe I'll start tomorrow.

Chapter Twenty-Six

The day of the royal visit from the prince and duchess has finally arrived. Bunting is hanging from every available space on the high street. Crowds of people are already forming in every open space, with families looking to make a day of it. Ice cream vans and hotdog stands line the streets, and pop music is coming from somewhere, causing people to sway their hips to the beat as they wander around. With the sun shining in a cloudless sky, the atmosphere has a carnival feel to it.

'It's going to be a red-hot day.' Joe takes hold of my hand as we make our way through the throngs of people. 'Fancy an ice cream?'

'Sounds good,' I say, and we head over to the nearest ice cream cart.

'Emma?'

I turn around. 'Dad!' I say in surprise as he pulls me into a tight hug. 'I wasn't sure if you and Margaret would make it.'

'We wouldn't miss it.' Margaret appears at Dad's side, dressed in a shocking-pink floral suit and a bright-pink hat with a brim so large I have to take a step back to avoid it clipping the side of my head. I wonder how long it will be before Margaret causes serious injury to some innocent passer-by with that thing.

'Wow, Margaret,' I say, 'you look…great.'

Margaret beams and does a little twirl. 'It's a little much, I know, but it is a wonderful occasion.'

Joe appears at my side and hands me a cone filled with mint-choc-chip ice cream. 'Hi, Michael,' he says to dad and then they wonder to one side as they engage in a conversation about some sport or another.

'Is Sophie coming today?' Margaret asks me. Clearly she has no desire to join in the sporting conversation either.

'Yeah, her and Matt should be here anytime now.' I glance around but can't see anything other than swarms of colours.

'And she's doing well? Both her and the baby?'

'Yes.' I smile 'Both are doing fine.'

'Not too long now is it?'

'No, only two months or so to go.'

'Isn't it making you broody Emma?'

Ah, here we go again. I knew this wasn't just some innocent conversation by Margaret to enquire about Sophie's health. It was the opening line of the "lets hit Emma over the head" conversation. I'm sure there's more to follow.

'No, I'm not broody in the slightest Margaret.' I say, a smile firmly fixed on my face.

Her expression falters for a second then her own smile is back 'You shouldn't leave it too long before you start a family Emma. You're in your mid-thirties now.'

'I'm thirty four.' I state flatly. I may not be a maths genius but I'm pretty sure that's closer to thirty than to forty so I haven't made it to my "mid thirties" quite yet. Hmm.

'We're very excited about the arrival of our first niece or nephew.' Joe rescues me from this conversation., which I fear was heading towards uncomfortable, and I couldn't be more grateful. He's much better at deflecting Margaret's interrogations than I am. 'and Emma has been spending more time with Simon and James's little boys, haven't you?' Joe squeezes my shoulder.

'Yes, that's right,' I say. 'See, Margaret, I have the best of both worlds. I get to spend quality time with my friends' children, and then hand them back when they're tired and cranky.'

'Let's leave these two alone, shall we?' Dad links arms with Margaret. 'How about we go and get some tea and cake?'

Margaret nods.

'We'll come and find you again.' Dad kisses me on the cheek and he and Margaret saunter off at a slow pace. Dad's arthritis isn't getting any better. His movement is decreasing and he's almost at a shuffle now. I watch them go with a heavy heart and a lump in my throat.

'Your ice cream's melting,' Joe says, taking a huge lick of my mint-choc-chip.

'Hey!' I whisk the ice cream cone away from him, laughing. 'You've got your own.'

'Emma!' Jenny appears in front of me, looking stunning and bohemian in a long, floaty dress. Confidently holding her hand and dressed sharply is a tall, dark and handsome stranger who, I assume, is Scott.

I hug her loosely, careful not to smear ice cream on her shoulder. 'Hi, Jenny.'

'This is Scott,' Jenny states proudly as she looks up at Scott.

'Nice to meet you.' Scott holds out a hand.

Thankfully, Joe leaps in and shakes it. 'I'm Joe.'

'We're going to grab a beer,' Jenny says, still swooning at Scott. 'Would you like to join us?'

'Oh, we'd have loved to, but we're waiting for Matt and Sophie.'

'No worries. Maybe we'll see you later.'

'Yeah, we'll be here for the rest of the afternoon.'

I watch as they walk away. Jenny leans in as Scott says something and then she giggles girlishly. This is a side to Jenny I've never witnessed.

'They seem very happy,' Joe says as I turn back around.

I frown. 'He's very formal.'

'It was only a handshake.'

'It was unexpected. I didn't know what to do.'

'Shake his hand.'

I pull a face. 'Very funny.'

Joe chuckles and then nods to my right. 'There's Matt and Sophie.'

I turn to see them walking towards us through the crowd. Sophie is dressed in a flowing blue maxi dress which shows off her now-somewhat-prominent baby bump. She looks stunning as her coffee-coloured curls bounce in the sunlight. Matt's clutching what looks like a picnic basket and a blanket, which comes as no surprise – he's as prepared and organised for every occasion as Joe.

'Hi.' Sophie hugs me awkwardly as I try not to squish her bump. 'Was that your dad and Margaret I just saw?'

'Oh, yes. I'm sure you'll see them later and Margaret will interrogate you then too.'

'Emma.' Sophie shakes her head at me. 'Margaret's always lovely. She was asking about the baby when I saw her last month in the supermarket.'

'Yeah, well, she will be nice to you. You're pregnant and following the social rule of reproducing before your "mid-thirties". I, on the other hand, am a disappointment, as I continue to flaunt my lack of maternal instinct at her when she's desperate to coo over a baby.'

'Don't be silly.' Sophie waves her hand at me. 'Come on. Let's find somewhere to sit down.'

Matt and Joe follow behind as we walk over to the gardens at the top of the street. It's busy, but we manage to find a spot to put down Matt's colourful picnic blanket, and we all sit down in a circle, admittedly Sophie with a bit more difficulty than the rest of us.

'I'm not sure I'll be able to get back up,' she giggles as she makes herself comfortable.

'So what's in the basket?' I ask, intrigued.

'Everything you could want for a picnic, Emma,' Matt says proudly. He opens the basket and takes out bread and olives, cream cheese and cucumber sandwiches, a selection of crisps, a variety of mini cakes and, finally, a chilled bottle of cloudy lemonade. 'Oh, and a few beers.' He hands a bottle of beer to Joe. 'Help yourselves.'

'Wow. This all looks great,' I say, reaching for a sandwich.

'Emma.' Sophie points. 'Isn't that someone wearing one of the dresses you designed?'

I look to my left and see a petite, dark-haired woman wearing the dress with the tulip bottom in navy. It looks fabulous, and I smile instinctively as my heart swells with pride. 'It looks good,' I say modestly.

Sophie points in the opposite direction 'And another one there?'

An attractive woman strolls by wearing the beige version with the a-line skirt. It looks really classy.

'They look more than good,' Joe says. 'You should be extremely pleased with yourself. We're all proud of you.'

'Stop,' I say, blushing. 'I only designed one dress.'

'It may only be a couple of dresses, but it will be the start of many, I'm sure,' Joe says, ever my champion. 'We should have a toast.' He pours cloudy lemonade into two plastic cups and hands them to me and Sophie. 'To Emma.' Joe raises his bottle of beer and we all clink drinks.

'To Emma,' Sophie and Matt say together. Sophie's grinning almost as much as I am.

I'm touched to have such wonderful, supportive friends, and of course Joe; and seeing a dress that I designed on a real human being, not just a manikin in a window, has overwhelmed me. It's something I hoped to see one day, but I didn't know if I ever would.

'Hey. Any room for four little ones?'

Simon's cheery tone booms from behind me, and I turn to see him and James each pushing a pushchair towards us. Simon is dressed in an outrageously patterned shorts-and-T-shirt set which, to be honest, you could see from the moon.

'Hi, honey.' Simon leans down and plants a kiss on my forehead. 'Mind if we join you?'

'Not at all,' I say, scooting round to make space on the picnic blanket.

'Don't worry, we brought our own food,' Simon says, unloading Fitz from his pushchair. 'Well, when I say "we" brought our own food, I mean James thought ahead and packed some nibbles.'

'Hi, James,' Joe says, standing up to give him and Simon room to sit down.

Sophie rolls herself to a kneeling position in front of Theo's pushchair. 'Don't they look cute,' she gushes. 'I love their matching outfits.'

Simon has dressed the twins in matching sailor outfits, and I shake my head at him.

'What?' Simon grins. 'They have hint of Jean Paul Gaultier about them.' He reaches down and pats Fitz's striped T-shirt, which Fitz seems intent on rolling up in his chubby little hands to reveal his cuddly tummy.

'Simon.' I look more intently at the baby clothes. 'These *are* Jean Paul Gaultier,' I say, astounded.

Simon shakes his head dismissively. 'Okay, so they're just a little treat for the boys from Paris.'

'It's a miracle that we made it out of the Gaultier shop without Simon bankrupting us,' James laughs as he gently takes Theo out of the restraints of his pushchair and sits down beside me, holding Theo tightly. Theo gazes at me with huge blue eyes and I pull a silly face. He giggles at me and points, before blowing a raspberry in my face.

'My thoughts exactly.' Simon nods at Theo. 'Your daddy James is such a spoil sport, isn't he.'

James cocks his head to one side. 'Simon, you made that exact noise in the Gaultier store as I took three outfits from your grasp.'

We're all laughing now, and I'm so pleased to see Simon and James relaxed and happy after the tension they've had over the last few months. It looks like a couple of days away together was just what they needed to get back on track.

We spend the next hour nibbling food, drinking lemonade and the occasional beer, and chatting the time away. The noise of the crowd seems to be intensifying as the time nears for the arrival of the prince and duchess.

'Maybe we should think about making a move.' Matt starts to pack the leftover food back into the picnic basket. 'If you want to catch a glimpse of William and Catherine as they cut the ribbon to open the new hospital wing, we'll need to head up towards there soon.'

'You're right.' I get to my feet, which are slightly numb from sitting down for too long. I help Simon and James get the twins back into their pushchairs, as Joe helps to ease Sophie to a standing position.

We stroll, in what seems to be a herd of people, towards the new hospital wing. By the time we get close, the prince and duchess are expected any minute. To be fair, it took us longer than we all anticipated to walk up with two pushchairs and a pregnant lady in tow. There's no sneaking between people in the crowd with that kind of convoy!

'Over here.'

Joe points to a slightly elevated area to the side of the building. There are too many people near the front of the gathering, pressing against tape which has been used to create a makeshift cordon in front of the building. I'm guessing they don't want people within touching distance of the royal couple, just in case someone goes a bit crazy and tries to get a 'selfie' with them. Or worse. I suppose they have to take security seriously.

The six of us, plus the two little ones, take up residence on the grass mound. The high position gives us a great view of two huge black cars pulling up in front of the hospital wing. The crowd noise reaches fever pitch. As the cars halt, the rear door of the first car is opened and the prince steps out, smiling and waving at the people gathered around. I have to say he looks much better in the flesh; the photographs of him don't do him justice.

Then Catherine steps out of the other side of the car. Glamourous, smiling and incredibly stunning. I stand, open-mouthed, in awe – not only at being in the physical presence of Catherine and William, rather than looking at them on a television screen - but at the sheer beauty of them both. As a country I think we're privileged to have such an accessible royal family.

'I can only aspire to achieve a smidgen of her allure,' I sigh, watching Catherine float seamlessly from person to person, shaking hands and chatting, as she makes her way towards the entrance to the new hospital wing. William follows, also shaking hands with people, completely at ease with the crowd.

The people in the crowd are all waving and making comments amongst themselves:

'Isn't she friendly!'

'He's so handsome.'

'What a lovely couple.'

The royals stop in a prominent position at the entrance to the hospital and address the crowd.

Catherine makes an inspiring statement about protecting communities, providing the right medical care, everyone being entitled to the best health service, and everyone listens intently.

Although only some of the people at the front actually met the prince and his beautiful wife, and the rest of us only got to admire them from a distance, there seems to be a collective feeling in everyone here that we're somehow closer to Kate and William than we were, and that on some level we know them.

As the royal couple wave their goodbyes and enter the building, the crowd loiters for a few moments before starting to disperse. We wait for a gap to appear before Simon and James negotiate the pushchairs back down from our viewing position.

'She looks amazing.' Sophie sighs emphatically. 'So elegant.'

I smile at Sophie, who looks immaculate, without a hair out of place. 'You're elegant too.'

'There's nothing elegant about being six months pregnant, Emma. Isn't that right, Matt?'

We all stop in our tracks and stare at Matt. There's no right answer to that question.

Matt glances at us all, clearly realising his predicament, before simply saying, 'You always look elegant to me,' as he squeezes Sophie's hand affectionately.

'Well played,' Simon chuckles as we all walk back towards the park near my flat.

'It's been a surreal day,' I say to Joe as we walk together, 'seeing two of the dresses I designed, the street party atmosphere, seeing the royal couple.'

'I know. It was good to see so many people turn out for it. I'm guessing there'll be some council bigwigs who'll be entertaining Kate and William tonight.'

'It's a shame we didn't see them for longer.'

'I know,' Simon chips in. 'I mean, it was a lot of fuss for a fleeting moment.'

'Come on, Si, it's not every day that royalty visits the city you live in,' I say. 'It's not like you were going to get to have a beer with the prince in your local pub.'

'I know that, Em.' Simon whacks me playfully on the arm. 'It's just...'

'That you quite fancy him,' I add.

'I do not!' Simon protests as he blushes crimson.

James laughs. 'It's okay, Simon. I'm not jealous.'

'You have nothing to worry about, babe.' Simon winks emphatically at James. 'Anyway, you're allowed a celebrity crush. It doesn't mean anything.'

I raise my eyebrows at Simon. 'Really?'

'Yeah, it's like you get a free pass.'

'A free pass? So if, for the purpose of this conversation, His Royal Highness just happened to come on to you and ask you out on a date, it would be alright, because he's your designated celebrity crush?'

'What's this?' Sophie and Matt catch us up.

'Simon's saying it would be okay for him to cheat on me with Prince William, if Prince William asked him out on a date,' James states perfectly calmly, as though that's the most ordinary thing to be having a conversation about.

'What?'

'Exactly.' I nod.

'Come on, Soph, help me out here.' Simon stops walking. 'I'm talking about your celebrity crush.'

'Oh.' Sophie looks at Simon. 'Then absolutely, that would be fine.'

'See?' Simon looks at us all smugly. 'Sophie knows what I'm talking about.'

'Soph?' I look at her, alarmed.

'Of course. I mean, it's not like it's ever going to happen in real life.' She laughs. 'It's just pretend.'

'Okay. So do you have one of these celebrity crushes that you'd have a free pass to sleep with?'

'Brad Pitt,' Sophie says without a second thought.

For some reason, we all simply accept this and continue the short walk to the park in silence. Perhaps we're all contemplating who our own celebrity crush is, or maybe we just all know better than to argue with a pregnant woman.

We hug goodbye at the entrance to the park, and I gently kiss the twins on their forehead, careful not to wake them, as they're both fast asleep, probably from listening to our crazy conversation.

Joe and I walk into our flat two minutes later.

'Fancy a glass of wine?' I ask as I kick off my shoes.

'So who's yours?' Joe asks.

'My what?'

'Celebrity crush.'

'Oh no, Mr Stark. You must think I'm crazy if I'm going to enter into that kind of conversation.' I grin.

'Really? You don't agree with Simon?'

'I think Simon, as per usual, likes to be controversial. And that's my final comment on the matter.'

'Spoilsport,' Joe calls after me as I head towards the kitchen.

As I pour myself a glass of chilled white wine, I could kick myself for not asking Joe first who his celebrity crush is. Although that's probably for the best, as whoever it is I'll just spend an unhealthy amount of time imagining him with her and wondering why I'm not as pretty/skinny/glamourous as her, while drinking wine to drown my sorrows. Oh, who am I kidding? I'm going to do that anyway.

I huff loudly. Damn Simon and his stupid ideas.

Joe comes into the kitchen just as I'm taking a gulp of wine. 'I think I will have a glass of wine actually.'

Taking a second glass from the cupboard I pour Joe some wine and hand him the glass. He smiles before taking a drink, and I silently curse myself. I wonder if she's blond or brunette?

Chapter Twenty-Seven

After Sophie's comments about baby showers, I abandoned the idea of a group gathering and instead decided on a small, intimate afternoon tea for just the two of us, but with a personal twist. It was Joe's idea to do something different which gave me the inspiration.

'Do something in your own unique way. Something that's meaningful to you and Sophie,' he said.

So, with Joe as my technical assistant, I went through all of the old photo albums I had as a child, filled full of far too many pictures documenting mine and Sophie's childhood – from our first day at school together to joining Girl Guides, and then our terrible fashion sense in our teenage years – and I created a 'documentary' as such, a flowing film of the last thirty-two years of our friendship. Sophie has no idea. She thinks she's coming over for a catch-up and a cup of tea, that's all, but instead she's getting afternoon tea and a home-made movie. I hope she likes it, although if the last thirty-two years have taught me anything it's that if there's cake involved, Sophie's usually pretty happy.

I think Sophie will get a real kick out of it. I know I did when I looked back through the photos. The worst part of it was having Joe see me in all my younger glory days. In fairness to him, he only laughed at a few pictures – well, that I saw anyway.

I have the laptop set up ready and connected (somehow) to the television screen. I pre-ordered and collected afternoon tea sandwiches and cakes from a lovely deli in town, and now I'm waiting for Sophie to arrive. Joe, thankfully, has gone out for a few hours to allow Sophie and me time to indulge in memories of our past and stuff ourselves with cakes (who really cares about the sandwiches with afternoon tea?).

I stare at the mini cakes presented on a stand and hover my hand over a lemon macaroon. They smell so amazing. I'm sure Sophie won't know if I eat just one now. My stomach grumbles in encouragement.

The intercom buzzes, making me jump a mile and nearly knock all the cakes flying. Sometimes I get the feeling that some higher force is watching over me and attempting to keep me in line.

I open the door to greet Sophie.

'What are you up to?' She stops and looks at me mid-hug.

'Me? Nothing.' I shake my head. I must still have a guilty expression on my face from the near miss with the macaroon theft. 'Come in and I'll get you a cuppa.'

I usher Sophie past the living room and into the kitchen. 'Sit down while I make a drink.' I nod towards the table.

'So what's happening with your mum's wedding? When do you fly out to New York?'

'Not long now – a couple of weeks. Mum keeps saying it's just a relaxed affair and all I need to do is wear a nice dress, while Joe wears a suit. Other than that, she's keeping quiet about the plans, which is kind of frustrating.'

'What are you getting them as a wedding gift?'

'That's been tricky too,' I say as I make the tea. 'As you know, my mother has everything and then some, so thinking of a unique present wasn't easy. We've decided to get them a voucher for an overnight stay at some fancy spa.'

'That sounds lovely. I really need a spa break, but you can't do those steam room things while you're pregnant. Apparently, I'll have no time for that once the baby's born.' Sophie rolls her eyes.

'Then you'd better make the most of today.' I smile handing Sophie a mug of tea.

'Emma?' Sophie says cautiously. 'What's going on?'

'Nothing bad, I promise. Just go through to the living room and take a seat on the sofa.'

Sophie eyes me up for a minute before reluctantly shuffling towards the living room.

'Oh, wow!' she exclaims as she enters the room. 'Are all those cakes for us?'

See? Nobody cares about the sandwiches.

'They are,' I say as I follow her in. 'Today is your mini baby shower. Just the two of us.'

'Oh, Emma. I told you not to make a fuss.'

'I know. But you're having a baby, so we should do something to mark the nearing arrival.'

'Thank you.' Sophie smiles as she reaches in and takes one of the very tempting lemon macaroons.

'Make yourself comfortable.' I grab the other lemon macaroon. 'We've got a movie to watch.'

'Ooh, which one?'

Sitting down on the sofa, I hit the return key on the laptop on the coffee table. A picture of me and Sophie from last New Year's Eve, looking slightly worse for wear from prosecco, appears on the television screen, and I breathe a sigh of relief that I didn't manage to break the technology in the half an hour since Joe left.

'Oh, wow. What's this?'

'It's our movie, Soph.' I shrug as a lump forms unexpectedly in my throat. 'I thought it would be nice to see us through all the years of our friendship, and it will be nice to show your child, my god-child, when they're old enough to appreciate it too.'

'That's so sweet.'

The picture on the screen changes to one of Sophie and me on our first day at nursery. Both dressed in cute pink dresses, we must have been about three years old. Sophie stands slightly forward of me, a confident smile on her face as she clasps my hand. I look slightly bewildered as I cling to Sophie. And that's pretty much been the dynamic of our friendship since we were three. Sophie, always my protector as I fumble through life.

As the pictures roll, we laugh, gasp and, on occasion, cry with emotion as we remember the different parts of our journey together. Things we'd totally forgotten about. Things we'd tried to forget about. But as we eat the cakes and drink numerous cups of tea, I'm so glad I decided to do this. It's been a great experience for me as well as Sophie, and it's made me appreciate our friendship even more, if that's possible.

By the time Joe comes home, we're both stuffed full of cake and blissfully reminiscing about the last fifteen or so years of our lives, in particular the long list of ridiculous things that have happened to me, whether instigated by me or not. I hadn't realised there were so many. I guess I never counted and documented them. When Sophie reels them off, it sounds like the script for a comedy.

Joe pops his head around the living room door. 'I take it you two have had a good afternoon?'

'Perfect,' Sophie says, still laughing.

'What's so funny?' Joe asks.

I look at Sophie and plead silently with my eyes. Joe, thankfully, only knows limited stories of my crazy existence prior to meeting him.

'Nothing.' Sophie shakes her head. 'Just remembering some of the things we've got up to over the years.'

I knew I could count on Sophie's discretion.

'That's okay.' Joe smiles at me. 'It's probably better all round that I don't know these things.'

Hmm. He knows me so well.

'Can I get either of you a cup of tea? I'm putting the kettle on.'

'No, thanks, Joe. I'm so full of all the lovely sandwiches and cakes that Emma got, I don't think I could fit anything else in.'

'I'm fine thanks too,' I say.

'Okay then, I'll leave you two ladies to it. I'll be in the kitchen.'

Sophie turns back to face me. 'Thanks for doing this, Emma. I've had a great afternoon.'

'Me too, and I had a lot of fun putting it all together.'

'You're going to be a great godmother.'

'You think?'

'Absolutely.'

'What makes you so sure?' I bite my lip.

'Because you care.'

'Come here.' I pull Sophie towards me and hug her tightly.

'What do think our story will look like?' Joe asks, nuzzling my neck as we lie in bed later that evening.

'Our story?' I ask into the darkness.

'Yeah, after thirty-two years.'

I feel a broad smile stretch across my face. I mean, I think about stuff like that and daydream about our future together, I just wasn't sure that Joe did too.

'I don't know,' I say quietly. 'Do you think we'll make it through the next thirty-two years without killing each other?'

'We might come close,' Joe says humorously, 'but I think we'll make it.'

'Yeah?'

'Yeah. And I'm looking forward to the journey.'

'Me too.' I snuggle in closer.

We lie quietly, and not long after I hear the soft sound of Joe's rhythmic breathing and I know he's fallen asleep, but I'm now wide awake. I am looking forward to the next thirty years of Joe and me together, but will it just be the two of us? If so, will we have enough in common to still be happy? Do people drift apart if they don't have children to bind them together for the rest of their lives? Maybe it's all about making the effort to spend time together and share your lives. Having children can work both ways – look at Simon and James recently. The pressure of putting your children first can put a different stress on a relationship.

I guess there's no easy answer either way, and the only people who know the right path for them are the two people in a relationship. So why isn't the choice to have children or not an easier decision to make?

Chapter Twenty-Eight

Two weeks later

The time has arrived for our trip to New York for Mum and Parker's wedding. It's five thirty a.m., not my favourite hour by far, and I'm feeling grumpy as we're herded like cattle through a maze of barriers. I think the entire population of the UK has descended on the airport today. I'm concerned there's a serious political issue or something else of which I'm completely oblivious that's requiring a mass exodus.

Once we've queued up to go through security, I feel like I've walked across the Sahara Desert. I'm almost relieved when I'm requested by the security staff to remove what feels like the majority of my clothing. I take off my coat and go to step towards the full-body scanner.

'And your scarf, miss.'

'Sorry?'

'Your scarf and shoes, please.' The security man smiles.

'Oh. Right.' I glance behind me at Joe, who already has his shoes and coat in his hands. 'Why don't you go in front?' I say as I load a large plastic tray with my handbag and coat.

Joe steps ahead of me, placing his coat and shoes in a separate tray, and walks swiftly to the body scanner and out the other side without incident.

I bend down and remove my shoes, but as I go to place them in the tray, I see the security man is holding my handbag.

'Any liquids in here?'

'Um, yes, but they're in a plastic bag,' I say.

He offers the bag back to me. 'Please remove any liquids and any electronic equipment.'

I open the bag, ignoring the huff of the passenger in the queue behind me, and pull out my mobile phone, the plastic bag containing my toiletries and, finally, my tablet. I never fly without the tablet; I need a distraction on the aeroplane, as I hate flying and detest being in such close proximity to a complete stranger. I usually get the chatty one who wants to engage in small talk, so I always have my headphones handy.

I place them in the tray with my coat and shoes, and then unravel the scarf from around my neck.

'They need to go in separate trays,' the security man says. His tone suggests he's becoming frustrated, and I can sympathise: I'm becoming increasingly annoyed by this process too.

I reach down to the shelf below and grab a further plastic tray and separate the items.

'Okay?' I ask.

'That's fine, miss. Step across to the body scanner, please.'

I am beckoned through the body scanner by a female security guard, and I stand facing the scanner and hold my hands above my head as instructed. As I exit the scanner I hear a buzz above my head, and as I look up I see a red light flashing.

Great.

The female security guard waves her hand. 'Step over here please, miss.'

At this point I'm wearing only my underwear and a thin knitted dress. Feeling slightly vulnerable, I stand in front of her and take in her latex-gloved hands. I pray they're purely to prevent the spread of germs and not for a more intimate search than a simple pat-down.

'Raise your arms, please.'

I hold my arms out at shoulder level and bite my lip as I'm frisked.

'You're fine, thank you.'

I breathe a sigh of relief and make my way to collect my handbag, but my relief is short lived as out of the corner of my eye I see a burley security man holding a grey plastic tray with my handbag placed inside.

I approach the desk with trepidation.

'Is this your handbag, miss?' the big man asks.

'Yes,' I say, feeling my stress levels start to elevate.

'Could anyone have interfered with your bag?'

'No.' I shake my head.

He inspects the small plastic bag containing my lip-gloss, my hand cream (the air on planes is very drying) and my mini deodorant (it's a long flight).

I force a smile. 'Is everything alright?'

'We need to look further, I'm afraid.'

'Oh. Um. Right.'

He then proceeds to rummage through the remaining contents of my handbag. I stand there feeling annoyance over the interrogation – and fear. It's stupid really. I know I haven't got anything that I shouldn't have in my handbag, and certainly not something that –

He pulls a lipstick from my handbag and holds it high in the air, as though presenting a trophy.

'This is a liquid,' he states. 'It needs to be in the plastic bag.'

'Really? It's not a liquid. A lipstick is a solid.' I glance over my shoulder at Joe, who's waiting over in the corner, and I see him shake his head and close his eyes.

'It's a liquid, miss, and we're going to have to scan the handbag again and take a swab.'

'Seriously? A swab because I have a lipstick in my handbag, which is a usual item to find in a woman's handbag.'

'But it wasn't in the plastic bag.'

'That's because it's not a liquid,' I protest.

I bite my lip, trying to remain calm. This is why I hate airports. I know they have a job to do in security and I'm really glad that they want to keep us all safe, but the majority of people who pass through here are simply en route to a holiday destination and have no intention of doing anything other than getting on their flight. You're made to feel like a criminal simply for being here.

I watch as the security man takes my bag away and I tap my fingers on the cold metal surface of the counter and simply wait, as I have no choice but to do exactly that.

'You can't beat them, you know,' a voice to my right says knowingly, and I turn to see a short, chubby middle-aged man nodding at me as he pulls on his jacket.

'Excuse me?' I say, raising my eyebrows.

'I work in pharmaceuticals,' he continues.

So? I want to say, but my overriding need to be polite keeps my tongue in check.

'A lipstick is actually ninety per cent liquid.'

I glare at him, trying to decide on an appropriate retort that won't result in me getting arrested, just to finish off this charade.

'You should read the airline guidelines before travelling,' he goes on.

Is this man serious? What a ridiculous thing to say to someone at an airport when they're experiencing security challenges. He's either very brave or stupid. I decide it's the latter, and just about to launch into a whole speech about the dangers of provoking a woman, who's already stressed at an airport from lack of sleep after getting out of bed at three am, by debating the liquid content of a lipstick when Joe appears out of nowhere at my side, swiftly taking hold of my hand.

'Is everything okay, Emma?' He looks me right in the eye and I can see him imploring me to remain calm. He glances from me to the man at my side.

'Everything's fine,' I tell Joe. 'Have a nice flight,' I say to the man, and turn away from him. Joe watches over my shoulder and I presume the man walks away.

The big security man returns and hands over my handbag. 'Your bag is clear, miss. Make sure you put all liquids in your plastic bag in future.'

'Thank you.' Joe takes hold of my handbag before I can say anything. 'Come on, Emma, let's get a coffee.' He leads me away.

We remain silent as we queue and order lattes. I'm still seething over that man's audacity in discussing the content of a lipstick. I mean, as if that's the appropriate time for that little bit of information. 'Read the airline guidelines.' Seriously?! Clearly this man has no wife or girlfriend, or he wouldn't have even considered making such a stupid comment. As we sit down, I open my mouth to speak, but Joe beats me to it.

'I can see why you might think he was out of order.' Joe slides my latte across the table towards me.

'But?'

'I think he was only trying to be helpful.'

'Helpful?'

'Yes, helpful.'

I scowl.

'Why do you always encounter such controversy when you fly?'

'I don't,' I say emphatically, 'and I really can't understand what the big issue is. I mean, yes, airport security people have a job to do, but why we have to put liquid things in a small plastic bag is beyond me. And if we do have to display all liquids then why can't we have more than one small bag? Quite honestly, if I've figured out how to put a bomb in my toothpaste tube, whether it's in my hold luggage or in a plastic bag in my hand luggage is probably irrelevant.' I take a gulp of my coffee.

Joe glances around nervously. 'Um, you probably shouldn't use the word "bomb" in an airport, Emma.'

'What? Oh, right.'

After what feels like the longest flight ever, we finally arrive at Newark Airport. Both Mum and Parker are there to greet us, waving frantically, as Joe and I lug our cases out of the arrivals hall. Well, I say Joe and I, but I really mean just Joe. I have my hand causally on the trolley carrying our cases, giving the impression that I'm somehow guiding it in the right direction. The truth is, it weighs a ton and I'm doing little to assist. We twenty-first-century women don't need a man, right? Sure we don't.

'Hi, darling.' Mum smothers me in a huge hug as Parker politely relieves me of trolley duty. 'I thought we could all grab some lunch once we've dropped your cases off at the apartment, and go over the plans for tomorrow.'

'Sounds great.' Joe kisses Mum on the cheek.

Lunch sounds very good to me. It feels like breakfast was last week, and the so-called "food" on the aeroplane has done little to appease my hunger. Lunch doesn't seem like the appropriate meal-time; I keep forgetting that New York is five hours behind the UK, and so in a way we've gone back in time. If only that meant that I could erase the idiocy at the airport this morning.

Mum and Parker, it turns out, have decided to get married at City Hall. I had expected The Plaza or somewhere equally as grand. For some reason I envisaged Mum saying her vows in some elaborate ceremony, followed by an extremely expensive five-course meal. Instead, we're simply heading down to City Hall in the morning to line up with all the other expectant brides and grooms and wait our turn. Apparently Mum would prefer the West Chapel and for it to be some guy with a moustache who marries them (he's some renowned marriage officiant in the Manhattan Marriage Bureau). In all honesty I'm intrigued to meet him – a guy who can perform hundreds of marriage ceremonies each week with a smile on his face; now that's an interesting perspective on the sanctity of the marriage vows. I bet he sees some interesting couples come through his doors.

I've already been warned by Mum that we need to get there early to be at the front of the queue, which means she will have prepared with military precision. I will, for once, do as I'm asked without question. This is Mum's day, and I will respect that. I'm actually looking forward to it, a lot more than when I thought it was going to be some huge, theatrical performance. I think it's quite sweet that she and Parker want to keep things low key. At the end of the day, how you get married is irrelevant; it's whether you're committed to the marriage that counts.

'Are you ready to celebrate your last night as a single woman?' I joke that evening, as I find Mum standing in her living room looking out at the stunning view over Central Park.

'I am.' Mum turns around, smiling. 'How about we start with a glass of bubbly?'

'Sounds good to me.'

'Where's Joe?'

'He's popped out for an hour to give us a bit of time on our own.'

'Then we'd better make the most of it.' Mum giggles girlishly. 'I'll grab a bottle.'

Parker has decided to spend the night at a hotel so Mum can spend her last night as a single woman without him. Half of me thinks this is romantic, and the other half thinks it's pointless, as they've been living together and sharing a bed (don't go there, Emma!) for a while now. I stand looking at the view and feel a familiar tightening in my stomach. I never get tired of looking at Central Park, lit up and stunning in the evening. It looks so magical, like a film set, and I feel inspired just standing here.

'Emma?' Mum nudges me and hands me a glass of fizz. 'Are you okay?'

'Of course.' I raise my glass. 'Here's to you, Mum, and to your future happiness.'

'Thank you, darling.' Mum clinks her glass on mine and we both take a sip of champagne.

'Do you ever get tired of looking out of this window?' I ask as we stand side by side.

'Nope.' Mum shakes her head. 'This is possibly the best part of living in New York.'

'What could beat this?' I look over at Mum.

'Being able to get Chinese food at four a.m.'

I laugh out loud. 'Like you get Chinese food at four a.m.'

Mum laughs too. 'You might be surprised, Emma.'

I raise my eyebrows skywards.

'What?' Mum shakes her head, seemingly amused. 'Why do you find that so shocking?'

'Um, because you're you.' I take another sip of champagne. 'You're my mother, and you're so...'

'So?'

'So smart, and accomplished, and why would you need Chinese food in the middle of the night?'

Mum takes a sip of her champagne. 'You don't think I ever come home from an event having had a little too much wine, and find myself with the munchies?'

I stare, open-mouthed, at the woman in front of me and wonder who she is and what she's done with my mother.

'Don't look so surprised, Emma,' Mum smiles. 'Hangovers don't get any easier as you get older; in fact, they're worse than ever.'

I laugh, shaking my head. 'Are you excited about tomorrow?'

'I'm excited about what it means,' Mum says. 'Formalising our relationship.'

I nod.

'It's different this time around,' Mum continues. 'Your father and I were so young when we got married. That was a long time ago.'

'But it was right at the time?' I ask.

'Absolutely, Emma. I have no regrets about marrying your father. We were happy for a long time.'

'Do you ever worry about, um, what society expects of you?'

Mum shakes her head. 'No, Emma. I worry about what I expect of me, that's all.'

I drink the last of my champagne.

'You don't agree?' Mum asks.

'I wish I didn't worry so much about it.'

'What do you have to worry about, Emma?'

I shrug. 'I'm thirty-four. I'm not married. I have no kids.'

'Do you want children?'

'Not right now.'

'Are you happy?'

'Yes.'

'And you love Joe?'

'Yes.'

'Then there's your answer.'

'I guess.'

'Nobody has a crystal ball, Emma. People make choices, and they might make mistakes – and if they do, they adapt and move on. It's life. All you can do is make decisions based on how you feel at that moment in time,' Mum says, and drinks the last of her champagne too. 'The worst thing you can do is make a decision based on somebody else's opinion.'

I take a deep breath and exhale.

'More champagne?' Mum shakes her glass with a smile.

I smile too. 'Sounds like a good plan.'

Chapter Twenty-Nine

I wake snuggled in the warmth of Joe, his arm wrapped around me as he sleeps. I can't believe Mum and Parker are getting married today. I mean, it's great for them, and I'm really happy for Mum, but I can't help but feel a little weird. Weddings provoke mixed emotions for me, since Joe and I were getting married and then we weren't. I got overwhelmed by the whole thing, started seeing it as a huge production, instead of concentrating on the most important thing: the two of us making a promise to love and cherish each other, for better or for worse.

I sniff back tears.

Come on, Emma, pull yourself together. You have a whole day of loved-up wedding stuff ahead of you and this isn't the best start.

'Hey,' Joe mumbles into my hair. 'Are you okay?'

'Sure,' I say over-brightly. 'Just excited about the day ahead.'

'Good.' Joe kisses my forehead.

I wriggle out from his grasp and slide out of the bed. 'I think I can hear Mum up and about. I'll go and check on her and make some coffee.'

I pull on my dressing gown and pad barefoot through to the kitchen, where I find Mum dressed in pale-grey jogging bottoms and a sweatshirt, looking casual but still with more class than I possess on any given day.

'Morning, Emma,' Mum smiles. 'Sleep well? Do you want coffee? Where's Joe?' she babbles.

'Mum? Are you alright?'

'Yes, darling. Of course. Why wouldn't I be?' Mum flaps her hands wildly at me.

'Well, for starters it's your wedding day, so you're bound to feel…' I pause and Mum raises her eyebrows at me. '…nervous,' I continue. 'And secondly, you're behaving rather erratically.'

Mum reaches for the coffee pot.

'Maybe you should avoid any further caffeine for the moment,' I suggest, prising the cafetière from her hand.

'You're right,' Mum states, heading towards the fridge. She leans in, retrieves a bottle and waves it at me. 'Buck's Fizz?'

I'm not sure whether that's a question or a statement, so I simply nod, and Mum proceeds to take champagne glasses from the cupboard. As the cork pops, I can't help but wonder if alcohol at eight thirty in the morning is a good idea. Although if it were my wedding day, I think I'd need a shot of something stronger than coffee to calm my nerves.

Mum hands me a glass of Buck's Fizz. 'Here's to marriage.' She raises her glass to mine.

'Here's to you, Mum, and to your future happiness with Parker,' I say.

'Oh, Emma.' Mum sniffs. 'I am doing the right thing, aren't I?'

My heart skips a beat and the Buck's Fizz seems to stick in my throat. Is this just pre-wedding jitters, or is Mum seriously asking if she should be marrying Parker? And if she is seriously asking, how the hell am I supposed to answer that? I take another gulp of Buck's Fizz while I try to formulate the correct response. So much for last night's words of wisdom from Mum. What's happened to that calm and collected woman?

'I'm not saying that I don't love Parker.' Mum downs her glass of bubbly and instantly pours herself a refill.

That's not giving me confidence.

'It's just marriage...it's a big thing, Emma,' she continues, seeming to inspect the contents of her glass.

'I know that, Mum,' I say, trying to keep my voice calm. 'I thought you knew that too, having been married before.'

'But that's just it, Emma. I have been married before, and that was a long time ago. I mean, should I be going down this route again at my age?'

'Okay, Mum, I don't mean to be rude...' I finish my own drink, take the bottle from the worktop and pour in a generous measure – given the subject of this conversation, I take back my initial reservations about drinking at eight thirty a.m. 'But I think it's a bit late to be contemplating whether you should be getting married again at your age.' I glance up at the clock on the wall. 'You should be heading down to City Hall in about two hours.'

Mum follows my gaze to the wall clock but remains silent.

I press my lips together and exhale. 'You know what, Mum? If you don't want to do this then no one is forcing you to.'

Still silence.

'In reality nothing will change between you and Parker, whether you get married today or not. Your relationship is what it is, because you're both committed to it.'

'Right.' Mum nods.

'The only thing you need to ask yourself is whether you want to get married today – and who cares how old you are? Marriage doesn't have an age ceiling. It's about two people only, nobody else. Remember all the things you said to me last night?'

'Oh, Emma.' Mum pulls me into a hug. 'Thank you. I'm just being silly, I know that.'

'So you're okay?'

Mum holds me at arm's length and looks right at me. 'Yes. I'm fine, and I do want to marry Parker. I'm going to marry Parker today. In fact, like you said, in about two hours, so we'd better get a move on.'

Honestly I can't keep up with this woman.

'I'll go and get in the shower,' Mum says.

'With all due respect, Mum, we've just glugged half a bottle of Buck's Fizz between us on an empty stomach, and we've got a long day ahead of us.'

'You're right. Some toast first, then the shower.' Mum walks over to the bread bin just as Joe walks into the room. 'Morning, Joe. Emma and I are having some toast. Would you like some?'

Mum's back to her usual cheerful self, the last three minutes of conversation that nearly upended this day apparently forgotten as she busies herself preparing breakfast.

'That sounds great, Rosalind,' Joe answers as he looks questioningly at the half-empty bottle of alcohol on the kitchen side. 'Everything okay?' he mouths silently at me.

'Don't ask!' I mouth back.

And we carry on as normal: Mum makes toast, I make some tea and we make small talk over breakfast.

I figure that something must go awry on most wedding days, and if this is the only hitch for today then it's not all bad – a few minutes of last-minute panic is perfectly acceptable. Maybe, to be on the safe side, I'd better keep Mum away from anything else alcoholic until she and Parker have exchanged their vows.

We sit in a line, Mum, Parker, Joe and I, waiting for our turn in the chapel, and I can't help but smile as I look around. We're surrounded by people in love, happy faces full of optimism for the new chapter in their lives that's starting. It makes me feel all warm and fuzzy – although that could just be the effect of Buck's Fizz at eight thirty this morning. It's just the four of us for the ceremony; that's all Mum and Parker wanted. Joe and I will witness the marriage, and then some of their friends will be joining us for food and drinks at a wine bar later.

Mum looks immaculate, as ever, dressed in a cream Dior suit. She's glowing from head to toe, and if I didn't know better I'd think she was ten years younger than her fifty-eight years. Parker sits close to Mum, his hand clasped tightly around hers as he stares ahead. I have to admit Parker scrubs up well too. He always looks smart, but today his thick chocolate hair has extra body and shine and his navy suit also looks like it's designer and probably cost more than my monthly rent.

I'm dressed in a beautiful pale-pink dress, which is sleeveless and has a fitted bodice, pulling in at my waist, and a full flowing skirt, like the famous picture of Marilyn Monroe. (I actually had a "Marilyn Monroe moment" as I got out of the taxi earlier and a huge gust of wind came around the corner, blowing my skirt up uncontrollably. Thank God I'm wearing big pants, or it could have been much worse!) Joe looks incredibly handsome in his dark-grey suit, so much so that despite my usual rule of behaving impeccably around my mother, I was almost inclined to take Joe back to bed before we left the apartment. It's probably in everyone's best interests that there wasn't time for that.

'Rosalind Storey?'

A small black woman hovers near to the row of chairs and we all stand. For some reason I feel more nervous than either Mum or Parker look; my heart is beating a little faster and I can feel a tightening in my stomach.

Joe leans in close. 'You okay?' he whispers in my ear.

'Sure.' I nod. 'Here, Mum, let me get that for you.' I reach down with my other hand and pick up Mum's bouquet of cream roses.

We follow the woman to the West Chapel and are greeted by the registrar. He smiles warmly and instantly I feel at ease, like he's exactly the right man to marry Mum and Parker. As he leads us to the front of the chapel, he explains how the service will go. Mum and Parker stand at the front with Joe and I slightly behind, and the registrar begins the ceremony. Joe slips his hand into mine and I smile at him. This is surreal, watching your mum get married. It's the wrong way around; it's something that you don't think you'll see, but at the same time it's wonderful to be a part of it.

It feels like a hush descends on the whole building as we stand in the chapel facing the registrar and Mum and Parker prepare to take their vows. Joe squeezes my hand and I squeeze it back tightly. I'm always one to feel over-emotional at weddings, but I think today I've gone into overdrive because it's Mum. That's silly really, as I was absolutely fine when Dad and Margaret got married years ago. Maybe I feel more protective over Mum? I contemplate. Why, I don't know. She's proven that she's a strong, capable woman on many occasions, particularly over the last few years.

I glance at Parker. He's staring intently at Mum, a huge smile on his face, and I know he definitely loves her. I'm happy for Mum, I really am. She's made a great life for herself here in New York, but as I can remember her saying to me once, there's a lot to be said for having someone to come home to.

The registrar smiles. 'Are we all ready?'

Mum and Parker both nod in unison as I wipe a tear from the corner of my eye.

The ceremony is over in only a few minutes (which we were warned about; the number of weddings carried out each day in these chapels means they have to keep them short). As the registrar announces 'I now pronounce you man and wife', Parker pulls Mum into a close embrace and kisses her passionately, causing me to blush. I glance around, trying to look every which way but directly at them, and I can't help but giggle as I notice Joe is looking discretely down at his feet.

Mum turns to face me, beaming. 'Oh, Emma, I'm married!' she declares.

'I'm so happy for you, Mum,' I say into her hair as she hugs me.

'Come on, let's go celebrate!' Parker takes Mum by the hand. 'There's champagne chilling that has our name on it.'

We head out of the chapel and back past the other couples waiting to take the plunge into married life. It's nice that so many people want to make that commitment to each other, even in this day and age when virtual relationships are on the increase with couples Skyping and Face-Timing, texting and having conversations using only emojis (I have no idea what half of them mean – I know the happy face, sad face and angry face, but beyond that I'm completely lost). I'm somewhat surprised, in a good way, that the traditional arrangement of marriage is still so popular. It's heart-warming, although maybe I won't research the current rate of divorce, which might burst my idealistic and romantic perception.

'Emma?'

'Yes?' I glance up at Joe.

'You were miles away.'

'Oh, sorry. What did you say?'

'Never mind.' Joe shakes his head.

Back out on the street, we walk the short distance to the wine bar where the "simple" reception will be held. As Mum explains it, there'll be 'lots of lovely nibbles and plenty of champagne', which sounds good to me.

'It should be interesting, meeting some of your mum's friends,' Joe says as we follow Mum and Parker into the wine bar.

'Yep, should be interesting,' I whisper. I'm imagining a room full

of posh women in their fifties with whom I'll have little in common;
I'll have to spend the entire time trying to make awkward small talk.

'Congratulations!' shout a group of men and women who look
like they've barely made it into their thirties as they rush over and
make a huge fuss of Mum and Parker.

I stand, open-mouthed, as I take in the young women dressed in
the latest spring/summer lines from Versace and Gucci.

'So much for old fuddy-duddies.' Joe nudges me, grinning.

I close my mouth and compose my face as a stunning brunette
makes her way over to me. Instinctively I tighten my grip on Joe's
hand.

'You must be, Emma,' the brunette gushes. 'I'm Miranda.'

'Hi,' I say, wondering if I should shake her hand or something,
but I decide against it.

'Your mother is an amazing woman,' Miranda says. 'She has us all
in fits of laughter at work.'

'You work with my mum?' This is so not how I imagined my
mother's work colleagues.

'Oh, yes. We have a great time. She's so much fun. Come on, I
know everyone is looking forward to meeting you. Rosalind has
told us so much about you.'

'Really?' I say. I wonder which bits. Hopefully only the good bits,
not all the random, crazy things.

'And you must be Joe.' Miranda leans in and kisses Joe on the
cheek. 'Very nice to meet you.'

Oh, I see. I don't get so much as a handshake, but Joe gets a kiss.
Hmm.

Miranda turns and heads back to the crowd, where Mum's handing out champagne.

'Come on.' Mum waves us over and hands us both a champagne
flute, before she's whisked into another conversation by an overex-
cited trendsetter on her left.

After the Buck's Fizz for breakfast, I'm about ready for a top-up.

'Don't let me have too many of these,' I say to Joe. 'I don't want to
end up drunk and disorderly.'

'I don't know, I quite like the idea of that,' Joe says, kissing me on the cheek. 'Then I can have my wicked way with you.'

'Not a chance while we're staying in Mum's apartment. You'll have to wait until we get back to England, I'm afraid.' I'm standing firm on this after my near miss this morning, when I saw Joe looking extremely handsome in his suit.

Joe strokes my arm gently with the back of his hand. 'But you look so sexy in your dress, Emma.'

My body shivers instinctively at his touch. 'No,' I say. 'Not under Mum's roof.' I sip my champagne.

'We're not teenagers, you know.'

'I know that. We're grownups, which means we should have more control.' I raise my eyebrows at Joe.

'Spoilsport.' He chuckles.

A very smart-looking couple suddenly appear at our side. 'So, you two must be Joe and Emma.'

'Yes,' I smile.

'I'm Poppy, and this is my husband Robert. We're friends of Parker's.'

'Ah, I see. Nice to meet you both.'

'They're such a lovely couple. We couldn't be happier for them.'

'They're very happy,' Joe says.

'So...' Poppy looks down at my left hand. 'No wedding bells for you two then?'

Oh my God. How rude! You don't just say something like that to people! Her blatant lack of social awareness stuns me into silence. Thankfully Joe rescues us.

'We're very happy just as we are,' he says politely. I have to refrain from adding a profanity to the end of that sentence.

Poppy and Robert excuse themselves and I quickly down the last of my champagne.

'Are you alright?' Joe asks.

'Sure.'

'I don't think she meant to offend you.'

'She didn't.' I try to sound nonchalant.

'So do you want to talk about it?'

'About what?' I look at Joe, feeling a tightness forming in my chest.

'Well, perhaps we should talk about the fact that marriage, and the fact that we're not married, seems to be a reoccurring topic, particularly given that people around us keep getting married.'

'Sophie and Matt aren't married.'

'No, that's true. But they are having a baby.'

I exhale deeply, unsure where this conversation is going but very sure that I don't want it to continue right here.

Joe takes hold of my hand and leads me to a tall table with two stools set slightly away from the wedding party. Once we're seated – which takes some doing in a fitted dress and heels – Joe finally speaks again.

'Look, I just don't want it to be something that you're worried about.'

'Why would I be worried about not being married? We've talked about this before.'

Joe shrugs. 'I don't want you to worry either way.'

'What are you saying? You don't want to be married ever?'

Joe presses his lips together and pauses for a moment. 'I used to think that being married was important to me.'

'Right.' I nod.

'But over the last few years, I've realised that actually being married isn't the most important thing to me.'

'Oh?'

'I love you, Emma, more than I thought I could love anyone.'

I gulp, feeling overwhelmed with emotion.

'And if you want to be married one day then I'd love that, but if you don't...'

I hold my breath.

'Then all that matters is that we're committed to each other and we spend the rest of our lives together.'

'Are you sure?' I say quietly.

Joe nods. 'Absolutely.'

'I'm not saying I want to, but I'm not saying never either.'

'Okay.'

'And I love you too.'

Joe leans in and kisses me.

'Everything alright, darling?'

The sound of Mum's voice makes us jump apart like two school-kids being caught making out, and I laugh.

'Everything's perfect, Mum.'

'Are you having a good time?' Joe asks.

'Brilliant.' Mum looks completely content. 'It's lovely to have eve-ryone here to celebrate with us, and I loved the fact that it was just you two with us during the ceremony. I couldn't have asked for a nicer day.'

The rest of the day goes by in a surreal blur, until we find ourselves back at Mum's apartment later that evening, exhausted and giddy and a little tipsy.

'What a fabulous day.' Mum collapses into an armchair.

I sit down on the huge, squashy sofa and almost slide into a horizontal position. 'It really was, Mum. Joe and I had a great time meeting all your friends.' I try, and fail, to prop myself up into a more upright position. Clearly this settee is purely for slouching on.

'You didn't think I was that cool, did you?' Mum smiles at me, eyebrows raised.

'I don't know what you mean.'

'You were expecting a load of old people, weren't you?'

I bite my lip. 'I would never call you old,' I say, grinning.

'We should have a nightcap,' Mum says, standing up just as Joe and Parker come into the room.

'One last toast to the happy couple.' Joe hands me a glass as Park-er hands one to Mum.

'What's this?' I sniff the contents. 'It smells fruity.'

'Cheers.' Parker raises his glass and we all follow suit.

I take a cautious sip. 'Oh my God! This tastes amazing.'

'I know,' Joe says. 'It's rhubarb and ginger gin with tonic.'

'It's like alcoholic rhubarb and custard sweets,' I say, before taking a much larger sip. This could be very dangerous, but it's too good not to drink. In fact, this might just be my new favourite tipple. 'We must get some of this when we land back in the UK.'

Joe just shakes his head at me.

The following day, we all head to the airport like it's some kind of road trip, but Joe and I are heading back to England, and Mum and Parker are jumping on a plane to St Lucia for their honeymoon. I don't blame them. They may have had a low-key wedding, but that's all the more reason to have a fabulous honeymoon somewhere exotic.

Mum hugs me goodbye as we arrive outside departures. Mum and Parker are flying from a different terminal.

'It was so lovely to see you both.'

'It went so quickly.' I hug her back. 'Have a great time in St Lucia.'

'Don't worry, we will,' Mum smiles. 'All-inclusive and in a hut on stilts right in the sea – what more could we want?'

That's a very good question. That scenario sounds like perfection to me.

'We'll call you when we get home,' Mum says. 'Have a safe journey.'

'You too.' Joe takes hold of the suitcases and we start to walk towards the doors.

We turn before entering the building and wave back at Mum and Parker, who are standing, holding hands, and waving frantically at us. They look so cute.

'Let's hope we have a less eventful airport experience on the journey home.' Joe raises his eyebrows at me.

'I don't know what you mean.' I shrug.

'Is your lipstick in a plastic bag?'

'Don't even go there!'

Chapter Thirty

I fiddle with the stem of my wine glass. 'Can I ask you a question, Si?'

It's been a couple of days have since mum's wedding and I'm having a catch up over wine with Simon at his flat.

'Of course, Emma. You can ask me anything, you know that.'

I bite my lip, wondering if the conversation I'm about to initiate will make me look like a heartless ice queen.

'Come on, Ems.' Simon places his hand over mine and gives it a little squeeze. 'What's bothering you?'

'When did you realise that you wanted to be a dad?'

I take a nervous gulp of my wine. Usually I feel like I can talk to Simon; that he will never judge me. But for some reason the whole marriage and children conversation has evaded us until now. I can't help but wonder if that's because I choose to avoid the topic, as I don't want to face the niggling thought in my head that I might not be cut out for motherhood. Or maybe Simon has always known this about me and so he never starts a conversation about my lack of maternal instinct.

Simon shrugs. 'I always knew.'

Oh. I wasn't expecting that. That's not helpful. Now I just feel worse about myself.

'Why are you asking me this?'

'I don't know.' I shake my head gently, but Simon just looks at me with a raised eyebrow. 'That's not true.' I take another sip of my wine. 'I guess because of Sophie being pregnant, and you and James getting the twins, I feel like...'

'You're being left out of something?' Simon sits down next to me at the breakfast bar.

'Maybe.'

'Maybe?'

I exhale. 'I suppose what's really bothering me is not that I'm not included in the gang of new parents, it's more that I don't know if I ever want to be.'

There. I've said it out loud. I glance across at Simon, waiting for his response.

'That figures.' He nods, taking a drink of his wine.

'That figures?'

'I get that vibe from you. I guess I always have, which is why I've never really pushed you on the subject.'

I don't know if I'm relieved or hurt by this. At what point did Simon come to the conclusion that I wasn't "mum material"?

Simon senses my change in emotion. 'Don't be upset, Emma. You are who you are and you can't change that, so why does that worry you?'

'Because I'm a woman. I'm supposed to want marriage and babies, and so far all I've managed in my thirty-four years is expecting a marriage proposal when my boyfriend of two years was actually breaking up with me...' That fateful evening with Chris still haunts me occasionally. I stupidly thought we were going to spend the rest of our lives together, and he'd actually been cheating on me with someone barely out of college. 'And then Joe did propose to me, in the most romantic way at the top of the Empire State Building in New York. But I freaked out so much at the idea of planning a wedding, along with all the other changes that were going on in my life, that I called off the wedding and ruined my relationship.'

'But you got Joe back. You're happy together – happier than ever. Aren't you?'

'Of course. I love Joe, more than anything.'

'So is he putting pressure on you to have kids now his brother and Sophie are expecting?'

'No, absolutely not. He says he's not in a rush, and if it's not right for us then he's fine with it just being us two.'

'So what's the problem, Em?'

'I don't know. Me. Maybe I'm the problem, because I'm having this inner fight with myself, wondering why I don't feel the need to get married and have children. I mean, don't get me wrong, I love other people's children...'

'That's evident when I see you with Theo and Fitz.'

'Really?'

'Are you kidding? They love their Auntie Emma.'

I swallow back tears.

'I feel bad for my mum and dad too.'

'I can't quite envisage your Gucci-clad mother as a grandma in a knitted twinset.' Simon cocks his head to one side thoughtfully.

'I don't think my mum would ever wear a knitted twinset, Simon. I've barely seen her in casual clothes since I was sixteen. Now she lives in New York, one of the trendiest cities, I don't think she owns anything that I'm not envious of. But I hear it in her voice when I talk to her about Sophie, her desire to be a grandmother. It's there, even if it's unsaid.'

'Oh, Emma, you shouldn't give yourself such a hard time, you know. It's your life and no one else's. You can't make decisions as serious and life-changing as having children based on someone else's desire.'

'Isn't it selfish to not want children? To say, "I like my life the way it is"?'

'No. What would be selfish is bringing a child into this world without it truly being what you want. It's far less selfish to be true to yourself. Having children or not is a lifestyle choice. A choice only you can make.'

'I worry about myself. I worry why I'm in my thirties and I'm not following the conventional life.'

'Who is?' Simon grins. 'I'm hardly the greatest example of conforming to the ideals society insists on trying to force us into.'

'I guess not.' I giggle. 'However, you did get married.'

'To a man, though, darling.'

'That's true.' I take a drink of my wine. 'Did you ever think you would get married when we were kids?'

'I never doubted it.'

'You didn't?'

'No. What can I say, I'm a true romantic.'

'Did you always know you would marry a man?'

'Don't be stupid, Emma. I'm gay. I've always been gay. I never imagined I'd be walking down the aisle ready to marry a petite brunette in a fluffy meringue.'

'Oh.'

'Stop worrying about what you think people expect you to be, and just be yourself. Joe seems to love you just the way you are, and if he's not putting you under any pressure to be married with two-point-four children, then you really should ease up on yourself, okay?'

'Okay.' I nod, although I'm not sure I feel a whole lot better. Simon seems pretty sure that marriage and babies would always have been part of his life, despite the less "traditional" lifestyle that he leads. Yet here I am, undecided, with the clock apparently ticking down loudly, if you listen to what society has to say. Who would have thought that I'd be reaching my expiration date at the grand old age of thirty-four?

'You make a fantastic aunt, Emma. And let's face it, if you ever feel like you want to experience having children, you can borrow Theo and Fitz for the weekend and see if you survive!' Simon grins.

'That good, hey?'

'I wouldn't change them, believe me; I love being a daddy. But my God it's hard work, harder than I ever imagined. And I never thought I would be so keen to put someone else's needs before my own, but they change you. They change your priorities. That's why you've got to be one hundred per cent sure before you go down that road, because once you do, there's no going back.'

'I know you're right.'

'Of course I'm right.' Simon winks. 'Now, I'm going to check on the two little sleeping monkeys. You pour another glass of wine.'

Chapter Thirty-One

'I'm so fed up. I'm huge and fed up, and I never go anywhere. I haven't been anywhere in months!'

I'm slightly taken aback by Sophie's rant, although more shocked by her appearance. Her coffee-coloured curls are swirling around her face, Medusa-like, taking on a life of their own. When she asked me over for lunch, I wasn't expecting a tirade like this; she seemed perfectly calm on the phone. I've not even stepped through the front door. This is how she's greeted me.

'I don't think that's entirely true now, is it?' I say, trying to placate her so she'll at least let me past the front door, and her considerable baby bump. 'And I thought you loved being pregnant.'

I'm met with a deep frown and a screwed-up mouth. Apparently this is not the appropriate response. Sophie wasn't looking to be placated; she was looking for me to agree with her.

'Come on, Soph.' I cock my head to one side. 'I brought cupcakes.' I wave the pink-striped box under her nose and she relents and steps back from the door.

'Now, what's wrong all of a sudden?' I ask as I step into the hallway.

'I'm fat and unattractive and I'm fed up of being pregnant. Nothing fits, I have permanent indigestion – and I've got five more weeks of this crap!'

'Okay…cupcake?' I hand her a vanilla cupcake with sparkly pink frosting. She snatches it from my hand quicker than a monkey taking nuts at the zoo and starts licking the frosting. 'Why don't you go and sit down and I'll make us a cup of tea. Are you still drinking that, um, ginger tea?'

'Don't you dare bring me a cup of that!'

'Earl Grey it is then,' I say, ushering Sophie into the living room and then heading into the kitchen.

As the kettle boils, I wonder what could have sent Sophie over the edge. Once she got over her morning sickness (which came in the evening), she had been glowing and perfectly at ease in her pregnancy. Overnight she's morphed into a version of herself that, thankfully, I've never seen before. I'm actually a tad scared. I make two cups of Earl Grey tea and cautiously head into the living room.

'Here you go.' I place the cups down on the coffee table and hesitate before taking a seat next to Sophie on the sofa.

'I'm sorry if I seem a little...' Sophie pauses.

Monstrous? I want to offer, but think better of it.

She goes with, 'Tetchy.'

Who am I to argue? Although if this is "tetchy", I want to be several miles away if she's ever really angry.

'That's fine,' I say dismissively. 'I'm sure every pregnant woman feels "tetchy" at some point. But you're not fat and unattractive, Sophie, you're pregnant, and that's beautiful.'

'Beautiful? Really? I can tell you lots of things about being pregnant that aren't beautiful,' Sophie continues, and I pray that I'll be spared the full details, especially before lunch.

'Swollen ankles, indigestion, back ache.'

Apparently I'm not going to be spared the details.

'Surely all of that pales into insignificance compared to the fact that you're carrying a small human that you and Matt have lovingly created.'

'Hmm.' Sophie chews her lip. 'I am excited about that, honestly. It just feels like I don't do anything anymore other than eat. I can't drink alcohol or go clubbing –'

'Seriously, when did we last go clubbing, Sophie?'

'Well, at least dancing in a bar.'

'Okay,' I concede, 'we have done that in the last year.'

'Exactly, and now I can't, and I just want to do...something.'

I have a sudden moment of brilliance.

'Why don't we go to the coast?' I say excitedly.

'What?'

'The seaside.'

'I know what the coast is, Emma.'

'Joe took me to this amazing cottage on the cliffs. It was so picturesque, and relaxing. We could take face masks and the foot spa my mum bought me years ago that's still in the box, and have a pamper weekend.'

Sophie's face brightens a little. 'That does sound quite nice.'

'And it's a lovely stroll along the seafront into the town.'

'How far?' Sophie glances down at her ankles and I follow her gaze. I hadn't noticed until now, but Sophie's ankles look like footballs.

'We can take it steady, and stop for fish and chips along the way.'

'And doughnuts?'

'Of course.'

'Okay. I'm in. Let's see if we can get booked in.'

'I'll call Joe now and get the details before we head out to lunch.'

'Great.' Sophie finally smiles and starts to look less like Medusa and more like her usual self.

Chapter Thirty-Two

'Jesus, Simon, how long do you think we're going for?'

I stare, open-mouthed, at the huge suitcase Simon is carrying, with great difficulty, towards my car. I can see Sophie giggling in the passenger seat. As soon as I mentioned that Sophie and I were heading to the seaside, Simon instantly invited himself – not that either Sophie or I mind.

'What?' Simon pauses, wiping his brow.

'You've got more luggage than me and Sophie put together.'

'Don't whinge, Em. There's plenty of room.' Simon launches the suitcase into the boot of the car and then slides into the back seat as I climb into the driver's side.

'I hope you're not going to be this grumpy the whole journey,' Simon says, fastening his seatbelt and grinning from ear to ear.

Sophie glances behind her. 'What are you smiling about?'

'I'm so excited. I haven't been to the seaside in ages,' Simon says. 'Can we have candyfloss?'

'Simon, I'm not your mother. You can have whatever you want,' I say as we set off towards the dual carriageway that leads out of the city. 'But if you eat so much you make yourself sick, you have no one to blame but yourself.'

Sophie chuckles and looks out of the window.

'Stick some music on then, Em, and let's get this party started.'

'This is supposed to be a chilling-out weekend for Sophie, Si, not an eighteen-to-thirties mini-break.'

'Don't be such a spoilsport, Em. Sophie might be nearly eight months pregnant, but she can still have a boogie in her seat while we drive, can't you, Soph?' Simon taps Sophie on her shoulder.

'What music do you want, Simon?' Sophie asks.

'Here, I'll connect my playlist. You do have Bluetooth, don't you, Em?'

'Of course,' I say convincingly but with no knowledge at all in answer to that question. I needn't have worried as Simon's already connected and we all jump in our seats as some frantic clubbing track starts booming out of the speakers.

'Sorry, sorry.' Simon waves his hands at us.

'Something a little calmer, please,' I shout over the thumping beats.

'Hang on…nearly there,' Simon shouts back, and then finally the hideous sound stops and the more placid beats of an old Stereophonics track fill the car. We drive along, all singing in time with the track.

We're not half an hour into the journey when Simon takes a break from reading snippets from the *Financial Times* to us (which is clearly falling on deaf ears, as neither Sophie nor I have any idea what he's talking about) to demand that we stop at the next Starbucks drive-through.

'Simon, we'll be there in an hour.'

'So? The journey is the start of the holiday, Em.'

'Honestly, Simon, it's like taking a child out for the day,' I say, exasperated.

'I could eat a muffin,' Sophie adds.

'Okay, you both win. We'll stop at the next Starbucks.'

Once we've located coffee and muffins, the rest of the journey is unhindered, if you excuse the two toilet breaks for Sophie. She can be forgiven, though. I think I'd need to constantly wee if I had a five-pound baby lying on my bladder.

We pull up at the cottage just over an hour later, and I'm still in awe at how beautiful it is – especially the view from the cliffs, which is breath-taking.

'Wow, this looks lovely,' Sophie says as she eases herself out of the car.

We all stand looking at the view of the ocean, breathing in the fresh sea air.

'So what's first?' Simon asks.

'Well, for starters you can lug that suitcase of yours, and mine and Sophie's bags, into the cottage,' I say. 'There's a double bed and a single room.'

'I'll have the single bed if that's okay,' Sophie says, walking towards the cottage.

'Whatever you're most comfortable with, Soph.'

'It's for your own good. If I don't wake you up every hour on the hour as I go to the loo, then I'm likely to knock you out of bed as I toss and turn, trying to get comfy.'

Simon chuckles as he heaves the bags towards the cottage. 'Matt must be loving this special time in your pregnancy.'

'Shut up!' Sophie whacks Simon on the back of the head.

'Not fair. I can't defend myself against a pregnant woman.'

'Seriously, though, Soph, have you actually knocked Matt out of bed?'

There's a pause. 'Just the once,' Sophie says dismissively as she walks through the front door.

We dump the bags and then take a steady stroll along the seafront, stopping for doughnuts, fish and chips, and then candyfloss along the way. I feel the size of the Michelin Man and slightly sickly as we start our return stroll back to the cottage. Sophie and I walk along the sand, while Simon runs in and out of the sea like a giddy Labrador. It's quite sweet how over-excited he is today. I wasn't wrong with my first analogy this morning – it is like taking a child out.

'I don't know how James copes.' Sophie smiles. 'It must be like having three children.'

'I know, but he adores Simon, and somehow they make it work.'

'They do, and it's lovely to see Simon settled down. There were many times when I seriously didn't think it would happen.'

'Me too. He dated a different man each week, and by dated I mean had alcohol and casual sex with.'

Sophie giggles. 'You are cruel.'

'I am not, I'm just telling the truth. I'm his best friend so I'm allowed to. Plus, have you forgotten how I first met James?'

'Oh, yeah.' Sophie raises her eyebrows.

'It was barely six o'clock in the evening on a Friday when I let myself into Simon's apartment with his spare key, as he hadn't answered the door after I had knocked. I was treated to Simon's bare arse and a naked stranger.'

'Stop it.' Sophie is clutching her stomach as she laughs loudly 'You'll make my waters break.'

'Oh God! Really?' I say panicked.

'No.' Sophie shakes her head at me 'Don't be silly Emma. Your waters break when your body is ready for the baby to be born, not because you're laughing too hard.'

'Oh, that's good to know. I can do without having to deliver my godchild in a remote cottage with no medical provisions, or any idea of what to do.'

Sophie stuffs the last of the candyfloss into her mouth. 'Believe me, that's not a scenario I want either. I don't know who would panic more, you or Simon.'

We make it back to the cottage and all collapse on the sofa, tired from the long walk and fresh air. Or, more likely, on a massive carb and sugar "come down" from the doughnuts, chips and candyfloss!

'I'll make a cup of tea,' I say, dragging myself up from the sofa. 'Then we should do the face masks and foot spa.'

'Good idea.' Sophie nods. 'I'm going to get my pyjamas on.'

'Me too,' Simon adds.

A short while later, we're all sitting in our nightwear, a green face mask plastered on our faces, and Sophie with her feet in the foot spa. She seems unwilling to relinquish this, and given the circumstances I'm going to allow her to monopolise it.

'Thanks for bringing me here,' Sophie says. 'I'm having a lovely time.'

'Me too,' I smile. 'And I'm sure tomorrow we'll all look suitably refreshed from all the sea air and whatever magic ingredients are in this green gloop. It must be good for our skin; it smells weird.'

'Is that how you judge a product?' Simon looks at me, amused.

'For things like face masks – yes,' I say confidently. 'In the past this theory seems to have been proven right.'

'I agree.' Sophie nods.

'It's good that you aren't put off by things that smell bad,' Simon says knowingly to Sophie. 'Once you have a baby, you have to get used to smelling things that turn your stomach.'

'I guess I hadn't really thought too much about that.' Sophie looks at me.

'Well, it's not just the smell, it's that you get covered in that stuff too – baby sick, pooh...'

'Simon!' I interrupt. 'Do we really have to talk about this?'

Simon shrugs his shoulders. 'I'm just saying, Sophie's going to have to get used to a variety of smells, that's all. Oh, and never being alone ever again.'

'What do you mean?' Sophie looks back at Simon.

'It's not so bad when they're babies, I guess, but once they learn to walk, they follow you everywhere. You can't even go to the bathroom in peace without them wanting to talk to you while you're trying to go to the toilet.'

I'm laughing now at the mental image.

'Don't laugh, Emma, I'm being serious. And forget your sex life,' Simon continues. 'If you do have the energy and inclination to try to get it on –'

'Get it on?' I laugh harder, and now Sophie's laughing too.

'If you do try to get it on, they'll immediately wake up and demand your attention by screaming the place down, and even I can't perform sexually under those circumstances.'

'Oh dear,' I manage to say through gulps of laughter.

'I'm being serious, Em. Although the worst thing is...oh, no, I can't say.'

'Come on, Si, you're amongst friends,' Sophie coerces him, although she's still laughing.

'No, it's awful. I...we...we were, um, you know.'

I help Simon along: 'Having sex?'

'Yes, we were having sex, and – oh God, I don't know how long he'd been standing there, but Theo had somehow got out of his cot and into our bedroom.'

'Oh my God! Had he seen you two...?'

'Naked and intimate? Probably.' Simon hangs his head. 'We've probably scarred him for life.'

This story has the complete wrong effect on both me and Sophie: instead of being serious and placating Simon, we just laugh even harder.

'Don't be silly, Simon. Theo is too young to know what he saw.'

'I hope so.'

'Well, what did you say to him?'

'Not much. I mean, we were under the bed covers for most of it.'

'Most of it?' Sophie looks astounded.

'Well, it didn't scar me for life to see you and James naked and having sex,' I say. 'Actually, I take that back – I think it has scarred me for life.'

'Shut up, Emma, you're a grownup who knows that I like having sex with men. He's a small child.'

'Simon, Theo is two years old. He'll be fine. I, on the other hand, may know that you like to sleep with men, but that doesn't mean I want a front row seat at a live show.'

Sophie's laughing again now and I join in.

Simon looks wounded. He tuts and says, 'Some friends you two are,' which just makes us laugh harder.

'Ooh.' Sophie stops laughing.

'What's "ooh"?' I ask, taking in Sophie's shocked expression.

'Um.' She looks around warily.

'Soph?' I prompt.

'Um, I think my waters just broke.'

Simon and I jump up from the sofa in unison.

'What? What do you mean your waters have broken?' I flap wildly as Simon just stares, gobsmacked, at Sophie. 'I thought you said that laughing wouldn't break your waters?'

'It can't,' Sophie shrieks, struggling to her feet.

'But the baby isn't due for another month!' Simon wails.

'Don't you think I know that?' Sophie shouts.

'Okay, okay. Everybody calm down,' I say, trying to take the edge off the atmosphere.

'Calm down?' Sophie gasps. 'I'm having a baby, for God's sake, Emma, and I'm not ready. I'm just not ready. It will have to wait.'

Sophie sits back down on the sofa defiantly, as though that's going to have any effect on the baby arriving early. Simon just stares at her, open-mouthed.

'Um, Soph. I don't think it works like that,' I say. 'It will be absolutely fine. I'm going to call an ambulance and we'll get you –'

'What? No, I'm not having a baby here at a remote cottage in the middle of nowhere with just a paramedic with a paracetamol.'

'Sophie!'

'I'm not kidding, Emma. I want to give birth in the hospital I've arranged to give birth in, and I want Matt to be by my side. I want Matt,' she sobs.

Simon is still standing in stunned silence as he looks at me, wide-eyed.

'Soph, I understand that, but I don't think there's time to get you back to the city.'

'Well, there won't be if we waste any more time debating the subject.' Sophie stands back up and starts grabbing her belongings.

Simon finally finds his voice. 'Are you crazy, woman?'

'Emma, you either drive me back to the city now or I will simply drive myself!' Sophie states.

'Oh God. Sophie, you are impossible.'

'I'm not arguing about this, Emma.'

I stare at Sophie. She has that steely determined look in her eye that over the years I've learned means she's at the point of non-negotiation. I take a moment to think how I would feel right here, right now if I was her, about to give birth a month early and not in the environment I'd spent the last six months planning. In all honesty, I would be shit scared, and I'd want my boyfriend to be there too.

'Okay. This is what's going to happen.' I hand everybody a facial wipe. 'Remove the green face mask for a start. We can't go anywhere looking like this; we'll scare people. Simon, you get the bags from upstairs and put them in the car.'

'Emma, come on. Really?' Simon wails.

'Simon?'

'Alright, alright. I'm on it.' Simon hurries from the room and up the stairs.

I take Sophie's hand and squeeze it tight. 'Everything's going to be okay, I promise.' I wipe the green face mask off her as I talk.

She gulps back tears and nods. 'I'm scared, Emma.'

'I know you are. But we're here, me and Simon, and we'll take care of you. So come on, let's get you changed into some clothes that aren't covered in-' I glance down and have no idea what the appropriate word is.

'Water.' Sophie interjects.

'Thank you' I smile 'and then we'll get you in the car.' I usher Sophie out of the room and towards the front door. Simon is clambering down the stairs laden with our bags.

'Hurry up, Emma, we need to get going.'

'I know, I know, we're going, Si. Sophie just needs to change her clothes. Have you got everything from upstairs?'

'Yes, yes, let's just go.' He rushes past me and Sophie and heads out to the car with mine and his luggage leaving Sophie's next to the door.

With some difficulty, I manage to help Sophie out of her wet skirt and into a clean floating dress that resembles a small tent.

We follow Simon out to the car and I help Sophie into the back seat as Simon flings the remaining luggage into the boot and then climbs into the front passenger seat. I jump into the driver's side and pull on my seatbelt, glancing over my shoulder. Sophie's face is pale and her expression is strained.

'Hey, are you okay, Sophie?'

She nods. 'I'm fine. No contractions yet.'

I nod, but I have no idea at what point the contractions begin. I presume the clock is ticking down quickly, though, so I switch on the engine and then drive down the country lanes that lead away from the cottage and back to the main roads.

I hear Sophie on the phone to the hospital explaining that she's in labour. They must be asking her questions as she's giving quick one word answers.

'Right, okay, thanks.' Sophie hangs up the call 'The hospital said not to panic as I may be in labour for a while but given my waters have broken and we're miles away they've suggested we make our way to the labour suite so they can take a look at me. It is a month before I'm supposed to be giving birth.'

'We know!' Simon exclaims.

'Labour suite. Right.' I nod 'Simon, you need to call Joe. He and Matt should be at football practice, or at worst, in the pub after football.'

'How can you be so calm in this situation, Emma? Why aren't you freaking out?'

'Simon, just call Joe, please.'

'I mean...' Simon looks behind at Sophie. 'No offence, Soph, but what if the baby comes before we get to the hospital?'

'Simon, just call Joe, please,' I repeat calmly.

'I'm not cut out for that type of stuff,' Simon flaps.

'Simon!' My voice is louder than I intended. 'I have no intention of delivering a baby in the back seat of my car. This isn't a soap opera, this is real life, and that simply isn't going to happen. We are going to make it to the hospital and Sophie is going to have the baby in a perfectly controlled manner with medial staff surrounding her, and with Matt by her side. So for the last time, will you please just call Joe!'

'Well, there's no need to shout, Emma,' Simon huffs.

I press my lips together, not trusting that the next words to come out of my mouth will be in any way polite. We whizz down the country lanes at a speed that in any other circumstance would be completely unacceptable. I'm thankful that the roads are clear, and we make it to the A road just as Simon is dialling the phone.

'Um, hi, Joe.'

I hear Joe's muffled voice on the other end of the line.

'No, Emma's fine, we're all fine. It's just...'

Simon pauses.

'Simon, just tell him,' I urge.

'Um, are you with Matt?...Oh good. You need to get to the hospital...No, no one is hurt, it's the baby. The baby's coming.' Simon exhales and I hear frantic muffled conversation, then Simon huffs loudly. 'Of course I'm sure. Her waters broke all over the goddamn sofa, and now we're hurtling at speed back to the city – so can you please get both you and Matt to the hospital so you can meet us there.' Simon hangs up the phone. 'They're on their way.'

We make the rest of the journey in silence, broken only by me intermittently asking Sophie if she's feeling okay, and by Simon repeatedly asking if the baby is making an appearance yet. We reach the edge of the city and I feel so relieved to see the glaring lights of the hospital in the distance.

Sophie gasps in the back of the car. 'I think the contractions are starting.'

'Hang on, Soph, we're nearly there,' I say as I step on the accelerator.

Two minutes later, we screech to a halt outside the maternity department, having taken the final corner practically on two wheels. The car has barely stopped moving before Simon jumps out and charges towards the glass doors. I turn around to look at Sophie. Her face is red and screwed up, and she's panting heavily and mumbling something incoherent.

'We made it. Everything's going to be fine now,' I say in a voice that's a lot steadier than I feel.

She nods.

'Just keep breathing. In, and out. In, and out,' I say, as though I have any idea what I'm talking about.

I turn back around and see Simon hurrying towards the car followed by a man in a hospital uniform pushing a wheelchair. I breathe a sigh of relief as they approach the car, and I climb out and open the rear door.

'Hello, Sophie.' The nurse leans into the car. 'I'm Jason and I'm going to help you. How far apart are the contractions?'

'About five minutes.'

That sounds really close. It suddenly dawns on me how close a call this has turned out to be.

'Okay.' Jason's voice is calm and full of authority. 'If you can stand up slowly and sit yourself down in the wheelchair then we'll get you inside.'

As Sophie obliges, Simon and I stand to one side, looking on and feeling totally helpless. We follow in silence as Jason pushes Sophie towards the hospital. As we reach the glass doors, I grab hold of Sophie's hand.

'Do you want me to come with you while Simon finds Matt?'

'Yes, please,' Sophie says between gasps of air.

Inside, Jason pushes Sophie down a corridor to the right as Simon jogs to the reception desk.

'I'm sorry I made you drive me here,' Sophie says. 'That wasn't fair. I'm sure there was a much closer hospital.'

'Don't worry about that,' I say lightly. 'We made it to the hospital in time, and I'm sure Matt is here too, so he'll get to be with you when the baby's born and everything will work out how you planned it.'

'But it could have been bad, really bad, Emma. What if the baby had come sooner?'

'Then Simon and I would have stepped up to the mark,' I say confidently, although in reality I have no idea what on earth we would have done. Simon is hysterical in most situations that require him to function under duress.

Jason wheels Sophie into a small room 'I'll just pop and get the midwife.' He says as he flips on the wheelchair break.

Sophie squeezes my hand tighter. 'I'm scared, Emma, really scared. I don't think I can do this.'

'Don't be silly, Sophie. You're the strongest person I know. Of course you can do this.'

'Matt!' Sophie shouts, and I look at the doorway to see Matt and Joe bumbling in.

'Oh, thank God you made it.' Matt hugs Sophie, and I stand back, suddenly completely overwhelmed by the situation. Sophie is about to have a baby. This is real.

'Hey.' Joe wraps an arm around me and kisses my hair. 'Are you alright?'

'Yes,' I gulp, blinking back tears of joy and relief.

'Okay, okay,' the midwife's voice booms as she enters the room. 'Anyone who isn't the father of the baby needs to get out of the room and head to the family waiting area. There are too many bodies in here.'

'We'll be right outside,' I say to Sophie and Matt, but by this point the doctor is talking to Sophie and she doesn't even glance over in our direction as we're ushered out of the room.

Once out in the corridor on the other side of the closed door, I feel my knees sag.

Joe takes hold of my arm. 'Emma?'

I bend over and take deep breaths. 'What if we hadn't made it?'

'But you did, and Sophie and the baby are going to be perfectly fine.'

I nod as Joe pulls me to a standing position and we walk slowly to the family waiting room. As we walk in, we find Simon hunched in a chair, chewing on his fingernails.

'Oh, Em.' He jumps up and pulls me into a bear hug. 'Is she okay?'

'She's in the delivery room with the midwife. It's all okay, Simon.'

'Thank God for that.' Simon's still gripping me as though his life depends on it.

'I'll get us some tea,' I hear Joe say as Simon finally relents and releases me from his vice-like grip.

'I'm so sorry, Emma.'

'What for?'

'I was a complete lunatic back there. I was no help at all.'

'Don't be silly,' I shake my head, leading Simon back to the blue padded seats and lowering him onto one. 'It was a highly emotional and very challenging situation,' I say, sitting down beside him.

'But I completely freaked out.'

'I think we all did, Si.'

'I'm just not very good at high-pressured situations.'

'I know,' I say kindly.

'James is always saying I need to "man up".' Simon shakes his head and I stifle a giggle. 'Oi, lady.' He jabs me in the ribs. 'I may not be the man you want to come and save you from a burning building, but I have other skills.'

'I know,' I say, smiling. 'And I bet you're really good at them.'

Simon laughs and I kiss him on the cheek. 'If I was in a burning building, I couldn't wish for anyone better to rescue me – except Joe, of course.'

'Of course.' Simon grins. 'I love you, Em.'

'I love you too, Si.'

'I hope I'm not interrupting anything,' Joe says, reappearing in the room carrying three steaming plastic cups.

'Don't worry, Romeo.' Simon stands up and relieves Joe of one of the cups. 'You have nothing to fear. Juliet only has eyes for one man and it sure as hell isn't me.'

'Glad to hear it,' Joe laughs, handing me a cup. He peers at me and frowns. 'You have green on the side of your face.'

I glance at Simon and chuckle as a vision of the three of us sitting with face masks on prior to Sophie's waters breaking flashes into my mind. Simon shakes his head at me, and I press my lips together before saying, 'I have no idea why.'

Chapter Thirty-Three

Forty minutes later, Simon, Joe and I are huddled in the family waiting room sipping Starbucks coffees that I sent Simon out for – I didn't think my body could digest another cup of hospital coffee.

'Are your mum and dad on their way?' I ask Joe.

'Yeah, I called them while Matt rang Sophie's parents.'

'Good,' I smile, but inside I feel slightly uneasy. I haven't seen Joe's mum since we had dinner at her house and I, of course, did something stupid. I refer to the incident as Cakegate when I allow myself to think about it, and then die of embarrassment all over again. Joe and I don't talk about it, on my insistence (much to his amusement). As far as I'm concerned, if we don't talk about it then it didn't happen!

'My mum's over it, Emma. You need to let it go too,' Joe says before taking a gulp of coffee.

I stare at my feet.

'What did you do?' Simon asks, grinning and shaking his head.

The lie is instant: 'Nothing.'

Joe glances at me with a smile tugging at the corners of his mouth but he remains silent.

I don't know what it is, I really don't. I can be a perfectly normal human being, and then you put me in front of someone I'm supposed to impress, like my boyfriend's mother, and I go and talk about moist sponge and then flick my cake, in a complete accident, across the table. I mean, who does that?

'How bad was it?' Simon looks right past me towards Joe.

'It was bad.' Joe laughs.

'Hey, I'm still here, you know.' I tut loudly. 'A girl could take offence.'

'If she wasn't mortified,' Simon chips in.

'I daren't even mention cake.' Joe chuckles.

'Right.' I stand up, hands firmly on my hips. 'Since when did you two become co-conspirators?'

'We're just pulling your leg, trying to lighten the mood,' Simon says, slurping his drink. 'I mean, it's pretty tense. We've just driven down country lanes at speed like in *Wacky Races*, and Sophie's in a room down the hallway trying to push a human out of her –'

'Mum.' Joe jumps out of his seat and I turn around to see Joe's mum walking through the door.

Simon's mouth hangs open, and I cock my head to one side and raise my eyebrows at him for a second, smug that he's joined me on the shelf of embarrassment. Then I compose myself and turn around.

'Hi, Mrs Stark,' I say politely.

'Hello, Emma.' She embraces me. 'I wish you would call me Lorna.'

I smile and retake my seat next to Simon. 'Close your mouth,' I whisper.

It feels like we sit there for an eternity. Sophie's mum and dad arrive. Her mum says a brief "hello" before disappearing into the delivery room. Her dad and Joe's dad make small talk together in the corner of the room, discussing a sporting event or something, while patting each other on the back.

'Shall we do another Starbucks run?' Simon asks, wistfully waving his empty takeaway cup in the air.

I stand up. 'I'll come with you.'

'No, you wait here.' Joe stands up with me.

'I don't think Sophie's going to have the baby in the next five minutes,' I say.

'Still.' Joe pulls on his coat. 'I wouldn't want you to miss anything. Just in case.'

'Okay.' I force a smile, realising that once Simon and Joe leave the room, I'll be left on my own with Joe's mum.

I watch them go and then I turn back around to find Joe's mum seated next to me.

'It's hard to know what to do in these situations, isn't it?' she says, smiling kindly at me.

'I, um, I guess so.'

She glances at Joe's dad and then back at me.

'Look, Mrs Stark...'

'Lorna.'

'Right. Yes. Lorna. Um, anyway.' I clear my throat. 'Can I just say again how sorry I am about the cake incident.' I can feel my cheeks heating the whole room.

Lorna shakes her head. 'Emma, I wish you would stop worrying about that night. I don't give it a second thought.'

'Really?'

'Yes. I hope it doesn't stop you wanting to come over. I know we both' – she glances at Joe's dad – 'we'd both love to see more of you and Joe.'

'Oh.'

'You're good for him.'

I smile sheepishly.

'I mean it. Joe's happy, and it's you who makes him happy.'

Suddenly the door to the waiting room is flung open and Matt appears, a huge grin plastered on his face.

'She's done it! I'm a dad, and I have a beautiful daughter.'

We all erupt into whoops and cheers and embrace Matt in a group hug.

I push the door open and immediately a lump forms in my throat. Sophie is sitting upright in the bed cuddling her baby, with Matt standing over them, his arm wrapped protectively around Sophie's shoulders.

Sophie looks exhausted, but she's glowing. I've never seen her look so beautiful, and so happy. Joe squeezes my hand and I gulp.

'Emma, hey, come in.' Sophie beckons me into the room.

I let go of Joe's hand and I head to one side of the bed, while he heads to the other. Joe shakes Matt's hand, then they hug.

I stare down at the little bundle wrapped in a fluffy pink blanket. Huge blue eyes stare up at me.

'She's beautiful, Sophie,' I say in awe.

'Isn't she?' Sophie gazes down.

'I'm so proud of you.'

'Say hello to Florence,' Sophie says.

'Hi, Florence.' I stroke baby Florence's cheek.

'She likes you.' Sophie looks up at me.

'I doubt that. I'm sure she can simply sense my fear.'

'Do you want to hold her?'

'Oh, um, no. She's too small. I might break her.'

'Don't be silly, Emma. Here.' Sophie leans towards me.

I glance over at Matt and Joe, and see they're staring at me with some expectation. I realise I have no choice but to step up to the mark and hold the baby. I'm a woman: it's expected that I will have no fear and immediately be comfortable holding an hour-old baby.

'Okay.' I smile, trying to portray confidence. 'Come here, Florence.'

I take the baby and cuddle her – close to my chest, because I read some article about babies being relaxed when they can hear your heartbeat. Florence gurgles again and continues to watch me with her huge blue eyes, and as I look down at her my chest tightens and I realise I'm in love. I'll always protect you, I silently promise, and I'll do everything I can to help you become a strong, confident girl.

'She has your hair,' I say to Sophie as the blanket moves a little and I see the dark, soft curls covering Florence's head.

'I know. I just hope she's got Matt's chilled-out nature.'

'As opposed to your neurotic, over-organised –'

'Emma,' Sophie interrupts. 'I've just given birth and I feel like crap. You're not allowed to insult me for at least a month.' She smiles.

I cock my head to one side. 'I hope someone's told Simon that too.'

As Joe and I leave the hospital a few hours later, walking silently hand in hand, I can't help but feel a little overwhelmed – not just because of the last twenty-four hours, including our mad dash to the hospital from the cottage, but because Sophie's actually had a baby. I mean, I knew she was pregnant and that this day would come, but I wasn't prepared for how emotional I would be about it.

'Hey.' Joe squeezes my hand as we step outside the hospital building and into the morning air. 'Are you okay?'

I nod, pressing my lips together, unsure what to say that won't make me sound awful.

'Emma?' Joe presses.

'I'm fine, I promise. It's just that…how did we get here?'

'Here?' Joe frowns. 'What do you mean?'

'I mean, old enough to be settling down and having children. I still think of me and Sophie as being kids, not responsible grown-ups.'

Joe tries to hide a smile.

'Okay, I admit I'm not always responsible. Sometimes I'm just downright ditzy…'

'Come here.' Joe pulls me close into a hug and I wrap my arms around him tightly, burying my face in his shoulder, savouring the comforting smell of his aftershave.

'Everything changes, though, from this day onwards,' I mumble into Joe's jumper.

He kisses my hair. 'Of course things will change. Matt and Sophie have this magical little girl to look after and to dote on.'

I swallow.

'But you, we, get to be a part of that too.'

I release myself from Joe's arms. 'I know.' I nod. 'And I'm looking forward to being cool Auntie Emma.'

'Exactly.' Joe smiles. 'You get to be the fun aunt.'

'I know I'm being silly and over-emotional.'

'Your best friend just gave birth. Of course you're going to feel emotional. But the bond that you and Sophie have won't change; if anything, it will only get stronger. She's asked you to be her baby's godmother. That's a huge privilege.'

'You're right.' I wipe a stray tear from the corner of my eye. 'I need to make sure that I show Florence all the crazy things not to do in life. At least I have experience of that, and can help to protect her, even if it's by demonstrating how not to do things.'

Joe laughs. 'You can also show her how important it is to surround yourself with good friends.'

'I am lucky, I know that. It's just that Simon has James and the twins, and Sophie has Matt and Florence.'

'And I've got you.' Joe cups my chin and brushes his lips against mine. 'And I don't know about you, but I'm really excited to see what the future holds for us.'

'Yeah?' I look up into Joe's eyes.

'Yeah. I think it's going to be pretty great.'

When we arrive back home, the rush and crash of adrenaline from the last twenty-four hours hits me hard and I feel a little emotional. I'm so relieved that we're all okay. Suddenly I feel a great need to be close to Joe, to feel the bond that *we* share, to be desired.

Joe seems to feel this too, as we quickly reach the bedroom and fall onto the bed. He kisses me with a hunger that I share. I want to feel him next to me, his warm skin touching mine; I want to feel his caress; I want to feel wanted and loved. I pull my clothes off roughly and Joe follows, and then he's on top of me and I can feel my heart racing. I look up into Joe's eyes and the pull of him is as strong today as the first time we met.

'I love you,' I whisper.

'I love you too, so much.'

Joe leans in and his mouth finds mine, and we make love with a passion and fever that's all-consuming. I lose myself in Joe, in the moment, and give myself to him fully.

We climax together, and I collapse back on the bedsheets, light-headed and tingling all over. Joe snuggles next to me and wraps his arms around me. I feel safe and secure, and loved, and I'm so grateful that Joe and I overcame our issues last year and got this second chance to be together, as I know that there's nowhere else in the world that I'm meant to be. I belong here, in the warm, loving arms of Joe, and married or not, with child or not, this is where I'm staying for the rest of my life.

Epilogue

Gorgeous cream and yellow flowers hang from every pew, giving the church a sense of occasion. I look across at the rows of smiling faces, the joy of the day showing in everyone's expression, and I give Joe's hand a little squeeze as he kisses my hair.

Sophie is positively beaming, I don't think I've ever seen her look so content, and Matt stands proudly at her side. He's a good man, and he's already showing what a good father he is. I'm so proud of Sophie; she's took the daunting leap into motherhood and has embraced every second.

'Can the godparents step forward, please?' The vicar's voice is calm and polite, and Joe and I step forward in unison.

I kind of understand why Sophie has chosen us as godparents (besides the fact that she and I have been friends forever, and Joe is Matt's brother). Joe and I are polar opposites. I'm quirky and clumsy and slightly dysfunctional, but I'm working on that under Joe's influence. He's sensible and methodical, and thankfully quite easy-going, so he calms and organises my chaos effortlessly. I glance across at Joe. He's a good man too, a really good man, and sometimes I can't quite believe how lucky I am to have found him, and held on to him despite the slightly rocky road that we've journeyed down. Maybe that's exactly it – every other guy I've been out with has jumped ship at the first hint of a wave, but not Joe. He's my rock and also my equal. Together we bring out the best in each other.

As the vicar hands little baby Florence to me, I grasp her tightly, staring down into her deep blue eyes. Her face is a picture of innocence, and as she grabs my finger with her tiny hand, my heart flutters. I smile up at Joe, who's stroking Florence's head with such tenderness, and I realise that one day I might want this. I might want a whole football team of kids. But if I don't then that's okay too – it's our decision, mine and Joe's, and no one else matters.

I snuggle Florence's warm little body tighter to me, and I can't help but think of what a miracle she is. Sophie and Matt are beginning a new and exciting chapter of their lives, and although our friendship will need to adapt, nothing about our commitment to each other ever will – if anything, Sophie and I are closer than ever.

Right now, though, I'm also excited about the next chapter for me and Joe. I'm finally living my happy-ever-after with the man I love, the man who owns my heart, today and always, till death do us part.

Thank you for taking the time to read my book; I hope you enjoyed it. If you did, I'd really appreciate it if you could take a moment to leave me a review on your favourite retailers' website.

Thanks!

Sasha Lane

About the author:

Hi, I'm Sasha,

I love anything books, along with cats, wine, yoga, and jogging when I find the time. I write Chick Lit novels with a twist! They're Chick Lit style with a hint of darkness. I write in first person as I find it much easier to get into character and tell their story that way. I try to create characters that are just everyday young women so hopefully readers can find something about their personality or life that they can relate to, and fall in love with them as much as I have while writing about them.

Other titles by Sasha Lane:
Girl, Conflicted
Girl, Unhinged